The Misfit Bounty

Markus Matthews

The Misfit Bounty
Copyright © 2023 by Markus Matthews
Covers by Deranged Doctor Designs

All rights reserved. No part of this publication may be reproduced, distributed, or transmitted in any form or by any means, including photocopying, recording, or other electronic or mechanical methods, without the prior written permission of the author, except in the case of brief quotations embodied in critical reviews and certain other non-commercial uses permitted by copyright law.

Talent
vell.ca

8513-9 (Hardcover)
512-2 (Paperback)
14-6 (eBook)

Books by Markus Matthews

The Bounty Series
A Bounty with Strings
A Bounty of Evil
A Personal Bounty
Bounty Calls
The Sin City Bounty
A Bounty of Fury
A Bounty of Darkness
The Misfit Bounty

To my wife. Without her none of this would be possible.

Chapter 1

Sunday, November 20

"What the f—"

The word died on my lips as my sleep-addled brain began to understand why I was entombed in ice. The blanket and bed around me were covered in four inches of thick ice, pinning me in place and leaving only my head free.

My eyes began to well up as it dawned on me what had happened. I let out a string of frustrated curses that would have made a hardened sailor blush.

For the last twenty years of my life, I'd been an Air Elemental, with the power of Air and Electricity at my fingertips. I'd used those powers for a decade to fight crime by patrolling the skies over the city as my alter ego, the Hamilton Hurricane, until I was too broke to continue my hero ways. For the last six years, I'd been simply Zack Stevens, bounty hunter, and had taken down a number of dangerous Enhanced Individuals with steep prices on their heads.

Besides my Air Elemental powers, I also had a sliver of Ice Elemental ability, but if I'd tried to make a snowball, it would completely drain me. The only benefit I really got from my Ice powers was that I didn't feel the cold like most people did. It usually just got me odd looks when I wore a T-shirt and no coat on a cold snowy day.

At least that was the case until last month when my team and I took down a lich. During the battle, the lich hit me with a spell that messed up my powers. The spell stripped away my Air powers completely and now instead of being able to shoot powerful blasts of lightning, the best I could do was make a few lame sparks. My formerly weak Ice powers had changed into a potent force. I could shoot ice spears from my hands, freeze things solid, and dramatically drop the temperature around me. *And that's just the tip of the proverbial iceberg*, I thought drily.

These new Ice powers scared the heck out of me. I'd had twenty years to learn how to control my Air powers but knew next to nothing about how to safely wield Ice powers.

After the battle with the lich, a mage friend speculated that I might be able to recover my Air powers. His suggestion was that I avoid using my Ice powers and just keep using the small amount of Electrical ones I had left. The idea was that if I kept working my Electrical powers, they would grow stronger again, and by avoiding using my Ice ones, they would diminish. The hope was that eventually my Electrical powers would grow dominant again and I'd get my full Air powers back.

At the time, I'd had two choices: work towards getting my Air powers back or embrace these new Ice powers and learn how to use them. The idea of never being able to fly again didn't sit well with me. I loved the freedom of soaring through the air, and if there was even a slim chance I could fly again, then I was going to take it.

With my team off chasing their own pursuits, I had nothing but time on my hands to work toward getting my powers back. Bree, our Werepanther, was away on pack business for three months. Olivia, our vampire companion, was also gone for three months and was spending time at the English Vampire Court learning about her vampire heritage. Alteea, our pixie, had gone with Olivia. Stella and Blue were keeping busy too, helping a young Super named Emma learn to use her powers to project pain.

For the last month, I'd been working relentlessly. But my Ice powers yearned to be released. Each day I could almost feel them calling to me, begging me to use them, but I refused.

It seems, though, that my Ice powers had other plans, hence the wet, or rather *frozen*, dream I had last night and why I was now a human Popsicle in my own bed.

I was almost surprised my growing rage didn't melt the ice clear off of me. I fumed as I pondered how much this unintentional use of my Ice powers had cost me in my progress. Every day I'd been casting those pitiful sparks until my arms were numb and I was exhausted. This past week my hopes had grown as I swore the sparks seemed a bit bigger and brighter and I felt I was finally making progress towards my goal.

Now, as I looked at all the Ice around me, I wondered how much this had set me back—a day, a week, the whole month?

I pushed those negative thoughts aside and focused on the here and now. I tried moving my limbs, but they were completely locked in place. I was able to move my right hand a tiny amount, but as it was trapped under the blanket of ice, that wasn't much help. My iPhone was sitting on the bedside table less than a couple of feet away, but it might as well be a mile away for all the good it did me in my current state.

Karma is a bitch, I thought as I looked at my phone. I had turned the voice control feature off, as it had a bad habit of speaking at the wrong time during a mission. I was regretting the decision now, though. I swore I could hear that evil electronic vixen laughing at my current situation, but that was probably just my imagination.

At least hypothermia wasn't a concern. Thanks to my Ice powers, I wasn't even slightly cold despite being encased in ice. Oddly enough, I was strangely very comfortable. My body was tingling and almost humming with energy. A small part of me briefly considered just going back to sleep and waiting for the ice to melt on its own. Only the risk of water damage to the carpet and floor beneath me made me abandon that plan. I needed free myself and get this ice out of the house.

As I lay there trying to figure out how to get out of this mess I found myself in, I heard voices below me. My spirits soared as it dawned on me that Stella and Blue must be home. "STELLA, BLUE, HELP!"

Feet pounded up the stairs and approached my room. Blue threw open the door and the two of them stopped speechless at the threshold and gawked at me.

Stella recovered first and with an amused grin said, "If you were warm, you could have just turned down the thermostat . . ."

"Har, har. I didn't do this on purpose. Get me out of here."

Stella nodded and slowly moved closer, Blue cautiously following behind her. Their timid pace both embarrassed and annoyed me as it felt like they were treating me like a bomb about to go off. I'd lost control of my Ice powers when I was asleep, and now that I was conscious the risk of me suddenly losing control again was minimal.

Stella leaned over the bed and examined the ice around me.

Blue peered over Stella's shoulder and said, "I could cut him out with my Keetiyatomi blade."

"No, that would ruin the sheets. I have a better idea. Use your sword to cut out a handhold for me in the ice here," said Stella, pointing to a spot just below and in front of my neck.

I was on my side leaning slightly forward and facing them, and there was a void between the blanket and the bed where Stella pointed.

Blue drew her blade and ignited it and said, "Tilt your head as far back as possible and do not move."

Normally someone using a flaming sword inches from my bare flesh would have made me more nervous than a cat in a room full of rocking chairs, but Blue was a master with that blade, and I knew I was safe.

I leaned my head back and Stella and Blue switched positions. Blue deftly plunged the flaming blade into the ice in front of me. I got a bit nervous as I felt the red-hot heat from the blade, and the cloud of steam that appeared didn't help any. Blue twisted and moved the blade around and then pulled it back and extinguished it.

Blue slowly stepped back, and Stella examined her work with a critical eye before giving a slow nod. Stella's young form was suddenly replaced by her massive Hyde alter ego, and I swore I heard the floor start to groan under her weight. That concerned me. Between Stella's 600 pounds and the extra weight of all the ice around me, I started to wonder if the floor would hold.

Those fears were pushed aside as Stella jammed her huge deformed hand into the void Blue had created. Her bulbous right eye looked down at me and she grunted questioningly. *"Ready?"* she seemed to ask.

I nodded and said, "Do it."

Stella flexed and the room was filled with the sound of cracking ice followed by a high-pitched scream that came from my lips as all the hair on my left arm, leg, and some of my back and ass was ripped away with the ice.

Fuck me, that hurt! I thought as I rubbed my now tender outer arm. A small part of me, though, suddenly blanched as I realized that things could have been much worse if I'd been sleeping on my back rather than my side.

Stella tossed the sheet covered in ice to the floor and looked back at me in concern for a moment before pointedly looking away. She changed back into her normal human form. "Zack, are you okay?" she asked.

"Yeah, the ice just took some hair with it."

It hit me that Stella was trying to look anywhere but my direction, and I suddenly felt self-conscious as I wasn't wearing anything. Blue gazed at me with an amused twinkle in her purple eyes. I quickly, but carefully, got out of bed and searched for something to wear. I spotted my jeans on the floor and almost dove for them. I frowned as I lifted them about six inches before they stopped dead. The pant legs, along with my underwear, socks, and T-shirt, were locked in the sheet of ice covering the floor.

I shook my head at the ice that radiated out from my bed. I felt bad about my earlier anger at Stella and Blue for approaching the bed slowly. It wasn't out of fear of me losing control but to avoid slipping on the ice.

Stella gingerly wandered over to my closet and then frowned as she tried to open it. The lower runners were iced up. She turned and carefully fled the room.

I looked over at Blue and found her eyes on me. I glanced down and realized that lying on a bed of ice hadn't done wonders for my masculinity.

I opened my mouth to defend myself, but Blue held up her hand and said, "No need to explain. I'm sure your sexual organ is normally perfectly adequate."

It wasn't exactly an ego-boosting statement. I felt the heat rush to my cheeks and closed my eyes and hoped this was a bad dream that I'd wake up from soon.

"Heads up!" said Stella from the doorway.

I looked over and saw a pink bundle of cloth being tossed towards me. I caught it and realized it was Bree's fluffy bathrobe that normally hung on a hook in the bathroom. I hastily put it on and tied it around me, trying to regain some dignity, which was challenging while wearing a bright pink bathrobe.

Stella took pity on me and said, "Go get a coffee and something to eat. Blue and I will start cleaning up here."

I nodded and gingerly shuffled my way toward the doorway and fled the room.

Twenty minutes later, with food in me and coffee working its magic, I was starting to feel human again. I decided to head back upstairs and help with the cleanup.

As I approached the door to my room, I felt the temperature noticeably drop and frowned. Surely the ice in the room wouldn't lower the temperature that much.

As I entered the room, I saw that the window was wide open and Stella or Blue had removed the screen. The curtains around the window fluttered as the cool morning air blew through them, which explained the dip in temperature.

I watched as Blue tossed a large chunk of ice out the window and into the backyard. I mentally nodded in approval, as this was probably the quickest and easiest way to get the ice out.

Stella stopped in her work as she noticed me and said, "We got the closet open. Grab some clothes and get dressed. If you want to have a shower first, go ahead."

I stood there and glanced around and noticed that the two of them had made great progress since I'd been gone and more than half the ice had been removed. "You sure?"

Stella nodded. "Go, we've got this."

I shuffled over to the closet and picked out some clothes to wear.

A loud cracking sound filled the room as Blue drove the hilt of her sword into a patch of ice on the floor to break it up. The two of them picked up the pieces and tossed them out the window without a word.

I left them to it and retreated to the bathroom to have a shower.

I gritted my teeth as the hot water hit the areas of my arm and leg where I'd gotten my surprise Brazilian this morning. The soothing heat of the water over my body easily outweighed that small discomfort.

As I started soaping myself up, it dawned on me that Stella and Blue were being exceptionally kind to me this morning. A part of me figured that they both felt sorry for me due to my setback from my unintentional use of my Ice powers, but another part of me wondered if there was another reason.

I prayed to Odin that they didn't need my help with Emma. In her Hyde form, Stella felt no pain, so she was the best person to assist Emma in learning to use her powers. When Emma first came into her powers at a Home Depot, Blue and Stella had been there shopping. The pain Emma projected had been enough to incapacitate Blue. I shuddered to think how bad that must have been and had no desire to be anywhere near Emma while she learned to control her powers.

Hopefully whatever favor they wanted would be something much less painful.

Chapter 2

Sunday, November 20

By the time I was showered and dressed, Blue and Stella had cleaned up most of the ice. Blue and I carried my mattress downstairs to the basement and propped it up over the drain in the floor to allow it to dry out. The basement was unfinished and any water that leaked from the mattress would just drip along the concrete floor and into the drain.

Stella tossed my bedding into the washing machine in the far corner of the basement and said, "You'll probably have to sleep in Bree's room tonight, as there is no way that mattress will dry out by this evening."

I nodded. "I'm going to start wearing power-blocking cuffs at night so something like this doesn't happen again."

"That would be prudent," said Blue in agreement.

After doing a bit more cleanup and putting the screen back on my window, I had Blue shadow travel me to our secret lab under London.

Blue instructed me to call her when I wanted to return and disappeared into the shadows, leaving me alone in the lab.

The lab had been built hundreds of feet, if not deeper, under London by Sir Reginald Whitworth before the turn of the twentieth century. The fact that it was still intact and functional over a hundred years later was a testament to his genius. He'd been a Mad Scientist and was Stella's adopted father. He'd done unspeakable things to her and was the reason for the existence of her Hyde alter ego. I hoped wherever his blackened soul ended up that it would suffer until the end of time.

Even though I'd probably visited the lab over a hundred times, I was still awestruck by the place and gazed with interest as one of the two automatons shuffled by, cleaning the brass fixtures as it had been doing since its creation. The other one was at the far end of the room dusting the rich brown wood that lined the walls of the lab.

Taking a moment to appreciate things was something I'd been doing more of since losing my powers. I was now determined not to take anything for granted. The other day, I'd spent a good while just staring out the window at the trees in the backyard, admiring how pretty they were with their leaves changing color.

I shook my head and focused back on what I was here for. I turned my attention to the two large Tesla coils with powerful blue ribbons of electricity arcing between them. I moved behind them and sighed to myself at the ladder that stood there. The sight of it depressed me every time I came here.

Before losing my powers, I'd effortlessly use my Air powers to fly up between the Tesla coils to recharge my powers. Flying between them as the electricity danced in and across my body was one of my greatest pleasures. It was like a soak in a hot tub at the end of a hard day.

Now, I had to climb the ladder to get up there. I trudged up the steps and braced myself for what was about to happen. I clenched my teeth as I extended my arms into the blue bolts of electricity and felt the unpleasant sensation of pins and needles along my arms. I hated that something that had once brought me so much joy now caused me discomfort.

I focused and began trying to cast lightning from my hands but was rewarded with a pathetic display of tiny sparks instead. I exhaled heavily. They seemed smaller and duller than the ones I'd cast yesterday, which confirmed my fears about the unintentional use of my Ice powers setting back my progress.

The good news was that since waking up this morning, my Ice powers weren't calling to me as strongly as they had been.

The one issue with standing on the ladder and casting sparks nonstop was that it gave me time to think. Some days that was a good thing, but today, not so much. My thoughts kept returning to this morning and how I had set myself back. Yesterday I'd felt optimistic about the chances of regaining my powers, but now I wasn't so sure.

The idea that I may never soar through the air again under my own power wasn't something I wanted to dwell on, but it kept creeping into my mind.

I pushed those negative thoughts aside and focused on trying to make the sparks a bit bigger. I smiled when the tiny sparks seemed to grow a bit larger and brighter.

I tried to reassure myself that Rome wasn't built in a day and that I still had two months until Bree and Olivia returned. I wasn't sure if

I'd ever get my Air powers back, but it wasn't going to be from lack of trying.

***

By the time I called Blue to pick me up for dinner, my shoulders ached and my arms alternated between numbness and a faint tingling sensation. Despite that discomfort, I was proud of the effort I'd put in today and felt I'd made progress in repairing some of the damage that I'd done from losing control of my Ice powers.

"I checked your mattress before dinner and it is drying out quicker than I thought it would, but it still probably won't be dry enough to sleep on tonight," said Stella between bites of her dinner.

I swallowed a mouthful of burger and said, "That's good to hear."

"Your bedding is washed, dried, folded, and in your room if you want to use it on Bree's bed," she said.

"Thanks. I owe you one."

Blue gave Stella a pointed look at my comment and Stella gave her a slight nod in reply before turning her attention back to me. "Well, as luck would have it, there is a way you can pay us back . . ."

My mouth was full, so I lifted a questioning eyebrow at Stella.

"I know we agreed to take a three-month break from bounty hunting, but I couldn't help but keep an eye on the UN Bounty website, and I've found us a case."

My stomach knotted up at the idea of going out in the field without my powers, but before I could voice my objections, Stella continued, "The bounty is a werewolf named Conner Baker; he lives in Brampton and is part of the Mississauga pack. He is wanted for assaulting a Mississauga police officer. The officer is still in hospital in serious condition. The bounty is fifty thousand."

About a thirty-minute drive from Hamilton, Mississauga was close enough that I considered it local, and I never liked hearing about an officer who'd been hurt in the line of duty. I decided to keep my objections to myself for the moment and hear Stella out.

"We've been monitoring him for the last week. He makes his living as a courier for drug dealers and has a drop this evening. We want to take him down tonight after he makes this drop. The apartment he is hiding out at is a bad location for a takedown, as there are young kids there. The drop location is the best place to nab him, as it's in a rough, quiet area of Brampton, which means less chance of a civilian accidentally getting in our way."

"Okay, but why do you need me for this? You and Blue are more than capable of taking down a Werewolf by yourselves."

Blue jumped in and said, "Conner will drop off his package at the front door of a townhouse. The door is steel-reinforced and bolted shut. There is only a small hatch in the door for him to drop his package, which removes that direction as an avenue of retreat. Due to his Were senses, we can't hide too close to the drop point, and there are no good shadows nearby. Once the drop is complete, there are three directions by which he can leave. We require your assistance to block the third direction."

I pondered Blue's words. It sounded like they'd scouted things thoroughly and this was their best plan. I hated that there were kids at the apartment and approved of their decision to avoid that route. "How am I supposed to stop a Werewolf with no powers?"

Blue said, "You don't need to stop him, just slow him down for us. You have gotten better at hand-to-hand combat this last month during our training sessions. This will be an ideal opportunity to put into practice what you have learned."

I almost laughed at that. When I had my Air powers, I never joined any of Blue's hand-to-hand training sessions, as most of my attacks were ranged. If I got into a fistfight with a perp, then something had gone badly wrong. Since losing my powers and not having the ability to fly above the fray, Blue had convinced me that close combat training was a good idea. The problem was the only skill I had mastered so far was the ability to faceplant into a mat better. I was not exactly MMA material at his point. Heck, I was pretty sure a dance troupe of young girls could probably wipe the floor with me.

My feelings of doubt must have shown on my face, as Blue added, "You can wear your armor, which will protect you from any serious injuries."

Blue had a point. My armor would probably prevent me from getting anything broken. The Were would also be in human form, which meant it wouldn't be as dangerous as its beast forms. Still, Weres in human form weren't something to take lightly; they were still stronger and faster than regular humans.

Part of me missed the excitement of bounty hunting. Over the last month, my days had been filled with casting pathetic sparks and training with Blue. The biggest excitement I got was training my foundation members every Sunday, which wasn't the greatest, as it served to remind me that I had no powers. Those training sessions were also a painful reminder that Charlie was gone.

Since her death, we'd changed the training to focus on defensive and delaying tactics and stressing that if they ran into any situation that seemed risky to call for backup. All the foundation members had been good with the new change in direction in the shadow of Charlie's death, but last Sunday and last night, my three teen Werewolves had started to chafe and pushed hard to get back to offensive training again. We had moved last night's training session because the Weres had a pack meeting tonight, which was odd, as the Mississauga pack usually met Tuesdays and Fridays.

That was a problem for another day. I focused back on the task at hand. As Blue mentioned, I didn't need to take down this Werewolf, all I had to do was slow him enough to let Blue or Stella get him.

I exhaled heavily and said, "Alright, I'm in. On one condition."

Stella lifted her eyebrow at me. "What condition is that?"

"That Bree and Liv never find out about my little ice problem this morning."

Stella suppressed a giggle.

"Deal," Blue said.

***

Two hours later, I stood in my armor in the living room, waiting for Blue to give me the signal to go. Blue was standing in a trance, gazing into the shadows and watching Conner. Stella was behind me, still in her human form.

We spent the time since dinner going over pictures Blue had taken of the townhouse complex and discussing where each of us would strike from. We'd gone over all the different scenarios of how the takedown would go, and I felt very prepared for this encounter.

It suddenly dawned on me that Blue and Stella hadn't given me a picture or description of Conner Baker. I was going to ask Stella about that but then figured I'd be able to identify him by his aura. All I had to do was spot a man with the purple, brown, and silver aura of a Werewolf and I'd found my target.

"He is approaching the drop site," said Blue, not looking away from the shadows.

My nerves and excitement grew, as I knew we were moments away from this going down. I did one last quick check to make sure my armor was on tight and that I had a pair of power-blocking cuffs on me.

Blue straightened and made a sharp hand gesture to open a new shadow portal. "Go!"

I stepped into the shadows and came out at the east end of the townhouse complex beside a graffiti-covered wall. I cautiously peered around the corner of the wall and looked deeper into the complex, hoping to spot Conner Baker.

About seventy feet ahead was a large purple, brown, and silver aura making its way up a half-height set of concrete stairs to the entrance of the drug den.

I cursed to myself and at my teammates. I suddenly realized why they hadn't given me a picture or description of Conner Baker. The man was a freaking mountain. He had to be every inch of six-four and easily a good 260 pounds. That weight wasn't the 'I eat chips and pizza all day while camped out on the couch watching TV' type; it was the lean, hard muscle-on-muscle type of weight.

My inner Han Solo was screaming *I have a bad feeling about this.*

I took a deep breath and tried to psyche myself up for this encounter. I reassured myself that no matter how big he was, he paled in comparison to Stella's monstrous Hyde form. Blue would also be able to take him down without breaking a sweat.

Well, the bigger they are, the harder they fall, I thought to myself before stepping out from behind the building to block his exit to the east.

A second later, I spotted Stella in her Hyde form appear down the street in front of me, blocking Conner's western retreat.

Blue appeared from the shadows in front of the townhouses across the street, directly across from the drop site.

In unison, we all started to close in.

Conner made his drop and then he turned and came down the small flight of concrete stairs. He stopped dead at the base of the steps as he spotted Blue's tall alien form. His head darted west and he saw

Stella lumbering toward him. He immediately swung his head in my direction and his eyes sized me up.

His attention was pulled to Blue as she ignited her sword and said, "Conner Baker, surrender or we may use lethal force."

Conner turned towards me, and my guts knotted as he suddenly charged in my direction.

As the Were freight train barreled towards me, I frantically went over all of Blue's hand-to-hand lessons in my head. *Use an enemy's momentum against them and let it guide your throw.* I kept repeating that advice as he got closer and closer.

He got within a few feet, and I started reaching to grab his arm to toss him over my hip and to the ground when he suddenly surged forward, completely messing up my timing. He slammed into me like a semi into a Honda Civic.

I was airborne before I even knew what had happened. A small part of me was amused that I had regained my power of flight, though this wasn't exactly how I'd pictured it.

I saw stars as I impacted the wall and staircase of one of the townhouses and bounced off it like a ping pong ball. I braced myself as I came in for a landing on the sidewalk and smashed my nose hard off the faceplate of the armor's visor and immediately tasted blood.

I'd barely landed when something heavy hit my armored side and then crashed down on top of me. I spotted Conner's prone form lying on the sidewalk and realized he had tripped over me.

He was starting to get to his feet when a familiar pair of black leather boots appeared in front of me and a flaming sword descended and stopped barely an inch from his neck.

"Do not move!" said Blue in a tone that had more cold in it than even my new mighty Ice powers could produce.

Conner froze and then slowly lowered himself back down to the sidewalk in surrender.

Stella appeared and reached down with a huge hand and lifted Conner to his feet. Blue sheathed her sword and quickly put the power-blocking cuffs on him.

Once Conner was secure, Blue glanced down at me with a twinkle in her purple eyes and said, "I do not recall teaching that particular move, but I cannot argue with the results."

Chapter 3

Sunday, November 20

"Another 'training' accident?" asked Marion, my longtime healer as she opened the door for me and Blue. Her grey eyes, which looked huge thanks to the glasses she wore, narrowed and locked on to the bloody nose I had.

My vision was blurry, and I was also nauseous which made me suspect that I'd gained a concussion from my impact with the townhouse. Head injuries were nothing to take lightly, and I had expressed my concerns with Blue and Stella while we waited for the police to arrive to take Conner into custody.

Blue volunteered to take me to Marion's for healing. A part of me had wanted to wait until the police arrived and took Conner from us, but Stella was more than capable of detaining him on her own for a few minutes until Blue got back.

I immediately felt a bit better being in Marion's presence. She'd been my mother's healer too and after mom died was probably the closest thing I had to family. A bit of guilt crept into my subconscious. Since forming the team, I mostly only visited Marion when I needed healing and made a mental note to improve that going forward.

I shook my head and winced at the movement. "No, takedown of a rogue Werewolf that didn't go as planned."

Marion studied me for a moment and then nodded and opened her door wider. "Come in and let's get you fixed up."

Blue said, "I want to return to Stella. Call me when you are done."

I thanked Blue and went into the apartment.

I'd barely entered when I spotted a woman with a light blue and silver healer's aura around her. The aura was the same as Marion's and only a touch smaller in size, which meant the mystery healer was potent in her own right.

"Zack, this is my niece and new apprentice, Cynthia Ryerson. She arrived here from out East a couple of days ago," said Marion.

Cynthia gave me a warm smile that lit up the room and a friendly wave from the couch.

Marion turned her attention to Cynthia and added, "Zack is my best customer, so you'll be seeing a lot of him."

I frowned at that, as being the most frequent patient of a healer wasn't exactly something I'd boast about, but I couldn't argue the fact. Cynthia seemed amused by Marion's statement.

My vision was still a bit blurry but that didn't stop me from checking out Cynthia. I guessed that she was close to my age—around thirty maybe. She had light brown hair that was fair enough it could have also been described as dark blonde. Her hair came down to her jawline and framed her slightly rounded face nicely. My attention was drawn to her grey eyes, which were a slightly lighter shade of grey than Marion's. The eyes, though, had some real depth to them as they studied me and a bit of sadness or worry in them that made me suspect that Cynthia had seen some darker things in her life.

Cynthia was very attractive and had a look that got to me. She was more girl next door than supermodel but was one of the most beautiful women I'd seen in a long time.

"Hi Zack, nice to meet you," she said in a warm tone that was almost musical.

Damn, even her voice is hot, I thought, and my nerves started to grow.

I suddenly had a feeling of déjà vu again. Between the nervousness, the elevated heart rate, and the butterflies in my stomach, though that could just be the nausea from the concussion, I realized that I was crushing on Cynthia hard. The last time I'd been this smitten was in eighth grade when I had my first crush on Wendy Kowalewski.

A flashback of Wendy's smiling face popped into my head. Twenty years later, I could still clearly remember her beauty and her smile. I remember being puzzled that none of the guys in my class showed even the slightest interest in her because they were all fixated on Michelle or Madison. Michelle had joined our class at the beginning of the school year and had moved with her family from Australia. The guys loved her accent, and it didn't hurt that she was a stunning brunette. Madison was like a Barbie brought to life and had the biggest boobs in the class. As far as I was concerned they could keep both, as neither girl held a candle to Wendy, my angel with braces.

Unfortunately, that admiration only went one way, and I alienated her with my awkward affection towards her. All that came out of it was me not being able to make eye contact with her throughout all of high school.

I mentally rolled my eyes at myself. Between crushes, wet dreams, and new uncontrolled powers it really was like I was going through puberty again. All I was missing was an outbreak of bad acne and I was there. With the way my luck was going, that would probably happen too.

Cynthia was looking at me with concern, so I gave her a small wave in response as I gingerly made my way over to the couch.

She got up as I approached, but I just focused on making my way safely to the couch and sat down. I took off my armored helmet and put it on the floor as Marion moved a small stool over and sat on it just in front of me.

"What hurts?" asked Marion as she gazed at me.

"I think it's just a nosebleed. My bigger worry is I think I have a concussion."

Marion placed her hands on the sides of my head and closed her eyes. She turned my head and that put Cynthia back into my view.

My eyes instantly locked onto her left breast. Oddly, I wasn't checking out her boobs but rather the white Rebel Alliance logo on her black sweatshirt had caught my interest. Cynthia frowned at me, and I realized where I was staring. "*Star Wars* fan?"

Cynthia's face lit up at that and she nodded. "Yeah, not a lot to do on the Island during winter, so we watch a lot of movies. Huge *Star Wars* fan but mainly the original trilogy."

It took me a minute before I remembered that all Marion's family was back on Prince Edward Island and that must be where Cynthia was from. Marion usually visited them every year during the summer for a couple of weeks. The last part of her comment had me liking her even more. "Marry me?" I blurted.

Marion clucked her tongue at me and said, "I only found a mild concussion, but after that comment, I'll take another look."

I felt some heat come to my cheeks and mentally facepalmed at my comment. *Smooth, Zack, really smooth.*

To my relief, Cynthia let out a peal of laughter that filled the room like a symphony. I swear that laugh was one of the most wonderful sounds I'd ever heard, and my interest in her deepened even more.

"Maybe we start with a coffee and see where things go . . ." said Cynthia, an amused twinkle in her eyes.

My heartbeat sped up. That response was certainly more promising than the 'get bent, loser,' I'd gotten from Wendy Kowalewski when I'd asked her out. "Coffee's good."

"Hold still," said Marion with an exasperated tone, as she was still examining me.

"Sorry."

My attention was pulled from my future wife, er, I mean Cynthia, when I felt tingling on the sides of my head as Marion started healing me.

After a minute, she dropped her hands and nodded in satisfaction. "That's the concussion taken care off. Let's deal with that nose."

She gently placed her fingers on the sides of my nose, and I felt her magic start to work again.

In less than twenty seconds, Marion removed her fingers and said, "Any other injuries?"

"Nope. That was all of them, thanks!"

Marion got up and pushed her stool back. "Even though I healed that head injury, I'd recommend that you don't go to sleep for a couple of hours. If you have any side effects or symptoms, call me right away."

I nodded but my attention was pulled to Cynthia again. In focus she was even more amazing than blurry Cynthia. I really wanted to get to know her better and didn't want to blow it. In my nervousness, a cheesy pickup line popped into my brain, and I was about to blurt it out but stopped myself.

Score one for personal growth, I thought with a mental grin.

Oddly enough, Liv's words when she broke up with me came rushing back. "If you do meet someone, don't try so hard. You have a lot of great things to offer; just be yourself," she'd said. My crazy vampire had actually given me sound advice, and I decided to take it. Rather than rush into something, I wanted to take time to figure things out. If Cynthia was going to be Marion's new apprentice, that meant she wasn't going anywhere, and I had plenty of time to get to know her.

"Thanks, Marion. I'll call Blue and get out of your hair. I'm sure you and your lovely niece have a lot of catching up to do."

A slight blush rose to Cynthia's cheeks. Marion nodded and I got up and moved to the side of the room to call Blue.

The call ended up being very short, as Blue and Stella were tied up with the police and getting a bounty claim number and wouldn't be free for at least an hour. I told her I'd get a taxi and that I'd see them when they got home.

I hung up and was about to call a taxi when Cynthia said, "Zack, hold off on the cab. You're just getting over a head injury, and you shouldn't be alone." She paused and with a smile said, "Besides, didn't you say something about coffee?"

I blinked at that and looked over to Marion. "I don't want to interrupt..."

Marion yawned and shook her head. "It's fine. It's getting close to my bedtime anyway. Cynthia and I have a long day together tomorrow. You two go get some coffee."

With that settled, I realized I had another issue. "Um, as much as I'd like to go for coffee, this armor isn't exactly low profile and I'm only wearing shorts under it."

Marion studied me for a moment and said, "I think I have a solution."

She got up and headed over to the closest by the door. Marion pulled out a green and white poncho. She came over to me and held it up for inspection. The poncho was basically a large wool blanket folded in half with a slit at the top for the head and sewn together at the sides with two arm holes. If I ditched my armor gauntlets and left my helmet off, the poncho would cover the rest and I'd be fine.

I removed my gauntlets and placed them and my helmet by the door. I thanked Marion as I took the poncho from her and awkwardly slipped it on. I popped my head through the slit at the top and looked down at myself. I wouldn't be winning any fashion awards, as I felt like I was wearing a giant carpet, but it did the job. It was certainly less conspicuous than my armor. I laughed to myself as I remembered I was in downtown Hamilton, which meant my current outfit probably wouldn't even get a second glance.

Cynthia made small talk as we walked down the hall and waited for the elevator. While I was slightly nervous about blowing my chance, I was also starting to feel strangely comfortable being with her.

We were both caught off guard as we exited the building and got hit by a strong gust of wind. Thankfully, neither of us went down. The multistory buildings around us acted like a funnel, so even on a night without much wind, you still got the odd powerful gust.

Cynthia laughed. "That wind makes me feel like I'm back home again."

I knew there was a Tim Hortons a couple of blocks from us, so I turned in that direction. The nice thing about Hamilton is that there's always a Tim Hortons nearby.

While I couldn't feel it, I knew it was a cooler evening, but Cynthia took it in stride and didn't complain about the temperature on our walk. Being from Prince Edward Island, she was almost certainly familiar with this kind of cold.

We reached Timmies and I was pleased to see it was mostly empty and quiet.

"Why don't you grab us a seat and I'll get us some coffees. What would you like?" asked Cynthia.

What I want isn't on the menu, I thought. I was glad I managed to suppress that cheesy line. Instead I said, "Coffee, one cream, and a chocolate glazed donut, please."

Cynthia smiled at that. "That's my favorite too. Better hope they have more than one chocolate glazed left . . ."

She walked away, leaving me amused at her comment. That simple statement said a lot of good things about her. I'd dated women who in the same situation would have let me have the donut. I loved that Cynthia made it clear I was shit out of luck if there was only one.

I found us a table in the corner and sat with my back to the wall out of habit.

I yawned as I sat down and was glad that coffee was coming; between the long day and healing session, I was almost wiped. The sugar high from the donut would help.

Cynthia returned with a red plastic tray with two coffees and two chocolate glazed donuts. "You're a lucky man," she said, referring to the donuts.

I looked her straight in the eyes and said, "I certainly am."

I smiled at the slight bit of red that colored her cheeks as she sat down.

We were quiet as we tucked into our donuts and then as she finished hers, she looked around and softly said, "Are you really the Hamilton Hurricane?"

"Was. I'm retired now. How do you know about the Hurricane? Marion talk about me on her visits or something?"

Cynthia nodded. "Yes, but you'd also made the news a couple of times. What was it like?"

I was surprised before I remembered that a few of my exploits back in the day did make the national news. I took a deep breath and talked about my hero days.

I rambled on longer than I meant to and was much more open about my hero history than I normally would have been. I think Cynthia being Marion's niece and Marion being almost family gave me comfort that I could be more forthcoming than usual. I even got into why I gave it up and turned to bounty hunting and my recent change of powers.

While I talked, I tried a few times to steer the conversation back to her and find out more about her past, but Cynthia quickly managed to turn it back to me without giving up much about herself.

The fourth or fifth time she did this, I pressed her. "So, what brought you to Hamilton?"

"I just needed a change. What are your teammates like?"

I shook my head. "Nope, I'm not letting you off that easy. I've monopolized this conversation; I want to hear about you."

Cynthia took a sip from her coffee as if to delay answering and then said, "Not much to tell. I'm just a simple girl from the Island. Why would you want to learn about me anyways?"

"Because I like you and want to get to know you better," I said without thinking about it, and I realized that I might have been a bit too direct.

Color rose to Cynthia's cheeks. "I'm flattered but I don't think we'd be a good match." My disappointment must have shown on my face as she quickly added, "It's not you, it's me."

I mentally sighed, as that line was up right up there with "let's just be friends," and this wasn't the first time I'd heard it.

There was a reason I wasn't a great poker player—I was terrible at keeping a neutral expression.

Cynthia rubbed her temples and groaned. "I'm making a mess of this. Let's try again, okay?"

I nodded and she glanced down at the table shyly. "I have a confession to make; I had a small crush on the Hamilton Hurricane back in university. I had part of my wall covered in newspaper clippings with your exploits." I felt my cheeks flush at that and she said, "I've long gotten over that, but you're different than I imagined."

"How so?"

Cynthia bit her lower lip for a moment. "You're more relatable and down to earth than I expected," she said.

I gave her a nod and small smile of understanding. A lot of people have these preconceived notions of what a superhero is like, but the truth of the matter is that most of us are just normal people. We have the same hopes, fears, and flaws as everyone else does.

"I do like you, Zack, but I have a past that I'm not proud of, and if this is to go anywhere, you probably should hear about it first."

I tried to be flippant about it and said, "Oh, a beautiful woman with a dark, mysterious past. I'm intrigued about where this is going . . ."

She laughed and shook her head. "I will tell you, but you need to make a promise first, okay? You can't repeat any of this to Marion."

I struggled with that, as Marion was like family and I owed her a lot. The idea of keeping secrets from her didn't sit well.

After a long silence, I decided it was worth the gamble and hoped I wouldn't regret this. "Anything you tell me is just between us. Promise."

Cynthia looked relieved at that. "I told Marion I wanted to come to Hamilton because I'd ended a toxic relationship and needed a fresh start, which was true but only half the story. I need to start at the beginning, and this might take a while. Do you want a fresh coffee?"

I thought about it, but the caffeine and sugar had kicked in and I was buzzing at the moment. "Probably not a good idea if I want to get any sleep tonight. If you want another one, though, feel free."

Cynthia shook her head and took a deep breath. "I came into my healing powers when I was twelve, and my mom helped me learn how to use them. I'd assist her with patients by healing minor injuries. When I was fourteen, I screwed up and ended up doing more damage than good. Mom managed to heal the patient, but it was touch and go. After that, Mom trusted me much less and didn't let me help as much."

That seemed unfair to me, and I said, "You were young and learning, mistakes happen. You should have seen some of the screw-ups I made with my powers when my mother was training me."

Cynthia smiled in understanding. "Anyway, this lack of trust between us caused a rift and I rebelled. Growing up in a healing family, it was always assumed that if I got powers I'd follow into the family business. When I was sixteen, I announced that I didn't want to be a healer and that I wanted to go into marketing. My parents were supportive, but I knew my mom was disappointed by my choice."

"Near the end of my second year at university, one of my friends in my program slipped and broke her arm and I healed her. She was in awe and asked me why I was in marketing if I had the power to heal. I dismissed her question, but it stuck with me. I'd already been having doubts about whether marketing was right for me, and at the end of the semester I decided that it wasn't my calling. I went home for summer break and had a long talk with my mother. She was overjoyed that I wanted to be a healer again and was fully supportive when I changed my degree to nursing."

I frowned at this. "If you have healing powers, why bother with a nursing degree?"

"You should know the answer to that. Powers aren't unlimited. The strong medical foundation a nursing degree provides means I can still help people even if my power is depleted."

"That makes sense."

Cynthia paused to take a sip of coffee and then continued. "The problem with changing programs was there weren't a lot of courses in common between the two degrees. So other than getting a few electives taken care of, I was looking at another four years in school. I enjoyed university and decided that it was worth it.

"When I graduated, I went home and joined Mom with her practice. At first it was okay, but Mom still saw me as that fourteen-year-old that almost killed someone and not as a healer with a degree, and old tensions quickly resurfaced."

Cynthia paused and looked off into the distance as if reliving old memories. "Anyways, I tried to prove to her that I was capable and earn her trust, but after almost two years of trying, my progress was minimal. I decided it wasn't going to work. I wanted to open my own practice, but PEI has more healers per square mile than anywhere else in the country and it's a hard market to crack. I decided to move to Halifax, as the city only has three full-time healers and I figured it would be a much easier market to make it in," she said, and I could hear the touch of bitterness and regret in her voice.

"Not as easy as you thought it would be I assume?"

She shook her head. "No. While it only had three healers, they were all long-established with large client bases. The city was also more expensive than I thought it would be, and all I could rent was a small one-room clinic with a tiny apartment above it. Those first six months were brutal. I went through my savings quickly and things got tight.

"I got to the point where I was having to decide between paying rent, utilities, or food and was considering crawling back home to Mom. Then one night just as I closed up, someone banged on my door. I opened it and was greeted by two tough-looking men carrying another man who had been stabbed and was bleeding badly. My healer instincts took over and I rushed them in and got to work.

"I saved him and when I was done, one of the men took out an envelope of cash and said, 'We were never here,' and all three of them left. Inside the envelope was $3,000 cash."

Her eyes welled up a bit, and she took a deep breath. "I knew those men were bad news and probably criminals, but that money was like a godsend. I didn't report the knife wound and just carried on.

"A couple of weeks later, there was a heavy knock on the back door of my clinic. It was the same two men, but they were carrying a different man than before, and he'd been shot twice. I healed him and they gave me another envelope and the same instructions but added that they'd have more work for me and I'd do very well out of this arrangement. This time they'd given me $10,000 in cash.

"I knew I was getting myself in deeper but justified it by pretending that they were just people in need of healing and that was my job. Deep down I knew better and that I was getting myself into something I should avoid, but I didn't feel I had much choice."

Cynthia went quiet but I sensed there was more coming and waited for her to continue. "Over the next six months, I'd get regular visits from them and more cash-filled envelopes. My legit business was also slowly growing, so things seemed to be heading in the right direction. Then I made an even bigger mistake. One of the men, Logan, began flirting with me and asking me out. I pushed him off, but he kept trying and I eventually gave in. I was a bit nervous about dating a Werewolf, but Logan seemed okay.

"The first year of dating Logan was fun. He always had nice cars and we'd go to expensive restaurants and clubs. He was handsome and kind to me and I had a good time. As things got more serious between us things started to change. Logan's true personality began to creep out. He got more possessive and controlling and his temper became quicker. I also found out more about what he did. He was a lieutenant for a local crime boss named Pierre LaPointe. Pierre is a mage and one of the scariest people I've ever met. He has this look in his eyes that just seems to go right through you.

"Over the next year things got worse with Logan and I was getting more and more unhappy about working with Pierre and his people. I had also been trying to end things with Logan for four months, but he didn't want to hear it. He had been coming around less and less and I hoped that meant he'd found someone new and was moving on from me.

"It all came to a head two weeks ago. A couple of Pierre's men showed up just as I was closing and had a young girl with them who was in rough shape, like someone had beaten her badly. I asked her age, and she claimed she was eighteen and offered to show me her ID. I declined because I knew Pierre's organization could get fake IDs. I healed her and got my usual envelope of cash, but this one bothered me. I knew that girl wasn't eighteen and suspected they were pimping her out.

"The next morning, I'd just opened and the two men and the young girl were back. She was in even rougher shape than before. I healed her again and they left. It hit me that they were conditioning her, and I was playing a big part in that. If I healed her, they could beat her into submission more often. The idea that I was involved in sex trafficking was the last straw.

"I called Marion and asked if she was looking for help and told her that I'd ended a bad relationship and was looking for a fresh start. She said she'd be happy to have me and that there was an empty apartment just across the hall from her that I could stay in."

I knew that apartment, as Marion used it to keep long-term patients. It was fully furnished and ideal for someone in Cynthia's situation.

Cynthia paused to take a sip of her coffee before continuing. "I spent the next week tying up loose ends, packing, and doing it all on the down-low, as I didn't want Logan, or worse Pierre, to find out I was leaving. I brokered a deal to break my lease and then packed up my Jetta and headed out. I got into town Thursday night; my trip took longer than expected because my car broke down in Quebec. Still want to date me?" she asked nervously.

I nodded. "Absolutely," I said. Cynthia smiled at that. "I think you're being too hard on yourself. The black-market healing was a bit of a grey area, but you were still healing people. The important thing is that when things did get ugly, you walked away. A lot of people wouldn't have."

Cynthia straightened in her seat at that and looked relieved. "Thanks, Zack. I've been dealing with all of this on my own for so long it feels good getting it out in the open."

"My pleasure. I'm assuming your reason for not wanting to tell this to Marion is that you're afraid of it getting back to your mom?"

She nodded. "I love my mom, but she does tend to dwell on things, and I didn't want to give her more ammo."

I could understand that. Sometimes it was easier talking to a stranger than those closest to you. We chatted for a bit and then decided it was getting late and headed back to Marion's.

We made small talk on the walk and as the apartment came into view, I gathered up my courage. "I had a good time this evening. Are you free tomorrow for another date?"

My heart sank when Cynthia shook her head. "No, Marion wants to spend the day going over her procedures and promised it would be a long day. I'm free Tuesday morning, though."

I perked up at that. "Cool, there is a decent breakfast place on the mountain I could introduce you to."

"Awesome, I love a hearty breakfast."

When we reached Marion's door, I leaned in to give her a quick goodnight kiss and was pleased that she leaned in and responded in kind. The kiss grew heated and went longer than I intended.

I reluctantly broke the kiss and said, "I should get going."

She nodded. "Thank you, tonight was fun. See you Tuesday."

I wished her a good night and turned and headed for the elevator. I made it about ten steps when Cynthia said, "Wait! Your armor."

I stopped and turned back to her. I gave her a small grin and said, "Thanks, I got a bit distracted there."

She smiled and unlocked Marion's apartment and disappeared inside. While she was inside, I stripped off the poncho, which was another thing I'd forgotten. Cynthia reappeared and I exchanged the poncho for my armor and wished her a good night again.

I had just reached the elevator when my phone rang.

"We're done with the police and are at home. Do you require transportation?" asked Blue.

It seemed my luck was rolling tonight, as I'd planned on just calling a cab. *"That would be great. I'll meet you in the shadows in the staircase at Marion's."*

"Roger," said Blue as she ended the call.

I turned and headed for the staircase with a spring in my step. Considering how poorly the day had started, it certainly ended better. We'd taken a violent Were off the streets and even better, I had a date with an interesting and beautiful woman in my future.

Chapter 4

Monday, November 21

It had been odd sleeping in Bree's room and wearing power-blocking cuffs, well, more like power-blocking bracelets, as there was no chain connecting them, but after my previous night, I wasn't taking any chances. I punched in the codes and removed the power blockers and felt the surge of my Ice powers return inside of me.

I stripped off my sheets and remade Bree's bed with her own bedding. I hoped by using my own bedding that her sensitive nose wouldn't catch my scent on her stuff, as that would lead to some awkward questions. She wouldn't be back for two months, so that helped my cause.

Thankfully, tonight I'd be in my own bed again, as my mattress had almost dried out last night and should be completely dry by later today.

After a quick shower and breakfast, I found myself back at the lab again. The climb up the ladder didn't even bother me. I stuck my arms into the electric field between the two Tesla coils and started casting sparks.

My thoughts soon drifted to Cynthia, and I began thinking about our date tomorrow. I spent the first couple of hours trying to figure out what to wear for a breakfast date at a diner. I found myself missing Liv and Bree; their fashion input would have been awesome. Stella, bless her heart, was always very dated and conservative and would be no help. Blue would probably recommend my armor or something in chainmail and be more concerned about which knife, sword, or other instrument of death would be best to bring in case something unexpected happened.

I finally settled on a pair of tan Dockers and a collared golf shirt, figuring that would be a nice balance of casual and formal.

I really wanted things to work with Cynthia. She was smart, beautiful, had a good sense of humor, and liked *Star Wars*. Even better, as a healer she was an Enhanced Individual, which meant my being an Air elemental—or an Ice elemental now I supposed— wouldn't be an issue for her. Don't get me wrong, I'd happily date an ordinary human, but things were just easier with someone who had powers.

I cursed to myself for dwelling on Cynthia, as I had a bad habit of taking things too fast too early in a relationship. If I wasn't careful, I'd start thinking of her as the future Mrs. Stevens before we'd even had a second date. Liv's advice not to try so hard came rushing back, and I decided to take a deep breath and stop planning a future with Cynthia and just see how our breakfast date went.

***

After dinner, I was back at the lab but this time in the hangar with Blue. Tonight was one of our twice a week hand-to-hand combat training sessions.

I smiled when I felt the sparring mat under my feet, as that was the only victory I'd ever achieved in my sessions with Blue. She wanted to train without the mats, as quote, 'Pain is a great teacher,' but I stood firm and said that there was no way I was doing this without them, and she reluctantly agreed to my demand.

Even with the mats, I usually had to visit Marion roughly every other session due to injury.

Blue gave me a bow and a pointy-toothed grin and said, "Begin!"

My adrenaline surged as we slowly closed the distance between us. I watched her like a hawk, trying to figure out where her attack would come from. The moment we got close enough, her right hand shot out towards my throat. I was ready for that and managed to block the punch. Her left leg immediately came in for a kick aimed at my groin, but I cheered to myself as I pivoted my hips and took the blow off my outer thigh. After our first session together, I now always wore a protective cup for this very reason; pain really *was* a great teacher.

The kick gave me an opportunity to go on the offense, and I made a swift jab at her midsection with my right hand.

I groaned a second later when I found myself lying on my back on the mat trying to get my breath back after Blue's lightning-fast throw.

She stared down at me and with a twinkle in her purple eyes said, "I told you that you were improving."

I frowned at that. "How so?"

"In our earlier sessions, you would not have gotten the chance to go on the attack."

I pondered that and nodded. She had a point. In the earlier sessions, I wouldn't have been able to block her attacks and would have been on the mat before I knew what hit me.

I got to my feet with a sense of purpose and began sparring with Blue again.

By the end of the session, I hadn't done much better and ended up on the mat more times than not, but I was satisfied I was making progress. That sense of purpose made the bumps and bruises from the session seem to hurt a little less.

***

The next morning, I was up early and shaved, showered, and dressed for my breakfast date with Cynthia.

A small part of me felt guilty, as I knew I should be using this time to continue working at getting my powers back. I promised myself that after the date I'd get to the lab right away and put the time in.

Blue shadow traveled me to the staircase in Marion's building, and from there, I made my way to Cynthia's apartment.

I was about to knock on her door but took a moment to calm my nerves and focus. I mentally reminded myself to not make a big deal about this date; we were just two people going for a hearty breakfast. We would see how the date went and take things from there.

I took a deep breath, and my hand shook as I knocked on her door.

I'd barely lowered my hand when the door swung open and the goddess that was Cynthia smiled and stepped out. I chided myself about thinking of her as a goddess, but I wasn't far off. She'd styled her hair with a few strategic curls and was wearing light makeup that made her light grey eyes pop. She wore a knitted light pink sweater that hugged her body, and a pair of form-fitting jeans. A small brown leather purse hung on her shoulder. She looked great.

Her smile widened as I said, "Wow! You look beautiful."

"You clean up pretty good yourself."

I had to admit that Dockers, a golf shirt, and the spring jacket were a better look for me than the walking carpet I'd worn for our last date. I gestured towards the direction of the elevator. "Shall we?"

She nodded and we walked together down the hall. "How did your training yesterday with Marion go?"

"Good. She is very different from my mom; it's hard to believe that they are sisters."

"Why's that?"

"My mom is more than a decade younger than Marion, but by how uptight my mom is, you'd think she was the older one. My mother is a lot more conservative than Marion, which also makes Marion seem younger. Marion makes things fun and I'm so excited about working with her."

I grinned at that. Considering Marion's love of hippie culture and the sixties, she certainly was a free spirit. While Marion was a bit odd at times, she was also a damn good healer and never took those responsibilities lightly. It was interesting how people could take different approaches to their jobs and still excel at them.

We made small talk in the elevator and in the lobby and came out to a lovely sunny day. The sunshine was certainly a nice change from the overcast skies that we'd gotten most of the month and I took that as a good omen.

Cynthia frowned as I pulled out my phone and called for a cab.

The moment I hung up, she asked, "You don't drive?"

"I could lie and claim that I don't drive due to my love of the environment, but the truth is I never saw the need for getting a driver's license because I could fly. I'm regretting that decision since I lost my powers though."

"I guess that makes sense; being able to fly would make a license redundant."

Cynthia tilted her head up to let the sun fully shine across her face and seemed to be savoring the heat on her skin. I was in awe at how she looked haloed by the sunlight but made a point of looking away. I angled my head up too and appreciated the sun like Cynthia was doing.

A few seconds later, multiple things happened at once. An older model white van screeched to halt just in front of us on the street and Cynthia let out a short scream that was quickly cut off.

My adrenaline spiked and things seemed to slow down as my thoughts began going at a million miles a minute.

I turned to help her and saw a large man with dark hair and short facial hair grab Cynthia and cover her mouth with his hand. He started dragging her towards the van. My stomach knotted as I noticed the five-inch purple, brown, and silver aura around the man accosting her. He was a Werewolf.

The van's side door was thrown open, revealing another man inside. This man also had an aura around him, but it was orange, brown, and mustard yellow. The orange meant Super class, but the brown and yellow combination were new to me, which meant I had no idea what his powers were. Out of the corner of my eye, I spotted another Werewolf aura around the driver of the van.

The odds were firmly against me. Weres were always tough to take down and adding a Super with unknown powers made the odds even worse.

The only good news was we were less than ten blocks from the Central Hamilton Police Station and this area had a frequent police presence. SWAT was also based out of Central, so their response time should be quick. I just needed to stall them long enough for help to arrive.

I decided the Super was the biggest threat and began calling on my Ice powers to hopefully send an ice spear at him. In the back of my mind, I worried that I'd probably encase and suffocate all of us in ice, but I didn't have any choice.

I'd barely lifted my hands towards the Super when something heavy and solid smashed into the back of my head and everything went black.

Chapter 5

Tuesday, November 22

I briefly opened my eyes and then instantly closed them again as the pain of the light drove into my groggy brain like an icepick. I suppressed a groan and tried to figure out what was going on. At first, I thought I was hungover, but then remembered I'd given up drinking and had been dry for a month, so that couldn't be it.

Slowly, flashes and images of earlier began coming back to me. Cynthia being grabbed, Werewolves, the van. My addled mind began slowly putting it together.

I could tell from the constant hum of a motor, the road noise, and the movement that I was in a vehicle.

I took a moment to assess my condition, which other than my throbbing noggin seemed to be okay. My right arm was stiff and sore from lying on my side, and my hands were numb from being secured behind me in cuffs.

Something else was off, but I couldn't put my finger on what it was. It hit me as I noticed the cool metal under me—I couldn't feel my powers. I realized that the cuffs must be power blockers, which was why I was noticing the cold.

In cuffs and without powers, I was in serious trouble, and my fear spiked. I'd obviously been kidnapped with Cynthia but had no idea why we'd been taken. My mind searched for someone from my past that had a grudge against me from my hero days or even from bounty hunting. I mentally shuddered as I recalled some of the people that I'd put away, and if it was any of the people I was thinking, I really hated being this helpless.

More details of the kidnapping came back to me and I realized I might be going down the wrong path. Cynthia had been grabbed first which meant she was the target and not me. There was a chance that Cynthia was just being used as a distraction to give whoever crept up and clocked me from behind their opportunity, but that felt thin. I'd been standing there oblivious to everything around me, so they could have jumped me without needing Cynthia as the distraction.

My concern for Cynthia's well-being overrode everything, and I needed to know she was okay. I steeled myself for the pain and slit my eyelids open. The pain wasn't as bad as I expected but it was uncomfortable. I gave myself time to adjust to the light and the discomfort started to recede with each passing second.

This was my second concussion this week and that probably wasn't doing my long-term mental health any favors.

My heart soared as my eyes came into focus a bit more and I began making out a pink and blue outline sitting across from me in the van. I took a deep breath and fully opened my eyes while trying to ignore the pain.

Cynthia came into full view. She was sitting against the far side of the van. Her head was down, and she had her legs tucked up close to her. She was also wearing power-blocking cuffs, and her ankles were bound together. I tried moving my feet and found they weren't tied up. I found it strange that they'd secure Cynthia more than they would me. I grinned, as that meant she probably managed to kick one of her attackers. I hoped she'd gotten one of them right in the balls.

I slowly shifted my head to look at the front area of the van and spotted that the driver's area was separated from the cargo area by a black metal mesh cage. Through the cage, I saw the dark-haired man who had grabbed Cynthia sitting in the passenger seat. He was eating what looked like beef jerky like he hadn't eaten in weeks. My stomach rumbled at the sight of the food, and I wondered how long I'd been out. The driver had a similar shade of hair, and by the arm I could see, he seemed to be of the same large, muscular build as the guy in the passenger seat.

The movement of my legs must have caught Cynthia's attention and she looked up. Her eyes were red, and I could tell she'd been crying. She gave me a weak smile. "Are you okay?" she whispered.

I was about to nod but thought better of it and said, "Other than a bit of headache, I'm fine."

Her eyes darted to the front of the van, and she mouthed "sorry" at me.

I made an awkward shrug and said, "Not the worst date I've ever been on."

Cynthia burst out laughing at that.

Her mirth was cut short when the Were in the passenger seat banged his hand hard enough on the cage to rattle it and said, "Shut it back there or I'll come back and make you shut up!"

Cynthia glared at the front of the van and it seemed she was about to make a retort, but then her shoulders slumped and she looked away and back at me.

A few choice smart-ass comments popped into my head as well but being handcuffed and a bit dizzy, I decided that discretion was the better part of valor for the time being.

The Were's voice had a maritime accent to it, which confirmed for me that this kidnapping was about Cynthia, and I had just been in the wrong place at the wrong time. I wondered if either of the Weres up front were Logan, her ex. I instantly dismissed that because if one of them was, I figured Cynthia would be more vocal with him.

There were four people involved in the attack but only two were in the van. The other two must be in a vehicle following us or up ahead. I assumed that Logan must be in that vehicle with the Super with unknown powers. It was probably Logan who knocked me out earlier as well, as he was the only attacker I hadn't seen during the kidnapping.

The silence made me notice my sore right arm again, and I decided to do something about that. I also wanted to take stock of what things I had available to me. I was pretty sure I could feel my wallet digging into my right butt cheek and was surprised that it was still there. I rolled over on my front, hoping to feel my iPhone in my jacket's inner pocket but was disappointed to find it gone.

I shifted around and with some effort managed to get to a sitting position with my back against the side of the van that faced Cynthia. I gently rotated my right arm in an effort to get the circulation going again.

I glanced over at Cynthia who watched me intently and noticed that I couldn't see her purse and assumed that our kidnappers had taken it too. What I really wanted to know was whether our phones were still in the van or if they had ditched them. If they hadn't, we might get rescued, as Blue was supposed to pick me up after my date. She'd get suspicious if I didn't show or call. Stella would be able to track my phone, and hopefully that meant the cavalry would be here shortly.

I gave Cynthia a pointed look and then tilted my head and mimed like I was talking on a phone. She gave me an odd look but then mouthed "phone?" at me. I nodded excitedly and then made an exaggerated slow head movement towards the front of the van.

She had a puzzled look on her face for a moment and then shook her head when she figured out what I was asking. She made a breaking motion with her hands, following that gesture with a tossing motion.

I gave her a slow nod of understanding. The phones were gone, and any hope I had of a quick rescue went with them.

***

The hours dragged by and now the sun was low enough in the sky that I could see it out the small tinted windows in the back doors of the van. The sun was setting behind us, which meant we were heading east. That brilliant deduction wasn't needed, though, as I had been watching the green highway road signs that would flash by the front windows every so often and knew we were close to Montreal.

I assumed that they were taking Cynthia back to Halifax.

I frowned for a second as I wondered why they weren't cutting through the US like a lot of Ontarians did when driving east. I mentally slapped myself for my stupidity—crossing the Canada-US border with two kidnapping victims in the back wouldn't have been a great plan. I tried to pretend that my recent concussion was the reason for my poor thinking, but I barely even had a dull pain left.

I shifted around, trying to get feeling back into my poor butt cheeks. Hours of sitting on the hard metal floor was starting to catch up to me.

My thoughts turned to my situation again. I wondered what their plan was for me. Cynthia, with her healing skills, was a valuable asset and I could see why they wanted her back. But why hadn't they just left me out cold on the sidewalk in Hamilton? They'd have been long gone by the time I'd regained consciousness. I realized that I'd been a witness, and that meant there was risk of their descriptions going out to the police. It would have also had the authorities looking for Cynthia. By taking me, no one was the wiser and it gave them more time to get away.

Kidnapping wasn't a small crime and not that far away from murder in terms of seriousness. I had to assume at some point they'd kill me and dump my body somewhere. Whether that happened on the way out east or once we got to Halifax remained to be seen.

I had to believe by now that Stella and Blue were searching for me. They were two of the smartest and most determined people I knew and would be turning over every stone they could to find me. Blue could cover a ton of ground spying via the shadows, but Canada was a big place and she'd need a starting place. I hoped that a camera on a nearby ATM or a store's security cam caught the kidnapping on video. If they could pull a plate, that would give them something to work with. I despaired a bit because even if they had a plate and description of the vehicle, a white Econoline van wasn't uncommon and there must be thousands, if not tens of thousands, of them in Canada.

I shook that doubt off, as I had to have faith in my teammates.

***

Once we passed Montreal, we pulled off the highway and slowed down. I spotted a familiar red and white Petro Canada sign as it flashed by the front window. The van came to a stop and the Were in the passenger seat jumped out.

I thought about spinning around and kicking and screaming to draw attention to the van and hopefully get some help. I ruled out that idea almost as quickly as I'd thought of it. Even if a police cruiser happened to be filling up with gas beside us, it wouldn't work. Four Enhanced Individuals would easily be able to take out a lone police officer, and ditto for any Good Samaritan trying to help. All I'd do is get innocent people killed.

Cynthia perked up, a look of hope on her face, and I assumed she had the same thoughts about yelling for help.

I shook my head and softly said, "Don't. Calling attention to us will only get people hurt or killed."

The gruff voice of the driver said, "Listen to your boyfriend, Toots. Don't be stupid."

Cynthia gave a short nod and slumped down in defeat.

I wasn't ready to give up completely and frantically tried to think of something I could do to help get us rescued. There was a slight gap in the backdoors that was just enough to slide something thin through. I remembered my business cards in my wallet. If I could fish one out, I could push it out through the gap. But if anyone found it, they'd probably just toss it or ignore it. If I had a pen, I could write on the back and hope that might encourage someone to pass it on to the police. I realized that even just bleeding on it might be enough to alert someone.

I started slowly shifting around, trying to reach my wallet without drawing the driver's attention to what I was doing.

Just as my fingers touched the edge of my wallet, I heard the fuel nozzle being removed and realized the Were had finished fueling us up. I was running out of time. I hoped he'd go into the store to pay and maybe get some more snacks, but I barely finished that thought when the Were jumped back into his seat and said, "Let's go."

He must have prepaid with a credit card at the pump. That actually gave me hope because if Stella and Blue could get a line on who kidnapped us, I knew they could track down credit card purchases. If they found this purchase, it would give them a better idea of where we were.

I cursed as the driver started the van. We were soon in motion again, and I'd missed my opportunity. I decided that the idea, though, wasn't terrible and slowly shuffled my way back until I reached the back of the van.

I fished out my wallet and awkwardly opened it. I felt around until I found the slot with my business cards and slowly pulled them out.

Cynthia was giving me an odd look and I gave her a small shake of my head to have her ignore me. She seemed to get the message and turned her attention away from me. I separated one of the cards and felt around for the small gap. When I found it, I put the card into it and gave it a good flick with my finger. I hoped that was enough to shoot it free of the vehicle.

I slid another one from the pile and repeated the process.

Ten minutes later, I was out of cards. I knew that this was a long shot and most of the cards would probably just end up in a ditch and would be destroyed by the elements long before anyone found them. At least trying something made me feel a bit better.

I shuffled back to my original spot.

Cynthia gave me an approving nod and a smile. I wasn't sure if she figured out what I'd done or if she just knew I'd done something, but at this point we'd both take any small victory.

A short time later, I noticed Cynthia was squirming around more than she had been. My first thought was she was trying to loosen up the bonds around her ankles. The slight look of distress on her face though clued me in: she had to pee.

I cursed, as the moment I thought that my own bladder woke up and began demanding attention.

Cynthia cleared her throat and said, "I need to use the bathroom."

The Were in the passenger seat just shrugged and said, "Hold it. We're not stopping."

"Please?" asked Cynthia in a distressed tone.

The Were sighed loudly. "Look, we aren't that far from where we'll be stopping for the night. Just hold on a bit longer."

The sun went down not long after that and put the time at around 5:00 p.m.

Cynthia and I both fidgeted around, trying to ignore our bladders. I almost laughed as I thought that at least we'd added dancing to our date.

With the sun down, it made it hard to guess the time, but it felt like hours had gone by and we were still driving. With each passing moment, I wished we would arrive at wherever we were going so I could get some relief.

Then the routine changed and my hopes soared as we slowed down and pulled off the highway. I hoped this meant we were close to our destination.

Finally, the van slowed down again and made a right-hand turn. We began bouncing around as we traveled down this new road, which was either gravel or a freaking goat trail by all the bumps we were hitting.

My bladder wasn't happy, and each bump was fresh agony. I could barely see anything out the front windows now, as it was pitch black out there. I thought there might be trees flashing by, lining the side of the road, but I wasn't willing to bet on it.

Wherever we were, it felt remote and out in the middle of nowhere. This remoteness suddenly gave me more concern than my bladder. Out here, they could kill us both and nobody would be the wiser. I hoped I was just being paranoid.

Chapter 6

Tuesday, November 22

After what felt like an eternity but was probably like twenty or thirty minutes, the van came to a stop and the driver turned off the engine.

We were finally here, wherever here was.

The Weres got out of the van, leaving us in the darkened cargo area.

I heard muffled voices approaching the van, but I couldn't make out what they were saying. I assumed the Weres with their enhanced hearing wouldn't have that issue.

The voices got quieter and then after a minute, the backdoors to the van were opened. Four men were standing there. Two were the Werewolves that had driven us here. Seeing their near-identical large forms standing side by side removed any doubts I had about them being related. I guessed they were brothers or, at the very minimum, cousins.

On the opposite side of the two Weres was the shorter dark-blonde man that I recognized as the Super with unknown powers.

My attention, though, went to the brown-haired man who stood in the middle of the group with a smug look of confidence on his face. I had no doubt that this was Logan. He was an inch or two taller than the two large Weres and probably had a good twenty-plus pounds on them as well. That weight was all muscle and, even if he wasn't a Were, I wouldn't have wanted to mess with him.

His intimidating size, though, wasn't what worried me the most. What concerned me was the wild look in his emerald green eyes. Those eyes told me that his beast was very close to the surface. I'd seen the same look when Bree was having control issues. It made me wonder if it was Logan or his beast that was in charge.

Cynthia glared at Logan. If looks could kill, Logan would have just been turned into a smoldering pile of ash.

The two Were brothers, at a nod from Logan, stepped forward and climbed into the back of the van. Cynthia and I were roughly hauled to our feet and pulled from the cargo area and out into the clearing.

I spotted a shiny black SUV parked about twenty feet back beside a small rustic cabin. I assumed the SUV must be Logan's. The cabin was dark other than the porch light, which was our only source of illumination other than the moon and stars. Weres had great night vision, so to them this semi-darkness was like daytime. I wondered if the Super had night vision as one of his powers.

The moment we were out of the van, the Were holding Cynthia pushed her towards Logan. With her feet bound, she stumbled and almost fell, but Logan's lightning-fast reflexes grabbed her and yanked her to her feet and closer to him.

The Super took hold of my right arm, and the Were gripped my left, his brother nearby.

"Hey, Babe, happy to see me?" said Logan in a taunting voice.

"Fuck you, asshole," said Cynthia, who paused to gather her breath, which I assumed was to continue letting out more obscenities at Logan.

During that pause, Logan gave a nod in my direction and said, "Choose your next words carefully."

The Were in front of me turned and drove his massive fist into my stomach. I felt like I'd been hit by a brick. The blow knocked the air out of me and would have knocked me off my feet if not for the other two holding me up. On the plus side, I was amazed that I somehow hadn't managed to piss myself.

Score one for self-dignity, I thought as I tried to suck air back into my lungs and stay conscious.

"Zack!" said Cynthia.

I tried to give her a reassuring wave with my hands but forgot that they were still cuffed behind me, so I probably looked like I was convulsing.

"Please, Logan. I'm sorry. I'll come back with you; just let him go. He has nothing to do with this," pleaded Cynthia.

I braced myself as the Were in front of me made another fist, but he looked over at Logan for direction.

Logan gave a slight shake of his head and turned his attention back to Cynthia.

To my relief, the Were lowered his fist and stepped back. I thought back to how many times in this past year someone had punched me. I was starting to get a complex. I must have a very punchable-looking face or something, as I always seemed to be the one getting hit.

"Cynthia, I'm not happy with you at the moment. Worse, Pierre isn't happy with either of us. Do you know what type of position that puts me in? Did we not pay you well for your services? Did I not take you out to nice places and show you a good time? And you reward that kindness by disappearing one day out of the blue." Logan shook his head at her. "Well, what do you have to say for yourself?"

"I have to pee," said Cynthia softly.

Logan threw his head back and laughed at that. My heart went cold at the sound of his laugh, which was mocking and cruel without a trace of mirth to it.

He stopped laughing and shook his head. "That is the least of your problems at this moment."

He studied her quietly for a moment and then turned towards me.

"Zack, wasn't it?" asked Logan in a mocking tone.

I nodded and matched his stare. I knew I was playing with fire by challenging him and his beast. I might be cuffed and helpless, but I wasn't going to cower to him.

Logan gave me a snarky smile and said, "You two dating?"

I didn't want to play whatever game he was playing and just stayed quiet. His eyes glowed for a moment, and he turned to Cynthia and said, "You bitch! Just over a week and you've already started dating again."

My stomach knotted up at the pure rage in his tone. From the look in his eyes, I could see his beast was closer than ever to becoming unrestrained.

My fear grew as he turned back to me with a smile on his face. The sudden change in demeanor threw me.

"You fuck her yet?"

I glared back at him and remained silent.

"No answer; I'll take that as a no then," he said. "You missed out. Cynthia here comes across as a nice girl, but she is a total freak. I know paid whores that won't do half the things she will."

My temper flared. "I guess she had to be creative to help with your little manhood issue. You know they have these little blue pills to help with that, don't you?"

The Were in front of me drove his fist into my gut again, but at least this time I knew it was coming and braced myself. Not that it helped much.

"Logan! Please! Let him go. He has nothing to do with this," said Cynthia.

I tried to make it look like I wasn't sucking in breath, but I doubt my act fooled anyone.

Logan jerked her around more, so she was facing me, and said, "You made Pierre unhappy, but you are too valuable to harm due to your skills. You know how Pierre abhors a waste . . ."

He made air quotes when he said 'abhors,' which made me think that phrase must be a favorite of his boss. Logan himself struck me as more of a single-syllable type of guy.

". . . but you need to be punished, so this is on you," he finished with a brief nod in my direction, and I tensed up waiting for more pain to come my way.

"NO! Please, Logan," pleaded Cynthia, but the rest of what she was going to say was cut off as a sharp crack filled the night.

The pain of my left knee shattering after a vicious kick from the Were beside me slammed home a moment later, and I went down hard. I hadn't even hit the ground yet and more kicks from the three of them were coming in.

The moment I fell, I turtled as best I could to protect myself but was hampered by my arms being cuffed behind me. I tucked my chin to my chest and curled up in a ball.

In the haze of pain and fear, my dark humor kicked in as I thought, *this is now officially my worst date ever.*

That humor disappeared a moment later as a boot viciously drove itself into my lower back with enough force to do real damage to my kidneys. Two things happened simultaneously after that: I felt my bladder let go and a flood of wet warmth began trickling down my legs, and I lifted my head and let out a scream of agony that Blue and Stella might have been able to hear in Hamilton.

That lifting of my head was a mistake, as another boot came in and caught me square in my temple. I mercifully blacked out after that.

Chapter 7

Tuesday, November 23

<u>Stella - Earlier that day</u>

"Fiddlesticks!" I said as I fruitlessly examined the power-blocking platform for the umpteenth time.

I was puzzled and frustrated due to not being able to figure out why the power-blocking field was leaking on one side of the platform. All the individual components were testing fine, so there was no logical reason for the issue.

I lifted my brass magnifying goggles and took a sip of now cold tea.

Overall, the power-blocking platform was a success. It was certainly easier just to place Emma on it rather than trying to put on her power-blocking bracelets when she lost control of her power. My ungainly Hyde hands weren't meant for such delicate work as closing tiny bracelets.

If I couldn't find the leak, then we'd have to live with it as is. There was some risk involved with that option as our last session aptly demonstrated. It was only luck that I'd already gotten Emma on the platform before the leak had forced me out of my Hyde form.

I shuddered as I thought about what would have happened if that sequence of events had been reversed. Emma's pain power would have incapacitated me, and it only would have ended if she'd passed out or died from the pain.

There is a mark on the platform on the side that had the leak, so as long as I don't approach it from that side, the leak will not be an issue, I thought, trying to reassure myself that the problem wasn't too bad.

I took a deep, calming breath and lowered my goggles again. I was studying the coils on the edge of the platform when something caught my eye. A closer look at one of the coils brought a smile to my face. I hurriedly reached for a pair of tweezers and used them to snag a piece of the long dark hair that was snagged under the coil. With the utmost care, I gently pulled the hair free and smiled in triumph as I held it up for inspection.

Ten minutes later, I'd tested the platform by standing near it in my Hyde form and was overjoyed that the leak was gone. I was just putting the protective cover back on the platform when Blue emerged from the shadows in the corner of the lab.

"Curious," Blue said, "Zack is not answering my texts or calls."

I tightened the final screw on the cover and said, "He's probably just lost track of time on his date with Cynthia."

Blue frowned and shook her head. "That was my initial thought too, but Cynthia is required to work with Marion at noon."

I lifted my iPhone off the bench and saw that it was just past noon.

That *was* odd. While I had never met Cynthia, she was Marion's niece, and if she had inherited any of Marion's work ethic, there was no way she'd be late for a shift.

"I'll use the Find My Phone application to locate where Zack is," I said, unlocking my phone. There were no bars showing on my screen, and I cursed the lousy reception down here. "Change of plans. Let's go home so I can get a decent signal."

Blue nodded. She waited for me to grab my stuff and then we headed to the corner of the lab. Blue made a sharp gesture with her hand and opened a portal in the shadows and stepped through. I followed on her heels, and we came out in the living room at our house.

The phone showed that I now had a strong signal, so I opened the app and attempted to locate Zack's phone.

"Odd, the app can't locate Zack's phone."

With a thoughtful look on her face, Blue said, "He might be engaged in amorous activities with Miss Ryerson and turned off the phone."

I snorted at the first part and shook my head. "The chances of Zack getting lucky on a second date are slim."

"I fail to understand why that is a remote possibility; he is a healthy male with all the necessary equipment. He is also reasonably—"

I held up my hand to cut Blue off and said, "We'll discuss human mating rituals at a later time. For now, just take my word for it. The more pressing issue is that the app couldn't find Zack's phone. It should be able to locate the phone even if it was turned off."

Blue nodded. "I will bow to your wisdom in these matters. Besides, even if I was correct, the duration of these encounters is not known to be one of Zack's strengths." I giggled at Blue's comment. "If the app can locate a phone that is turned off, then there are only three reasons why it could not be found: the battery is completely dead, the phone has been destroyed, or the phone is in an area with no cellular coverage," she said.

I pondered Blue's reasoning and said, "A dead battery is unlikely. Zack is religious about charging his phone each night, so he would have left here with a full charge."

"Then destroyed or lack of coverage remain as our only two options."

"Marion's apartment is downtown, and The House of Bacon is on Upper James. Both areas would have strong cell coverage."

Blue said, "By elimination, that leaves Zack's phone being destroyed, which does not bode well."

I wanted to argue that Zack was fine, but if Blue was correct about the phone, then Zack was probably in trouble. "Let's move up to the office."

When we arrived upstairs, I suggested that Blue call Marion. I called The House of Bacon.

My concern grew when the hostess said that she found the reservation for Zack Stevens but informed me that he and his party never arrived.

Blue ended her call and said that Marion was quite angry that Cynthia hadn't shown up for work yet and that she hadn't heard anything from either of them.

"I'm not liking this. Let me call Rob and see if anything odd has happened in the city. Can you check the Internet and see if there is anything local that might explain Zack's disappearance?"

Blue nodded and sat down at the other desk and began typing away at the computer.

Rob was a Hamilton police officer and Zack's best friend. He wouldn't be able to do anything officially, as Zack hadn't been missing long enough, but he would try and help.

He answered after a couple of rings and we exchanged greetings. I got right down to it and explained what was going on and asked him to look at the incident reports for this morning and see if anything stood out.

"I'm not seeing anything out of the ordinary so far. Hold on, there was a report of an abduction around nine this morning and the location is right by Marion's building." Rob groaned and then added, "Never mind, false alarm."

An abduction right by Marion's building sounded promising, and I was curious why he dismissed it. *"Was there a report or not?"*

"Yeah, there is a report, but the call was from Rosie Whitlock. Rosie is a bit of a legend around here. Last month she called 911 to report that squirrels were plotting to kill her. The month before that she called in a report of space aliens stealing her chocolate. Those are just a few of the many calls we've gotten from her over the years."

"Can you look at the details of the call?"

"Sure, hold on," said Rob.

He came on a few moments later and said, "It looks like Rosie might be right for a change. She reported a young couple being pushed into a van against their will by four men. Rosie is in her eighties, so Zack and Cynthia would fit her definition of young. I'll head over to her place for an interview and get back to you."

I thanked him and we ended the call. I told Blue about what Rob had said, and we decided to proceed under the assumption that Rosie really had seen a kidnapping. That meant it was time to find some clues so we could locate Zack.

***

A few hours later, we'd confirmed Zack and Cynthia had been abducted by visiting the scene of the crime. We bribed the manager of the building across the street from Marion's, which had gotten us access to video recordings from the security camera that clearly showed four men grabbing Zack and Cynthia and forcing them into a white van.

Rob had gotten access to the security cameras for Marion's building, which also had footage of the kidnapping.

Unfortunately, neither video had a clear shot of the license plate on the van. The footage of the kidnappers also hadn't yielded much. We had images of four Caucasian males in their late twenties or early thirties, with no visible tattoos or distinguishing marks.

One thing of note was the large man who seemed to effortlessly pick up Zack and toss him over his shoulder before dumping him in the van. Zack wasn't overly heavy, but a normal human would have needed much more effort to carry him than what was shown on the video. This meant at least one of the suspects was Enhanced.

Rob and I sent our videos to Bobby Knight at EIRT, and an alert of the suspects, the van, and Zack and Cynthia's descriptions had gone out to all law enforcement agencies in Canada.

Blue and I were now back home in the office to look through Zack's electronic case files for potential suspects. Between his hero days and bounty hunting, Zack had made a lot of enemies, and we were checking to see if any of them who might hold a grudge had been released from prison recently.

The search so far wasn't yielding any promising leads. I could almost feel the clock ticking, as I knew that the more time that elapsed, the less chance there was of the kidnappers being found. "Should we get Olivia and Bree back here to help?"

Blue shook her head. "No. The English Vampire Court will not allow Olivia to be released from their custody, and Bree is on an important mission for the Were Council."

Olivia had managed to get herself in hot water during her time at court. She was currently confined to the English Court pending her trial in a few weeks. Blue and I had argued about whether to tell Zack, but Blue insisted that we shouldn't. She was concerned that Zack wasn't handling his loss of powers well and worried that the news might drive him back to the bottle. He'd been sober for a month now, and while he tried to put on a brave face, it was obvious he was struggling to cope with his new situation. I deferred to Blue's judgment but knew Zack would not be happy with us when he found out. "I could talk to Sarah; she might be able to convince Elizabeth to release Liv to our custody until we've found Zack."

"The English Vampire Court is not known for its flexibility in these matters and your pleas would be a wasted endeavor."

I wanted to argue but knew that Blue was right. While Sarah and Elizabeth had a soft spot for me, it wouldn't be enough for them to override protocol. "What about Bree? We could just borrow her for a couple of days and then return her to her mission."

"That would not be advisable, as we would risk the wrath of the Were Council. Besides, Bree and Olivia would be of limited use at this moment. Neither is particularly proficient at research." I felt my shoulders slump at Blue's assessment and was about to get back to the files when she said, "If we find a solid suspect and locate Zack, we can discuss again borrowing Liv and Bree for the rescue operation."

Blue gave me a devious smile as I turned back to my screen. It hit me that Blue was planning on using our teammates if we found where Zack was being held. With her powers, she'd be able to sneak both of them out for a few hours with the court and council none the wiser.

I got back to my search with a renewed sense of purpose. Now we just needed to figure out who grabbed Zack and Cynthia before it was too late.

Chapter 8

Wednesday, November 23

The first thing I noticed when I became conscious was that every part of me hurt. Bile rose in my throat due to my nausea, and it took every ounce of willpower I had to force it back down.

I was in motion again, and every movement magnified the pain. I kept my eyes closed and just tried to figure out where I was and what was going on. I was pretty sure I had another concussion; at this rate, I was going to be brain-dead by the end of this year.

For a brief moment, I thought I was back in the van again, but that didn't feel right. The engine noise was too loud and not the right sound. The cold breeze and the damp, musty smell it carried clued me in that I was on a boat.

I remained still, eyes closed, the whole time I'd come to, not wanting to give away that I was awake. I took a moment to assess my injuries and instantly knew I was in bad shape. My left knee throbbed, and my legs felt incredibly heavy. It took me a moment to realize the heaviness wasn't due to an injury but rather because something with some weight to it was wrapped around my legs.

Images of bad mob movies came to me. My weighted legs reminded me of the scenes where mobsters threatened to fit people with concrete shoes to go sleep with the fishes.

A metallic *clunk* as the boat hit another wave clued me into what was weighing my legs down. They'd wrapped heavy chains around my lower legs.

My panic rose at that, but I pushed it back and returned to assessing my injuries. The sharp pain radiating from my lower back area had me the most worried, as I was pretty sure there was internal damage. My sides hurt, and I recognized the feeling of cracked ribs. My right eye felt swollen near where I'd been hit in the temple, and I was pretty sure I couldn't open that eye. My arms were numb, but that was probably from being cuffed in that position for so long and not due to an injury. Even through the numbness, I could feel pain from my ring and pinkie fingers on my left hand and assumed they were broken. Other than bruises and general aches over my entire body, I was pretty sure I'd found all the damage.

In short, I was in rough shape in a bad place, and things were looking pretty bleak. I doubted they were taking me out for a pleasure cruise and figured they'd soon stop the boat and toss me over the side.

"Is this far enough, Logan?" yelled a voice by my feet.

"No, keep going," said Logan from an area near my waist.

"C'mon, Logan, it's cold out here. I want to get back to the cabin and warm up," said another voice just ahead of me.

"We are in enough trouble with Pierre. We do this right and dump him with the others. Unless you want to tell Pierre that we dumped him in another spot because you were cold?"

The constant loud drone of the engine and the sounds of the boat cutting through the water were the only response.

The conversation confirmed my fears and my thoughts turned dark. I hoped that Stella and Blue would eventually rescue Cynthia and avenge me. I'd pictured dying a lot of ways but being trussed up like a turkey and dumped in a lake by some two-bit hoods hadn't been one of them. I'd always assumed I'd go out making a stand in an epic against-all-odds battle or due to a mid-air collision with a Canada goose.

My mind began trying to find a way out of this mess, but I wasn't seeing a lot of options here. With the busted knee and chained legs, I wouldn't be able to stand. Add in that my arms were still cuffed with power blockers, and things looked even grimmer. It wouldn't have surprised me if Blue had eventually gotten to taking out three Enhanced opponents with nothing but bites and headbutts in her training sessions, but we hadn't made it that far yet.

Bree and Liv popped into my thoughts, and I suddenly felt even worse. The last time I'd seen them was before they left. I'd been drunk and said some shitty things to them. I hated that that night would be their last memory of me and wished I'd gotten the chance to apologize.

The engine throttled down and turned off, leaving everything eerily quiet. My panic grew as I realized this was it.

The boat rocked around as the three of them got up, and I felt hands grab me.

"Wait, get the cuffs off him," said Logan.

"Why?" asked another voice.

"Because those cuffs are expensive, and you know how Pierre *abhors* waste."

I almost laughed, as I swore I could picture Logan doing freaking air quotes around Pierre's so-called favorite word again.

Hands roughly flipped me over on my front, and it took everything I had not to cry out in pain and reveal that I was awake. Letting them think I was out cold might just be the edge I needed to get out of this alive.

As someone fumbled with the power-blocking cuffs, my hopes began to grow. I mentally cursed about not having my Air powers, as I was limited in what I could do with my new Ice power. I started frantically thinking of options. Once the cuffs were off, I could try to attack with my Ice powers, but even if I could control them, there were three of them. If I missed any of them, I'd be a sitting duck.

Another option came to mind, but it was almost as bad as the first idea. Both were risky, but the second was probably the better of the two crappy options.

I felt my Ice powers come flooding back as the cuffs were removed. All my focus went into preventing ice from forming on my hands, which would expose my powers.

The three of them reached down and grabbed me in different places. I fought down a scream as my whole body cried out in pain when I was lifted off the deck. I managed to keep silent but felt sweat breaking out across my brow from the effort.

"On three?" asked one of the voices.

They began rocking me in the air, and a voice started counting. When the voice reached the count of three, I found myself flying out into the cool air.

I sucked in one last deep breath and hit the water a moment after that. I felt my body shift from the weight of the chains, and I was soon heading feet first towards the bottom. I tried to remain calm, but as I rapidly sank deeper into the dark waters, that became a supreme test of will.

My whole body tingled warmly, and it hit me that my Ice powers liked being in this freezing water. It reminded me of how I used to feel between the Tesla coils when I had my Air powers. The feeling calmed my fears, and I focused on what needed to be done.

The sound of the boat motor starting up came to me as a muffled echo through the water and added more reassurance that things were going to plan. Well, maybe it was less of a *plan* and more a desperate last-ditch gamble. My goal was to encase my body in enough ice that I'd float to the surface of the lake like an ice cube in a glass of water.

I called on my Ice powers and began coating my entire body below my arms in thick ice. A bit of panic bubbled up, as I was still rapidly descending to the bottom of the lake even as the ice around me grew in mass.

I hit the bottom unexpectedly and that almost ended me, as the pain of my busted knee had me wanting to scream out loud. If I'd screamed and expelled the air in my lungs, this adventure would have come to a quick end.

It was hard using my powers in the pitch black. I had no idea if I was actually still growing the ice around me or just shooting it off randomly into the water. But the feeling of comfort around me continued to grow and I took that to mean the ice was building.

I was also reassured by the fading motor noise of the boat. It sounded like the three goons were almost gone.

The need to exhale and take a breath grew, and I was becoming more and more aware of that with each passing second.

C'mon, c'mon, I thought as I kept applying more ice to my body.

The burning feeling in my lungs was starting to build, and I was getting lightheaded.

My hopes began to soar as I felt myself lift off the bottom. I continued releasing the ice around me, focusing on trying not to breathe and staying calm.

I mentally cheered as I began rising in the black water, but that victory was tempered by the growing agony in my lungs; every fiber of my being was begging me to take a breath.

It felt like I was picking up speed, but another part of me wondered if it would be enough.

I let out a small breath and immediately clamped my right hand over my nose and mouth to stop more from escaping. I was almost in a full-blown panic now, as I knew I had just seconds left before I started inhaling water.

It seemed like the darkness wasn't as absolute now, and I prayed that meant I was near the surface.

I couldn't take it anymore and let my hand slip away from my nose and mouth to let out my final breath. I fleetingly hoped that I might get a hot-looking Valkyrie to escort me to Valhalla so I could join my departed mother.

Those thoughts vanished as I suddenly breached the surface of the water like a whale and shot into the air. I gratefully sucked in air as tears of joy streamed down my face.

A moment later, I sputtered as I landed face down in the water. I frantically thrashed with my arms and then sighed in relief as I rotated around so that my face was out of the water again.

Floating there, I enjoyed the feeling of being able to breathe freely again.

I grew concerned as the faint noise of a motor reached me and glanced around in worry. If they'd noticed me exit the water and were coming back, I was a sitting duck. Eventually I relaxed, as I couldn't see them, and the noise of the motor continued getting fainter with each passing second.

After a bit, I'd recovered enough to realize that I couldn't float here all night. I began freaking out again as I looked around but couldn't see anything but water. I calmed, though, when I spotted a tree line way off in the distance.

I started to paddle with my hands to turn myself in that direction and let out a cry of pain. I lifted my left hand and blanched when I saw that my ring and pinkie fingers were bent and sticking out at odd, unnatural angles.

I brought my right hand up and focused on calling my Ice power again. In the back of my mind, I was chiding myself for using them so much, as this was yet another setback to getting my Air powers back, but I ignored those thoughts.

Survive first, worry about powers later, I thought.

I mentally nodded in satisfaction as I locked the broken fingers and lower part of my hand in thick ice to keep them immobile. The ice around them also did wonders for the pain.

It dawned on me that my ribs, kidneys, and knee also seemed very happy being surrounded by ice, as the pain from all of them had lessened considerably.

I tried my left hand in the water as I started paddling towards land and was pleased that the pain was now manageable.

After what felt like thirty minutes of paddling towards the shore, I tilted my head back to check my progress and was a bit underwhelmed by how far away it still was. It would have been nice to have my legs free so I could kick with them too, but that wasn't happening. I cringed at the thought of moving my left knee in that manner.

Thankfully, the lake was fairly calm, and the waves were small to nonexistent at times. It didn't feel like there was any type of current or undertow that I was fighting as I kept paddling.

Do lakes even have a current or an undertow? I idly thought and then mentally shrugged.

It was times like these that I realized I was too much of a city dweller and I was seriously out of my element at this moment. I giggled at that last part. My power was Ice and I was in a freezing cold lake; I couldn't be more *in* my element if I tried.

I just needed to stay awake and keep paddling. I caught myself drifting off a few times but managed to catch myself before falling asleep. I started singing sea chanties to keep myself conscious. I tried a few lines of "What Shall We Do with a Drunken Sailor" but felt foolish and stopped.

I wondered now if my fatigue and injuries were making me giddy, and that concerned me.

Have I traded a quick death for a longer, more drawn-out one? I thought.

My thoughts turned to Cynthia being stuck in Logan's clutches again, and that surge of anger helped fuel my alertness and put some more vigor into my paddling.

After what felt like forever but was probably only a couple of hours, I finally slid up on the shoreline. I used my leaden arms to drag myself up the beach until I was out of the water.

I heard Blue's voice in my mind, lecturing me that if I was in better shape a couple hours of paddling in a lake wouldn't have been an issue. She was probably right, but I ignored that and cursed when I realized I'd gotten stuck due to the weight of the massive amount of ice around my body. The ice, though, was mostly round, so rather than dragging myself forward, I slowly pulled myself around until I was parallel to the beach. I then awkwardly rolled myself farther up the rocky shore until I was a few feet from the water. I dragged a large rock that was just off in front of me around and down and wedged it under the ice to stop me from rolling back into the water.

I tried wiggling around to free myself from the ice, but I was completely stuck in place. I wasn't going anywhere soon. The weather was cool but the temperature was above freezing, so I knew nature would eventually take care of the ice for me.

By then I was so exhausted that rather than continuing to fight to get free, I just closed my eyes and blissfully drifted off.

Chapter 9

Wednesday, November 23

A loud *boom* woke me from my peaceful slumber, and I wondered what the heck was happening. I blinked my eyes open and was greeted by driving rain hitting me. It was still nighttime, and off in the distance the sky lit up with flashes of lightning from the approaching storm. Other than knowing it was night, I had no idea what the time was. I once again found myself wishing that I was more of a Johnny Woodsman. I was sure that someone with more outdoor experience would have a rough idea of the time by the position of the moon or the stars. Not that I could see either of them through the dark clouds.

My mouth and throat were parched so I opened my mouth and lay there drinking the rain. It wasn't coffee, but the cool wetness felt wonderful going down my throat.

After drinking my fill, I glanced down at the ice that was still around me. The rain had done wonders in reducing its mass, but I still couldn't slip its grip. I fished around and found a rock about the size of my hand that had an edge to it and got to work chipping myself free from my icy tomb.

Eventually I managed to break away enough of the ice around my chest that I was able to sit up. I gasped as I did this, both my ribs and my kidneys strongly voicing their objections to the movement.

A few calming deep breaths later, I focused on my next task, which was freeing my legs. I sighed and started chipping away again at the ice.

I eventually rescued my legs from the ice but the heavy chains around them meant I wasn't going anywhere fast, especially with my messed-up knee. I spotted the padlock that secured the chains. I reached down and wrapped my hands around the lock and focused on sending as much cold into it as possible.

I smiled as I swore I could feel the metal contract in my hands. I put the lock down on top of the chain links and picked up my handy rock. I took a hard swing and slammed the rock down on the lock. I cursed at how much the impact hurt in my hand. But the cursing was short-lived because I noticed the lock had popped open.

I slipped the lock from the chains and began unwinding them from around my legs, uttering curses the whole time. My knee radiated pain each time I had to lift my leg.

By the time I'd freed myself, my brow was covered in sweat and I was shaking. The storm was also getting louder and closer.

I supposed *free* was a relative term. With the busted knee, I still wasn't going anywhere fast. I moved my hands to my injured knee and called on more ice until it was covered by a makeshift ice cast.

With that taken care of, I focused on my surroundings. I spotted a downed tree branch about six feet away, which gave me an idea. I half crawled and half dragged myself across the rocky beach until I got to it.

I reached out and was pleased to find it wasn't stuck on anything and that it looked like it would suit my purpose, as it was about two inches thick, five feet long, and reasonably straight. I took a deep breath and called on my Ice powers again and formed a four-inch ball around one of the ends.

With that in place, I gingerly got to my feet using the branch for support. I tucked the ice-covered end of the branch under my left armpit and tried to hobble down the beach. It was slow going but doable. The two broken fingers on my left hand made gripping my makeshift crutch tricky, but thankfully they were the least used of my fingers.

I stopped to catch my breath and figure out a plan. I was sore, hungry, and exhausted. I looked around to figure out where to go but the only things around me were water and trees. I'd hoped to see a light or some sign of civilization to at least give me an idea of which direction to head.

The lightning lit up the sky in the distance and something gleamed in the temporary light about ten feet farther down the beach. I carefully made my way down the treacherous wet and rocky shoreline to investigate. The object turned out to be a slightly bent aluminum tent pole. I was about to toss it back into the woods but decided to keep it. The pole was light and easy enough to carry in my right hand and provided another bit of support.

The upside to moving down the shoreline was that just to the right there was a small stream—well, more like a trickle of water—that cut deep into the trees. The area around it was clear, so it would be easier to walk along than cutting through the thick woods.

Following the stream seemed like a better idea than staying along the shore. The whole area seemed incredibly deserted, and the lack of lights along the shoreline meant that the kidnappers' cabin might be the only structure along the entire lake. Wandering unknowingly up to that cabin would be a very bad mistake. The Weres would hear or smell me well before I would them. Worse, one or two might be out in their beast forms hunting deer or something. If they found me, I'd be dead before I even knew it. The best course of action was for me to find someone and get help for Cynthia. I smiled at the thought of Stella's Hyde form stomping the Werewolves into paste or Blue's magic flaming sword removing Logan's smug head from his shoulders.

Buoyed by those pleasant images, I hobbled along the side of the stream for a bit but soon started to tire and questioned how far I'd make it in my current condition.

I stopped as I came to a fork in the path. To my right, the stream continued, and to my left, there was a path that led to a rocky slope that turned into a hill. The hill was high enough that it was above the treetops, silhouetted by the flashes of lightning in the distance.

If I could get to the top of that hill, I'd be able to see for miles and possibly find some sign of humanity. The downside was that the trek up that slope was going to be brutal. I glanced right to the flat stream that led deeper into the woods as I pondered my options.

I suddenly felt like a character in a bad Choose Your Own Adventure novel. *Do you want to go right and follow the stream? Turn to page 49. If you want to attempt the dangerous rocky slope, turn to page 78.*

The cynical part of me figured the first one would end in disaster: *You wander deep into the woods for days until you collapse. The scavengers of the forest enjoy feasting on your dead flesh. The End.*

And the second probably wouldn't be much better. *You make it part way up the slope but lose your footing. You tumble hard down the hill and snap your neck at the bottom on impact. The End.*

Another bright flash of lightning pulled me from my dark musings and sparked an idea. The idea was so crazy that it showed how desperate I'd become. But the more I thought about it, the more I thought it was my only chance.

Well, Zack, sometimes you just have to roll the dice and hope you don't crap out, I thought as I turned to my left and began heading for the hill.

I tried to take things slow and steady, but the lightning storm was getting closer and I needed to act fast.

I gritted my teeth together and continued working up the hill as fast as I dared.

Walking up an uneven incline using makeshift crutches truly sucked. I moaned to myself as I kept climbing.

I lost count of how many times I almost went down after losing my footing, but by some miracle, I managed to stay upright. The effort was taking a grueling toll on me, though, and I'd needed to stop a couple of times just to catch my breath.

Six feet from the top of the summit, my luck gave out on me. The end of my improvised wooden crutch slipped on a wet rock, and I went down hard. The crutch and my aluminum pole slipped from my hands and began sliding down the hill. I disregarded the crutch and focused on saving the pole. The moment I landed on my butt, I ignored the pain of the impact and immediately lunged out with my right foot to pin the pole down to stop it from going any farther down the hill.

I exhaled slowly in relief, as I'd just managed to catch the very tip of it under my foot. I carefully shuffled down the slope a bit until I could lean forward and grab the pole with my shaking hand.

The moment I had it, a loud peal of thunder shook the night and made me jump. It also meant I was running out of time. With the pole grasped tightly in my hand like it was the most precious treasure ever, I started crawling and dragging myself up the last bit of the hill.

The sharp rocks made me very aware of every inch of progress. I cursed as I pulled myself higher with my bloody hands and hoped this idea was worth it.

I giggled like a madman as I realized that either the plan would work and I'd be saved, or it wouldn't and I wouldn't be in pain anymore, as I'd be dead.

I grunted as I crested the hill and rolled myself to the center of the flat plateau I found at the top.

A huge flash of lightning lit up the night, and I watched in awe as sparks flew from a tree it struck not 400 feet away. The deafening explosion of thunder followed not even a second later and shook me to my core. The same fear I had when I was sinking in the lake earlier returned. My heart was beating so fast and hard that I swore I could hear it.

I took a deep breath and raised the aluminum pole into the air with my right hand and realized again how insanely stupid my plan was. The pole wavered in the air a bit, but I didn't lower it. This was my one shot at getting out of this mess; I was going to kickstart my Air powers or die trying.

Now I just needed the lightning to find me.

Another bright flash lit up the night sky, but it was further away.

"ODIN, YOU BEARDED SON OF BITCH! FIX ME OR FRY ME!" I yelled into the storm.

Not ten seconds after that, I was blinded by a flash of light so bright I worried my eyeballs had melted. Those worries turned to screams as red-hot pain traveled down my arm and my entire body felt like it was on fire.

And then there was darkness.

Chapter 10

Wednesday, November 23

Waking up in pain was starting to become a theme for me and I really wasn't a fan. I blinked my eyes up at an overcast day. Some birds were chirping happily nearby, and I cursed them for it. I was lying with the top half of my body on the edge of the plateau, my legs hanging off it. Everything hurt.

I was puzzled about how I ended up over here when I'd been in the middle of the plateau to begin with. It dawned on me that the lightning strike must have blasted me over.

I raised my right hand to clear the sleep from my eyes and stopped dead. My hand was locked into a blackened fist of charred flesh. I swallowed in fear as I stared at it. From the look of it, I should be screaming in agony, but the truth was I couldn't feel my hand and that worried me more; the dangerous burns are the ones you can't feel, as that meant there was serious nerve damage.

It looks like I'll be using the European grip for a while in any late-night porn sessions, I thought with a dry chuckle.

Dark purple fractal patterns ran under my skin from my right wrist up to the sleeve of my golf shirt. I brought my left hand up. I mentally sighed at the sight of it as I realized that I was down to two working fingers and a thumb as the sum of my functioning digits. I carefully lifted my sleeve and the purple jagged marks continued. I wondered how far they went. The designs were actually kind of cool and looked like some sort of funky tattoo.

While I was in pain, physically as weak as a kitten, and more than a little concerned about my right hand, something else slowly started dawning on me. I was alive. But more than that, I felt alive for the first time since my fight with the lich over a month ago.

I held up my left hand and tried to cast some sparks. I cursed and cheered as a twenty-foot arc of lightning shot from my hand and into the sky. I giggled almost hysterically as I tried blinking away the spots in my eyes from the bright electricity.

The Hurricane is back, baby!

I broke out into a coughing fit and brought my left hand up to cover my mouth. My earlier glee faded as my hand came away bloody. I was coughing up blood, which I didn't think was a good sign and seriously dampened my excitement.

I ignored that for the moment, as I was able to sense that I was brimming with power. I felt I had enough power to both fly to the moon and power the whole of Toronto.

I quickly began thinking of a plan. I was in bad shape, but with my powers back, taking down a few Weres and an unknown Super was doable if I struck hard and fast.

The plan ended up being straightforward: find the cabin, take out the bad guys, rescue Cynthia, and get healed. There was no Plan B.

A smile came to my parched lips as I called on my Air powers and gently lifted myself into the air. Being off the ground instantly lessened the pain I was in, as I used the air around me to support my busted knees and ribs. I slowly rotated a full 360 degrees as I hovered in the air, making sure my control was good.

Oh yeah! I thought in satisfaction as I completed the turn.

I turned a bit more until I could see the lake and put some serious wind behind me. I felt my eyes well up a bit as I shot towards the lake and felt the wind on my face for the first time in over a month.

Flying sure beats hobbling my broken ass down that hill, I thought.

I was probably doing close to a hundred klicks an hour as I shot over the lake and let out a cheer as the surface of the water parted behind me in my wake.

Even narrowly avoiding the flock of ducks I'd startled didn't dampen my joy.

I eased up on my speed as a stray thought entered my mind. What if getting my powers back was just temporary? Hitting the water at a hundred kilometers from a height of sixty feet up would probably be the end of me if that was the case.

Because I could feel the power flowing through me, I pushed those doubts aside and put the pedal down again.

In the back of mind, I knew I was pushing my speed for another reason. While my powers seemed to be in peak form, my body wasn't. The sooner I got to Cynthia, the sooner I could get some much-needed healing. I was more concerned about my body giving out on me than I was about the threat that Logan and his gang posed at the moment.

When I reached the center of the lake, I banked left, remembering that was the direction the boat went last night.

After what felt like five minutes of heading in that direction, I started questioning my choice and sense of direction. What was odd was the lack of cottages along the lakeshore I'd been following for the last few minutes. In most lakes in Ontario, the shoreline would be packed with them, and I assumed that would be the same in Quebec. That either meant the lake was part of a national or provincial park and building wasn't permitted or someone owned a crap-ton of land around the lake and didn't want any neighbors.

Just as I was about to give up and turn back to try another direction, I spotted a cabin up ahead. Even better, there was a familiar white van parked in front of it. My unease grew when I didn't see Logan's shiny black SUV anywhere. If he'd left with Cynthia, I was in trouble. With each passing minute, I could feel my strength fading and knew I desperately needed healing.

I slowed down as I approached but gained some altitude. I readied my Electrical powers and did a flyover of the property to scope it out. I'd hoped that one or two of the bad guys might be out of the cabin and give me an easy target, but no such luck. The place was as quiet as a tomb.

I did a wide arc in the air until the front door of the cabin was in front of me and then went into a dive, heading straight for it. I began building up a charge for my Air powers and, twenty feet from the front door, released a concentrated blast of hurricane-force wind.

The wood door blew off its hinges like it had been hit by a giant sledgehammer. My heart almost stopped when it flew into the cabin like a deadly Frisbee and headed straight for the bed that I could see Cynthia was in.

She screamed as the door crashed off the wall a few feet above her head and bounced off to the right, which was thankfully away from her.

I entered the cabin and pushed air in front of me to bring me to a hard stop. I shifted the air beneath me so I could hover in place and frantically assessed the situation. I spotted the Super with the unknown powers getting up from the kitchen table. I noticed there was a black, wilted potted plant on the center of the table, which I thought was odd.

The Super cursed at the hot coffee that had spilled down the front of his shirt and pants. His eyes locked on my mine and went wide.

He began raising his hands in my direction, but I was quicker and lashed out with another powerful blast of air.

The blast sent him, his chair, and the table tumbling deeper into the cabin like leaves on a gusty fall day. A second later, all three hit the kitchen counter with a loud crash.

Before the Super had even hit the ground, I followed up with a lightning attack powerful enough to fry an elephant. The bright blue electricity slammed into him, but he didn't even cry out or stir. It was then I noticed that his neck was at an odd angle and realized that my lightning attack had been completely unnecessary.

No such thing as overkill, I thought with a grim smile.

I glanced around to find the Weres, but it was just the dead Super, Cynthia, and me in the cabin.

"Zack! You're alive!" exclaimed Cynthia, with pure joy in her tone.

I nodded and asked, "Where are the Weres?"

"Gone. They left a couple of hours ago. Pierre wanted them back in Halifax."

I released the power I'd been building up in preparation for another lightning strike. The threats were gone.

Cynthia shifted nervously around on the bed, and I saw the power-blocking cuffs she was wearing were secured to the iron headboard. "Is the leech dead?"

I frowned at the question, as I wasn't sure what leech she was talking about. I glanced around and spotted the dead Super and clued in. Leeches were Supers that could steal an Enhanced Individual's powers, and I shuddered to think how the fight might have gone if he'd attacked first. "Yeah, he's dead."

"Good," said Cynthia in an ice-cold tone that surprised me.

"Did he hurt you?" I asked in concern.

"No, but he'd been threatening to whither my fingers off one at a time."

Cynthia's comment made me realize that I'd mistaken his powers. The dead plant on the table made more sense now. The guy couldn't steal powers; he leeched life. The plant must have been a demonstration. This type of leech was even rarer than the type that could steal powers. He could literally suck the life out of any living thing. Usually they'd get stronger or faster or some sort of healing benefit from it. They were like the opposite of healers, and that type of power along with the Super's threats certainly explained Cynthia's frosty reply earlier.

Cynthia moved around again and the metal of the power-blocking cuffs rattling against the iron headboard brought my focus back to the here and now.

I hovered over to the dead leech and used my Air powers to lift his body from the floor, patting down his pockets with my left hand. I felt something hard and metallic in the right front pocket of his jeans. I slipped my two working left fingers into the pocket and extracted the keys that were in there.

There was a key fob for the van outside and five other keys attached to the key ring. Of the five keys, one was the small odd-shaped one that I'd hoped to see.

I flew over to Cynthia's prone form on the bed. Close up, she looked a bit worse for wear but seemed to be in good health and had no visible injuries, which was a relief. I tried the small key on the cuff around her right wrist and exhaled in satisfaction when it clicked open. I repeated this with the other cuff and freed Cynthia.

She gave a low moan of pleasure as her powers came flooding back and almost leaped from the bed. I cried out in pain as she embraced me in a tight hug.

Cynthia immediately released me. "Sorry."

She then looked over me with a critical eye that made me smile, as Marion had given me that same disapproving look many times. Her glance made the family resemblance between her and her aunt much more obvious. "Jesus, Zack, you look like shit. Lie down before you fall down."

"Yes, ma'am."

I hovered myself above the bed and then carefully lowered myself down. I grimaced when I landed on the firm mattress and the various injured parts of my body loudly voiced their objections. I settled and released my powers.

Cynthia, with a serious look on her face, was moving her hands slowly above my body to assess the damage.

Her hands moved over my face and I suddenly passed out again.

Chapter 11

Wednesday, November 23

I woke up and smiled. For once I wasn't in pain or nursing a concussion. My smile grew when I realized I was naked under the blankets and Cynthia was snuggled up beside me.

For a brief moment, I pondered if I'd died and gone to heaven. I also wondered if we'd had sex, but I hoped that wasn't the case because I had no memory of it.

Thankfully, my brain started making sense of my surroundings. I could feel that Cynthia was fully dressed beside me, which probably ruled out my sex concern. I was confused about why I was naked but then spotted my clothes hanging on a line in the corner of the cabin. I vaguely recalled that they had been more than a little damp from my swim in the lake and being out in the rain all night. The clothes seemed cleaner and in much better shape than I remembered them being. The golf shirt, though, was badly charred on the right sleeve and there was clearly no saving it. Cynthia must have washed them in the sink or something and hung them up to dry.

I brought my right hand up to rub the sleep out of my eyes and was pleased to see new pink skin covering it and that it seemed fully functional. The hand did itch slightly, as did various parts of my body where I'd been injured, which I thought was odd. When Marion healed me, it was common for the healed areas to tingle for a day or so. I speculated that Cynthia's healing technique was the reason for the itchiness. I'd happily take that small discomfort instead of the pain I'd been in.

I took inventory of all my previously injured body parts and was overjoyed to find each one working and whole.

My stomach rumbled loudly in the peaceful quiet. Between not eating for over twenty-four hours and undergoing the healing process, I was surprised that I hadn't started eating my pillow while I slept.

I was going to get up to see if there was any food in the cabin but realized that I'd have to disturb Cynthia's rest to do so. I ignored my hunger and took a moment to simply enjoy the feeling of her warmth up against me.

After a bit, my hunger prompted me to act. "Wake up, dear, we need to get the kids off to school soon . . ."

Cynthia stirred beside me. She slowly lifted her head and looked at me with sleepy grey eyes. Her hair was a mess, she wasn't wearing any makeup, and she had a tiny bit of dried drool on the right side of her lower lip, but my heart beat a little faster, and I thought she looked truly beautiful at that moment. She smiled at me and shook her head. "Kids? Did I miss a head injury?" she asked with a grin. "How are you feeling?"

"I feel great, thank you," I said as I leaned over and planted a chaste kiss on her forehead.

She quietly studied me for a moment as if making sure I wasn't just putting on a brave face, and I said, "Really, I'm good. Well, other than being really hungry. Any food in this place?"

"Yeah, but just canned food and jerky."

At this point I wasn't going to be picky as long as something with calories was around. I got up and Cynthia made a point of looking away as I got out of bed. I found that amusing because she'd undressed me in the first place.

I padded barefoot across the cabin and retrieved my clothes. I was surprised that they were mostly dry but figured being hung over the still-warm potbellied stove probably had something to do with that.

I noticed that the Super's body was missing, along with the broken chair and table, and as Cynthia handed me a bag of beef jerky, I asked about them.

"The body is outside the cabin with a tarp over it. I dumped the table and chair remains out there too. Take a seat and I'll make us some soup," she said, pointing at the couch off to the side of the cabin.

I already had a mouthful of jerky, so I just gave her a thumbs up and left her to it. I'd never been a huge fan of dried meat, but at this moment, it tasted better than steak. I plunked myself down on the surprisingly comfortable couch and stuffed another mouthful of jerky into my gob.

Cynthia pulled out a worn-looking cast iron pot, cracked open a large can of soup, and dumped the contents inside. I mentally nodded in approval as she grabbed a second can and added it to the pot as well. She carried the pot across the cabin and placed it on top of the stove.

Cynthia opened the front of the stove and tossed a couple more logs on the embers inside of it.

There was a slight breeze coming through the cabin and I wondered where it was coming from. I glanced around and spotted the cracked wooden front door propped up against the split door frame, which solved that mystery. Which reminded me of another mystery. "Sorry about falling asleep on you earlier."

Cynthia looked up from stirring the soup and said, "It wasn't your fault; I put you to sleep with my powers." The confusion must have been displayed on my face as she added, "By how badly injured you were, it was easier than numbing the nerves around each injury."

I nodded. "As long as it was just for healing and my virtue is still intact, it's all good."

Cynthia let out a delightful peal of laughter that warmed my insides better than anything else could and then said, "You caught me. I just knocked you out so I could undress you and take advantage."

"Don't let it happen again. Besides, you don't have to knock me out to have your way with me."

I smiled as heat rose to her cheeks and her stirring became a touch erratic. "Seriously, though, thank you for the healing and for whatever magic you did to my clothes."

"No problem."

A few minutes later, Cynthia joined me on the couch and we both tucked into our large bowls of beef stew. I noticed that her bowl was just as full as mine and figured I wasn't the only one starving.

The situation was a bit surreal. On the one hand, sitting on the couch with Cynthia while we ate soup together in the rustic cabin almost made it feel like a romantic getaway. And yet, there was a dead body outside, we'd both been kidnapped, I'd been beaten, drowned, and struck by lightning, and we'd barely survived the last twenty-four hours.

Once we finished the soup, Cynthia got a sad look on her face and said, "Zack, I'm so sorry you got dragged into this. If I thought Logan would follow me to Hamilton, I never would have left Halifax. The idea that I might have put Marion in danger . . ."

I shook my head. "Marion is fine. Her apartment has some very expensive wards around it, and she is well-loved in the community. Anyone attempting to go after her would regret it."

Cynthia seemed relieved at that and then asked, "How did you get away? The last time I saw you you were unconscious and being loaded on a boat with chains around your legs."

I took a deep breath and then told her about everything that had happened. I tried to gloss over some parts because I knew she already felt guilty, but that effort came to a crashing halt when she probed me about how I got my powers back.

Cynthia was aghast at my response. "You purposely tried to get hit by lightning?!? Are you insane?"

I was going to quip that my mother had me tested but wasn't sure if she was a *Big Bang Theory* fan or not and just shrugged. "It was a calculated risk. Besides, the important thing is it worked. I have my powers back."

Cynthia cocked a questioning eyebrow at me, and the look of disbelief on her face forced me to add, "Yeah, okay, it wasn't the safest of plans, but it wasn't like I had much choice."

With food in us, it was time to figure out a way out of here. There was still a chance that Logan and company might return here. If they'd made it to Halifax and then tried unsuccessfully contacting the leech, it would take them at least ten hours or so to get back here.

While I had my powers back and was reasonably sure I could take them, and a large part of me would have enjoyed frying Logan's smug face, three mature Werewolves weren't a threat to take lightly. We needed to get out of here before they returned. Blue and Stella would be worried, and I wanted to link up with them before taking on Logan and company. "Any chance the leech had a phone on him?"

"He did, but it was fried."

I cursed at that. I'd probably hit it in my unnecessary lightning strike. Being able to call Blue for a lift would have been nice. I could fly us both back to Hamilton, but that would be at least a six-hour flight. I was still brimming with power and could probably make the trip, but it would be a brutally cold flight for Cynthia. I also wasn't one hundred percent sure that my powers were permanently back. If they cut out while I had us both a couple of hundred feet in the air, I figured Cynthia wouldn't speak to me again, or that neither of us would ever be able to speak again in general.

I kicked around options. If we could get to a phone, Blue could get us home in minutes. I realized the solution was just outside. "Up for a drive?"

Cynthia frowned. "Where to?"

"We need to get to a phone. We'll take the van outside and try and find a phone booth or a store. Once we find a phone, Blue can have us home in minutes."

Cynthia nodded and we got up from the couch. We did a quick search around the cabin to make sure we had everything. Other than the clothes on our backs, we took the keys to the van, another bag of jerky, and a couple bottles of water and left.

When we got outside, I was relieved when Cynthia raised the fob and the van's lights flashed as the doors were unlocked. A part of me had been worried I might have fried it too with my lightning blast.

It was also a nice change to be sitting in the seats up front rather than being cuffed in the back. Cynthia started the van, and we headed back down the rough dirt road that brought us here.

The drive out from the cabin was infinitely better than the drive in. We were still tossed around on the uneven road but sitting in padded seats made the experience better than being on the hard metal floor we'd been on.

The area was actually quite pretty, thick trees lining the trail. The birch and maple trees had all mostly lost their leaves due to the lateness of the season, but there were lots of evergreens with their full green needles mixed in to add a bit of color to the starkness of the bare trees. This place in early fall must be a spectacular sight to see.

"Sorry," said Cynthia as the suspension of the van was tested by a particularly deep pothole.

I figured we weren't doing any favors to the resale value of the van, but if it got us off this trail and some place with a phone, I frankly didn't care. I laughed to myself, as my team and I weren't kind to vehicles. Between Bree's and Liv's cars getting destroyed by robots during the Master's attack on our house, Liv writing off her replacement vehicle after running into a zombie dinosaur, and the van we were in now, I doubted a good driver discount was in my future.

After a long thirty minutes, and dozens of potholes later, we finally reached the end of the dirt road. We idled at the entrance to the main road, both of us looking left and right for some indication of which way we should go.

"Which way?" said Cynthia.

The road was void of traffic and offered us no clues. I missed my phone; it would have been nice to Google directions to the nearest gas station or rest stop. I recalled that we'd made a right onto the dirt track and figured heading back the way we'd come would eventually lead us to Montreal.

"Left," I said.

Cynthia signaled and pulled out on the main road. She was a little aggressive with the gas pedal and fishtailed the van during the turn but recovered.

"Whoops, this thing has a bit more pep to it than my old Jetta," said Cynthia with a grin.

I noticed that she didn't let off the accelerator too much and wondered if women who drove like maniacs were an unknown fetish of mine. At least Cynthia eased off once we got to eighty kilometers an hour. Liv would have kept going. After driving with the speed-obsessed vampire, this was almost relaxing in comparison.

For the first ten minutes of the drive, traffic was light to nonexistent, and we passed nothing but rock formations and trees. We finally spotted a green road sign with an arrow and Montreal 135 KM on it.

Twenty minutes later, a sign for a gas station appeared on our right. Cynthia pulled us into the lot and parked out front of a convenience store and gas station combo.

She shut off the van, and I looked around and didn't see a phone booth. I wasn't surprised. As smartphones had become so common, phone booths were going the way of the dinosaurs. I hoped the store had burner phones for sale or that we could at least beg or bribe the attendant to use his phone.

The store was modern and clean. The bored attendant behind the counter gave us a quick dismissive glance and then went back to playing on his phone. I spotted a display of calling cards and phones just behind him and approached the counter.

As we stepped up to the counter, he looked up and said, "Bonjour."

My fake smile fell as I realized I might have a problem. The extent of my French vocabulary was 'Hello, do you have a red pencil crayon?' and I didn't think would be that helpful. "Do you speak English?"

Before the attendant could answer, Cynthia sighed and nudged me to the side. She let out a stream of fluent French and then the attendant laughed. I suspected she'd said something like, *Please excuse the ignorant baboon beside me but do you have a phone we could buy?*

I felt like a third wheel as they chatted back and forth, and the attendant showed her the different phones he had available. Another part of me loved hearing Cynthia speak French, and I was envious of her ability. I also realized that if our relationship went further, I could see her and Blue having side conversions that excluded me, as French was one of the multiple languages Blue was fluent in. I made a mental note to Google the French words for *small penis* at some point so I could at least catch that if it came up.

Cynthia selected a phone and a prepaid card for it and prompted me to step up and pay for it. I was still amazed that I'd managed to keep my wallet throughout my little adventure. Cynthia hadn't been as fortunate, as they'd taken her purse.

We took our purchase back to the van and I said, "Your French is impressive. Lots of French-speaking people in PEI?"

Cynthia shook her head. "No, but about a third of the population of New Brunswick speaks French, so it was a handy skill to have when I was in Halifax. My parents also loved vacationing in Quebec City each winter because my dad grew up there."

"Your dad is fluent too then?"

"Yeah, he was the one I practiced with when I was learning it in school."

I peeled the phone out of the package and was pleased that the battery had half a charge left on it. I dialed Blue's number, and she picked up after a couple of rings. *"Blue, it's Zack."*

"Zack! Where have you been? We have been searching for you. A witness saw your abduction but only got half the license plate number for the van. Marion is also very concerned about the health and wellbeing of her niece."

"Cynthia and I are fine. We could use a lift home though."

"What is your location?"

I froze for a moment and started looking around when Cynthia rhymed off an address with a coy smile. I began to wonder who was rescuing who here. I thanked her and repeated it to Blue.

"How did you end up in Quebec?"

"Long story. Can you open a portal nearby?"

"Hold on." The line went quiet, and I could picture Blue gazing into the shadows trying to locate us.

After a long pause, Blue came back on the line and said, *"There are shadows behind the convenience store. I will be there shortly."*

I ended the call, and we got out of the van and walked to the back of the store.

I turned to Cynthia and, with a grin, said, "There is one good thing that came out of all of this."

"What's that?"

"Our next date can't be any worse than this one was."

Chapter 12

Wednesday, November 23

The moment we stepped out of the shadows and into our living room, Stella hugged me and then punched my arm hard.

"What was that for?"

"For worrying us sick. Don't get kidnapped again!"

I blinked at that and wondered how getting kidnapped was my fault. I was going to argue that, but seeing the serious yet relieved look on Stella's young face, I just said, "Yes, ma'am." I was also in a bit of shock that Stella had actually hugged me. It was very out of character for her and showed how deeply worried she'd been.

She gave me an approving nod and introduced herself to Cynthia. Cynthia seemed a bit taken aback by Stella, and it dawned on me that she had no idea who Stella was. I realized Cynthia might be wondering if she was my daughter or something.

Before I could explain, Stella hit a button on her phone and said, "Talk to your aunt and let her know you are okay."

Cynthia took the phone from her and wandered off to the corner of the living room to get a bit more privacy.

In contrast to Stella's reaction, Blue just gave me a curt nod of acknowledgment. I was a bit disappointed not to see Bree and Olivia here as well. I figured that a kidnapping would have been enough for Blue and Stella to get the team back together to find me.

Before I could ask about them, Stella said, "Fill us in on what happened to you and Cynthia."

I took a deep breath and started with being knocked out and waking up in the van. Blue's purple eyes narrowed, and I knew she disapproved of me being taken so unaware. I wasn't overly proud of that either, but thankfully she let it go, and I continued my story.

When I got to the part where they tossed me into the lake to die, I glanced over to Cynthia to make sure she wasn't listening. The moment I saw her tears and heard her reassuring Marion over the phone she was okay, I knew I was good and went into full detail about my near drowning.

Stella looked horrified at how close I'd been to death. Blue's reaction was an approving twinkle in her eyes, and her tail began making happy circles behind her, which meant she was amused. I found Blue's reaction a bit odd but then figured she probably viewed it as a test of my warrior prowess or something.

I got similar reactions when I reached the part about trying to get struck by lightning.

"You did what?!" said Stella.

"I know, I know. But wait," I said, pausing to shoot sparks from my fingers and send a gust of wind through the room. Stella looked at me, stunned, her face lighting up with joy.

Blue just nodded and said, "I had deduced as much."

I was dumbfounded at that. "How could you have possibly known I had my powers back?"

Blue gave me a grin of pointy teeth and said, "Your posture announced it to me the moment I saw you."

I was going to call bullshit on that but then stopped myself. Blue was an expert swordswoman and part of that skill was reading body language to anticipate when an opponent would strike. The smallest twitch of muscle or shift of stance and Blue would pick that up. I'd tried to put on a brave face when I'd lost my powers, but if I was honest with myself, I knew my confidence had been false. Blue would have noticed that with ease, so she probably did know I got my powers back the moment she saw me.

I quickly went over my rescue of Cynthia and taking out the Super that was on guard in the cabin, her healing me, and our trip in the van to get to a phone.

Stella shook her head as I finished and said, "It is a miracle you are still alive, but I'm glad you are, and it's great to have you back."

"Your tale is worthy for the bards to inscribe and sing about. I informed you that you had a warrior's heart, and you did not disappoint me with your actions," said Blue.

I swear there were times Stella and Blue felt like my pseudo-parents. Stella was the caring but stern mom, and Blue was the hard-ass father figure whose main advice during any difficult time was to walk it off.

That thought made me smile, as I knew both cared deeply for me in their own ways.

Cynthia joined us and I looked with concern at her red eyes. "Is everything okay?"

Cynthia nodded. "I think the stress of what happened just caught up to me. Marion is relieved and wants to see me."

"We'll get you to Marion shortly, but first we need to figure out what to do next. Logan and the two other Weres are still out there, and by your description of Pierre, he doesn't seem to be someone who will take us getting away lightly."

Cynthia didn't reply and just slowly nodded at my assessment.

"I concur," said Blue. "The threat to both of you is not over and we need to figure out a course of action. In Pierre's position, I would opt to eliminate you both to avoid facing kidnapping and attempted murder charges."

Cynthia gasped at Blue's assessment. I'd been around Blue too long, so I'd been expecting a comment like that. I turned to Cynthia and said, "Don't worry, you're safe. Pierre and company would regret coming here."

Cynthia smiled and seemed to be reassured by my statement.

I shifted my thoughts back to Blue's remark. Pierre would know that dead men tell no tales. That's why they had tried to dump me in a lake in the first place. Blue's mention of charges had me thinking in another direction. The rough plan I'd been forming in my head had consisted of finding Logan, the two Weres, and Pierre and personally delivering some payback. While that held a lot of appeal, it wasn't the smartest route.

We needed to contact law enforcement and give our statements. Two kidnapping charges and attempted murder would bring the full weight of Canadian law enforcement down on Pierre and his gang. As all four of them were Enhanced, it would also put bounties on their heads, which meant we'd be able to go after them hard.

Involving law enforcement would also help with my main priority of keeping Cynthia safe. As much as I'd like to fry all four of them, if they were picked up by authorities and stuck in jail before I got to them, that would be ideal. The quicker they were off the streets, the safer Cynthia would be.

The other issue we had was a lack of information about Pierre and his organization. By the money Cynthia mentioned that they were throwing around, it sounded like they had substantial resources. I had no idea how many people worked for Pierre or if his organization extended across Canada.

I was suddenly feeling overwhelmed. Less than twenty minutes ago, my only concern had been finding a phone and getting home. Now I was trying to figure out how to protect Cynthia and take down a criminal organization. I was also not at my best, as I was still feeling the effects of all that healing Cynthia had done to me recently.

I smiled to myself as I realized I didn't need to figure this out alone. I shared my thoughts with Blue, Stella, and Cynthia and we discussed a course of action.

During the discussion, I brought up bringing Olivia and Bree home to help.

Stella shook her head. "No. Blue and I considered this when you were kidnapped. Bree is on a mission for her alpha and the Were Council and that is something we can't interrupt."

I sighed at that but couldn't argue. "What about Olivia? Having her presence here would drastically improve our nighttime security."

Stella broke eye contact and idly tugged on one of her long braids. "Um, Olivia is under house arrest by the English Vampire Court..."

"She's *what*? Is she okay?"

Stella nodded. "She is fine at this point. Her hearing is a few weeks away and she and Sarah are busy preparing her defense. Sarah wouldn't get into the details but mentioned that Olivia broke some sort of court protocol. Sarah didn't seem to be too concerned, but she said that if Olivia left before the hearing, she would face a lifetime banishment from the English Court and all its territories."

I rubbed my temples, feeling a headache coming on. The last part of Stella's statement was an issue because Canada was part of the English Vampire Court's territory, which meant if she was banned, she couldn't live here going forward. It would also technically bar her from our secret lab in London, but as Blue's shadow travelling was the only way to access that lab, we could still have her there and the English Court wouldn't be able to do anything about it.

My mind wondered what the heck Liv had done. Knowing her, she probably flipped Elizabeth the bird or ended up topless at a royal function or something equally crazy. I smiled at the thought.

I forced myself back to the here and now and silently cursed the Court and their protocols, as it meant we were denied Liv's services for at least the next two weeks. "I'm not happy about this, and once we've dealt with this mess, we'll have Blue spy on Olivia during the hearing and if she is in any danger. We'll figure out a rescue plan."

Cynthia's eyes bulged out of her head at the last part. "You would take on the entire English Vampire Court to rescue your friend?"

I smiled and nodded in response. "Liv's family, and there is nothing we wouldn't do for family. Sadly enough, that wouldn't even be the craziest thing we've done this year."

Cynthia's expression softened to one of understanding at my mention of family, but she shook her head at us over the last bit of my statement. She then grinned and said, "Well, at least you're not boring."

Blue cleared her throat. "It would be prudent for Cynthia to stay with us here or at our secret lab until the threat against you both has been dealt with."

I was about to agree when Cynthia said, "You have a secret lab and a daughter. Is there anything else I should know about? Batcave in the basement? You're an agent for the Illuminati? You have an upcoming comedy special on Netflix?"

I was taken aback by her statement. It made me realize how little we knew about each other. I'd felt the bond between us growing from our harrowing adventure and that made it seem like we'd known each other much longer than we actually had. "No to the Batcave," I said with a smile, "but I can't confirm or deny your second question. Zack's Windbag of Fun Special is still in the negotiation stage with my agent and Netflix, but I'm hopeful we'll get a deal done."

The sound of her laughter at my comment warmed my soul, and seeing a smile on her face reaffirmed how truly beautiful she was.

"Stella isn't my daughter; she is a teammate and a lot older than her appearance suggests. The secret lab is also hers."

Cynthia cast a look of doubt at me. I glanced between her and Stella and said, "Brace yourself." I gave Stella a nod.

Stella stepped back and then transformed into her monstrous Hyde form, instantly making the living room seem a lot smaller.

Cynthia jumped back and exclaimed, "SWEET BABY JESUS!"

Stella reverted back to her human form and said, "Sorry to have startled you."

Cynthia tried to say something but ended up just giving a slow nod in response to Stella.

Blue interrupted our demonstration. "Getting back to the task at hand..."

Returning to our earlier conversation, Cynthia agreed to stay with us until the threat was over and would take over Bree's empty room during her stay.

We'd barely settled that when Blue said, "With Cynthia here or at the lab, our enemies won't be able to reach her, but I am concerned that Marion or Cynthia's family will become targets."

Most times Blue's ruthlessness made me nervous or scared, but today I was glad for it. She brought up legit concerns. The house was heavily warded, and with Blue, Stella and me here, it would be hard for them to get to Cynthia. If we were extra cautious and moved to the secret lab, it would be next to impossible for Pierre to get to her. If they couldn't get to Cynthia, then they'd need leverage to force us out of hiding.

Cynthia interrupted my thoughts. "My family is fine. I will call them and warn them. Our house is warded. My parents' next-door neighbor is a retired EIRT officer. Also, my hometown is small and close-knit. With tourist season over for the year, any strangers will stick out like sore thumbs."

I ponder her statement for a moment. "Is the EIRT officer Enhanced?"

"No, but his wife is."

"What's her power?"

"Tank," said Cynthia with a smile.

I smiled at that too. Super strength and near invulnerability would be a bad match for Weres. "Okay, that takes care of your family. What do we do about Marion?"

"She can stay here too," said Stella.

We chatted for a few more minutes and came up with a plan. Stella and Blue would take Cynthia back to her apartment so she could shower, change, and pack. They'd get Marion to pack up too and come back here. I'd stay here, grab a shower, and then call my EIRT contacts.

Once they were back, we'd shadow travel to EIRT headquarters in Toronto to make our statements about the kidnapping.

Blue opened a portal and I waited until all three of them disappeared into the shadows before heading upstairs.

I stripped off my clothes and spied the laundry hamper in the corner. I sighed as I picked up my shucked clothes and decided that between the stains, the grime, and the other physical damage, there was no saving them.

I got into the shower. Normally, I waited for the water to warm up, but this time I stepped under the stream of water right away. I still wasn't one hundred percent sure my powers were back and was relieved that the water was a cold shock to my system. None of the comforting tingling feelings I'd gotten from the ice-cold lake were present, which helped reassure me that my Ice powers were still in the background where they belonged.

I sighed deeply as I felt the temperature shift and let the hot water dance across my skin. The heat working into my tired and sore muscles was almost as good as Cynthia's healing.

The last twenty-four hours came rushing back as I enjoyed the shower. I was elated that I had my powers back but was a bit shaken by how many times I could have died. A couple extra well-placed kicks by the Weres during my beating could have finished me. The near drowning in the lake and the lightning strike both easily could have killed me too.

The important thing was that Cynthia and I had survived.

A cold smile came to my face as I thought about Pierre and Logan. They'd had their shot—now it was my turn.

Chapter 13

Wednesday, November 23

Showered and freshly dressed, I felt like a new man. I retired to my office and used the landline to make some calls. The lack of a cell phone was the first thing I addressed with a call to my wireless provider. I was pleased that a replacement SIM card and phone would be sent to me tomorrow. On a whim, I added another phone to the order, figuring if Cynthia was staying with us, she would need a phone too.

I felt the loss of my missing phone when I had to look up Bobby Knight's number from a file on my computer. I dialed and prayed he was in, as I didn't have my other EIRT contacts in that file.

I was relieved when Bobby answered. *"Hurricane, are you okay? A lot of people are looking for you. There was a rumor you'd been kidnapped."*

I told Bobby I was fine but that a civilian and I had been kidnapped and eventually escaped. We both wanted to come down and give our statements. He asked me a few questions about the ordeal, and his voice sounded tired. I wondered if he was coming to the end of his shift. His entire tone changed when I mentioned Pierre LaPointe's name.

"There is a detective here who I know will want to take your statement. How soon can you get here?"

I told him that I was just waiting for Stella and company to return and that we could be there shortly after that. The call got a bit mysterious when Bobby vehemently stressed that we were to talk to only him or Detective Grissom. I asked about that, but Bobby said he'd explain when we got here and ended the call.

Bobby's reaction was odd. It sounded like EIRT was familiar with Pierre, which meant his organization might be bigger and more dangerous than I initially thought.

I opened a browser to do some research on Pierre and hopefully find out more about him and his enterprise, but the moment I did, I heard familiar voices downstairs.

I intercepted Stella, Blue, and Cynthia as they were coming out of the living room and frowned when Marion didn't appear. "Where's Marion?"

Stella shook her head. "She's not coming. She won't leave her place because she wants to be there for her patients."

I mentally cursed. I should have seen this coming. Marion took her responsibilities as a healer very seriously, and she'd view going into hiding as abandoning her patients. I tossed around whether it was worth paying her a visit personally, but Stella added, "She has promised not to leave her apartment and will have her friend Al get her groceries and stay with her."

Al was a hippie pot dealer, and I didn't picture him being able to slow down Logan or his Were companions if they went after Marion. The one piece of good news, though, was her promise not to leave her apartment. Marion had lived in the same place for decades and the wards around her apartment were top-notch. They were so good that they'd once deterred Drow from entering her place. If Logan or one of his people did go after Marion, the wards should hold them off long enough for either us or authorities to arrive.

The situation wasn't ideal, but it was workable. Marion wasn't the primary healer for the Hamilton Police Department, but she was their backup and had saved many officers over the years due to her skills. I'd reach out to my buddy Rob and my other contacts on the force to request some more police presence in her area. "Blue, please make a point of checking on Marion from the shadows on an hourly basis to make sure she is okay."

Blue nodded in agreement. I hoped that between the wards, the extra police, and Blue's monitoring Marion would be kept safe.

***

I found myself waiting in an interrogation room at EIRT headquarters while Stella and Blue were back at home researching Pierre LaPointe and his organization.

Bobby had met us in the lobby, and he was currently taking Cynthia's statement in another room nearby. Bobby had promised that Detective Grissom would be with me shortly. Just before he left with Cynthia, he said, "Detective Grissom comes across as a bit odd, but he has his reasons. He's a solid officer and you can trust him like you can me."

I was a bit annoyed that he'd dumped me in here and exited with Cynthia so quickly that he didn't have a chance to explain his mysterious demeanor on the phone earlier or what was going on. I took a deep breath and tried to be patient. There wasn't a better law enforcement officer than Bobby Knight, and I just had to believe that this would all make sense soon.

The door opened and my confusion grew as a shabbily dressed older man in a grimy T-shirt and ripped jeans came in. He had a long, unkempt beard that was dark brown with large streaks of grey in it. The hair on his head was also long and disheveled though it was almost entirely grey. My first thought was the guy was homeless and had picked the wrong room.

Before I could say anything, the man said, "Zack Stevens?" I nodded and he smiled. "I'm Detective Ted Grissom. Excuse my appearance. I did a lot of undercover work earlier in my career, and I've never been able to shake the habit of not looking like a cop."

The powerful and commanding voice he had and the glint of steel in his brown eyes had me quickly reassessing my first impression of Detective Grissom.

He crossed the small room and put the pad of yellow lined paper he was carrying on the metal table I was seated behind.

I rose from my chair and we shook hands.

A screech of metal filled the room as he pulled his chair back and we both took our seats.

"Sorry for the wait. I was off work today and tried to get here as quickly as possible when I got Bobby's call, but you know how traffic is in this city."

I nodded at that. Toronto driving is always chaotic, especially on weekdays. Every time I flew above the city, I was glad I didn't have a driver's license.

He glanced over to the camera mounted in the corner which I'd spotted earlier and then turned to me and said, "Time is short, and I need to ask for your patience. The monitoring equipment is off but will be back on soon. When it comes back on, I will take your statement. I'm sure you have questions about Bobby being cagey with you on the phone, and I'll explain all of that after the interview. Is that okay?"

I pondered his words and then nodded in agreement.

He was about to say something but paused as he looked over at the camera again and then said, "Thank you for coming in, Mr. Stevens. I'm Detective Grissom. When you are ready, can you give me in your words what happened to you?"

From the corner of my eye, I spotted a green light on the camera. I gathered my thoughts and then started from the beginning when Cynthia and I were outside her building.

The process of giving my statement lasted a good hour and a half. Detective Grissom was very thorough in his follow-up questions and had pages of notes by the time we were done. He gave me a quick wink at the end and said, "Thank you for coming in today, Mr. Stevens. I'll escort you to the entrance, and we'll be in touch."

I frowned at his statement, as that wasn't what he promised at the beginning of the interview, but then I recalled the wink and realized he was playing a role for the cameras. I nodded and we got up and left the room.

I was about to ask him about all this secrecy the moment we exited the interrogation room, but he shook his head at me and put a finger over his lips. I blinked at that. Surely off camera and in the heart of the EIRT headquarters building we should be able to chat. I mentally sighed in frustration, but once more gave him the benefit of the doubt and held my tongue as we walked towards the elevators.

Even on the elevator, he held up his hand to me to indicate that I should hold my questions. He hit the B5 button, and we began moving downwards. B5 was the very last button at the bottom, and I assumed it referred to basement level five.

The elevator opened and I was greeted by a plain and dirty hallway. This was odd, as the EIRT building had been renovated not too long ago and the rest of the building was a spotless and modern state-of-the-art affair. We passed several doors with numbers on them that gave no indication of the rooms' functions. If I had to guess, I would assume they were probably used for storage. Deep down the corridor, we passed a door that was marked Maintenance Personnel Only. There was a steady hum coming from the machinery within which was fairly loud.

We stopped at the first door after the maintenance room, which was labeled with the number twenty-seven. This door was painted in the same dull grey color as the other doors in the corridor but there were a few differences. Most of the doors we'd passed were cheap interior doors. On a good day, I could probably punch through their thin wood with my fist. They all had flimsy locks built into the doorknobs that a child with a paperclip could probably pick.

The door we'd stopped in front of was solid steel, like the type used as fire doors. It also had an imposing bolt lock positioned above the door handle.

I was puzzled when Detective Grissom crouched down and intently studied something at the base of the door that I couldn't see and then gave a satisfied nod. He stood back up and unlocked it.

I followed him into the darkened room. The fluorescent lights flickered to life, and I got a better look at my surroundings. The place was a bit larger than my bedroom at home but seemed smaller due to all the clutter. Lining two of the walls were battered file cabinets that had probably been in police service longer than Detective Grissom. The other two walls were filled with yellowed newspaper clippings, mug shots, headshots, and surveillance photos. One of those walls looked like a conspiracy nut's wet dream. He had head shots arranged in a pyramid shape with red string connecting each of the photos. I spotted a photo of Logan about midway down and on the right side of the pyramid.

Near the back of the room was a worn wooden desk that reminded me of the type some of my grade school teachers had back in the day.

Detective Grissom plunked himself down in an old leather office chair that rattled as his weight hit the seat. He gestured at the chair in front of the desk and said, "Get comfortable. This is going to take a while."

I sat down and asked, "What were you looking for on the door?"

He gave me a coy smile and said, "I placed a hair in the base of the door frame. If that hair had been disturbed, I would have had to sweep this office for listening devices before we could have this conversation."

A part of me was starting to think the good detective was a paranoid fruitcake, but Bobby's word about him being solid had me reserving judgment for now.

"Thank you for your patience, and I will answer your questions, but it will be more efficient if I tell you what led to me checking for a hair under my door."

He raised a questioning eyebrow at me, as though asking for my approval, and I nodded. "Twenty-two years ago, EIRT was building a money laundering case against a man named Alex Gray. Alex Gray was and still is the head of the largest crime organization in Canada. That organization is known as the Misfit Mafia. The name is appropriate, as unlike most mob families which come from certain ethnic and family backgrounds, the Misfits are a diverse collection of criminals with no family ties. A good chunk of them are Enhanced, which was why EIRT was investigating and not the RCMP. They have members from every Enhanced class—Were, vamps, fae, mages, Supers, etcetera."

My stomach rolled a bit at the implications of that. Organized crime families were dangerous enough; add Enhanced Individuals to that mix and things got even worse. The Master and his crime spree with his young Enhanced minions came to mind as a prime example of that danger. The fights we'd had against them had been brutal.

"The key witness for the case was an accountant that worked for the Misfit Mafia that wanted out. We'd just gotten a statement from him about some of the details of the money laundering when a day later, he and his entire family died in a house fire. The fire was thoroughly investigated, and the cause was determined to be faulty wiring. The autopsies came back and confirmed the cause of death for the witness, his wife, and two kids as smoke inhalation. No sign of foul play was found. With the accountant dead, so was the case."

Detective Grissom sighed and added, "I wasn't part of that case but the whole thing reeked to me. I believe that the family was murdered, and it was made to look like a tragic accident. This also wasn't the first time Alex Gray had ducked criminal charges. The Toronto Police had built two cases against him before this. The first one made it to court but fell apart when crucial evidence went missing from police lockup. The second case ended when their primary witness went missing and to this day has never been seen again."

I really didn't like where this was going. Logan's picture in the pyramid on the wall meant he and Pierre were members of this Misfit Mafia. Taking them down had just gotten much more complicated.

"Nine years after the accountant was killed, we got another shot at Alex Gray. He killed a rival mob boss by entombing him in ice in the rival's home. We had a witness, a landscaper who was working across the street, who spotted Alex Gray leaving the scene around the time of the murder. We had footage from an ATM of him two blocks away shortly after the time of the murder as well."

"Entombed in ice? So I'm assuming Alex Gray is an Ice Elemental?"

He nodded. "Yes, sorry, should have mentioned that earlier. He is known as 'the Iceman,' which is an appropriate alias for multiple reasons. It also refers to his ability to evade criminal charges, as nothing sticks to him. He is the most ruthless, coldhearted SOB I've ever met.

"Anyways, I was involved in this case. It fell apart before we even brought it to the Crown. Again, the witness disappeared and so did all copies of the ATM footage. Without those, we couldn't place him at the scene. He had two employees that gave sworn statements that he'd been in his office at the time of the murder."

I frowned. "How do a protected witness and video evidence disappear?"

"How indeed? We have a leak or multiple leaks inside EIRT, which is why we are having this conversation here off the record."

I rubbed my temples, as this whole thing was getting worse and worse with each passing minute. I'd come to EIRT to make it easier to take down Pierre and Logan, and if anything, I might have done the opposite.

"The two cases falling apart and the possible leak led to the brass putting together a secret taskforce twelve years ago. The goal of the taskforce was to arrest and convict Alex Gray and find out who was behind the leaks. I was selected to lead it, and I handpicked nine other trusted officers to work with. I report directly to the director himself.

"One of the officers I picked was a young female officer named Kim Bailey. She'd been working in Vice doing undercover and sting operations for two years. She was also an Ice Elemental, though with very limited powers. At best she could shoot a couple of small ice spears before draining her powers."

Grissom trailed off, a faraway look on his face.

After a moment, with a wistful smile and a sad tone in his voice he said, "She could make these incredibly detailed ice sculptures. They were no bigger than six inches high and didn't last long due to their size but were amazing."

He shook his head. "Anyways, I took her under my wing, and we spent six months training her and building her cover. I thought she'd be the ideal candidate to infiltrate the Misfits. As I'm sure you know,

Elementals enjoy being around their own kind. I hoped her being an Ice Elemental would make Alex Gray open up to her. I also thought they'd be less likely to suspect she was a cop compared to a man. She was sharp, quick on her feet, a great actress, and good at improvising."

His eyes welled up slightly, and I sensed this was difficult for him to talk about.

"Long story short, she disappeared after her first meeting with a Misfit contact. I still kick myself for not insisting that we keep her under surveillance for the meet, but she was adamant that there was too much chance of a tail being spotted and insisted that she go alone. The leak was the main factor in my decision to let her go alone. I trusted my team, but the more people involved in the meet, the more chance it might get leaked. Only Kim and I knew the meeting was happening. At the time, I was puzzled how her cover could have been blown.

"Three years later, we tried again with another agent. This time, rather than trying to get into Alex's Toronto operation, we went to Halifax to infiltrate the East Coast branch of the Misfits, led by Pierre LaPointe. We used a Halifax police officer who had spent a year working undercover as a minor drug dealer in the city. I thought using someone outside of EIRT would reduce the chance of a leak, and he already had an established cover.

"This time, I had a full surveillance and backup team on hand in case anything went sideways. The meeting happened, but when he arrived, he was instructed to give up his cell phone and get in a car. I wanted to stop the meet then, but the undercover agent made the decision to surrender his phone and was in the car before we could stop it. We tried tailing the car discreetly, but they shook us."

After a long pause, he continued. "The agent was found dead in an alleyway. He'd bled out from a knife wound. I can only surmise that something or someone startled the killers, as they left him before he died. The agent managed to use his blood to write part of a message on the ground before he died—T-E-L-E-P-A," Grissom said, spelling the message out.

I frowned for a moment and then said, "Telepath?"

"Exactly. We think that was how they knew Kim was a cop too. By using a telepath to screen new recruits, they took the risk of being infiltrated by an undercover agent off the table. The former director barred us from trying it again."

I thought about how I might beat a telepath. Enhanceds, like Elementals, mages, and vampires, were resistant to mental assaults. But resistant didn't mean immune. A good telepath, if they were touching someone, could easily get around those mental blocks. I suspected that if someone was able to block the telepath, they wouldn't be recruited. You would need to find someone who could fool a telepath, and that was much more difficult. Off the top of my head, no Enhanced I could think of could do that.

"Without an undercover agent, we couldn't be proactive in the investigation. The best we could do was to try to turn an existing member of the Misfits or catch Alex or one of his employees in the act of a crime. We did our best but had no luck. Each year, our budget got smaller and smaller, and officers were assigned to other duties. You are now looking at the entire Misfit taskforce. I should have technically been retired last year, but the director gave me a special dispensation to stay on. I couldn't leave until I brought Alex Gray and whoever killed Kim to justice to answer for their crimes."

I sat there taking in all Detective Grissom had told me. His paranoia now seemed completely justified and I felt for him. The man had spent more than twelve years of his life on this project with nothing to show for it but the death of two officers. The leak in the department had also made his job next to impossible. "I'd hoped bringing this to EIRT would make things easier, but with your leak issue, I may have made things worse."

"Look, I know things sound bad, but this is the best chance I've had at taking down the Misfits in a long time. Due to the leak, I'd recommend you and Cynthia pass on protection from us and just take care of that yourselves."

I hadn't been looking for protection, so this wasn't a big issue. I nodded in agreement.

"I'll discuss this case with Acting Director Cooper. What you've given us should be enough to get an arrest warrant for Pierre, Logan, and the two other Weres. The one good thing about working on this for so long is my list of possible people that could be the leak is down to six. I can prevent any of those people from being involved in the operation."

The term *operation* made me believe that he would get the warrant and then use a strike team to serve it and take Pierre and Logan into custody. I wanted revenge on Logan for the beating and his treatment of Cynthia, but I could push that to the side if it meant getting him off the streets sooner; keeping Cynthia safe was more important to me than anything else at this moment. "Okay, what are you asking of me?"

"Keep yourself and Cynthia safe and give me forty-eight hours before you do anything about Logan or Pierre. If all goes to plan, we should have them in custody and awaiting trial by then. If not, then they will be wanted fugitives with bounties on their heads."

The more I thought about his offer, the more I liked it. Stella and Blue had just started research on Pierre and company, so the forty-eight hours would allow us time to build a better picture of what we were up against. Also, while my powers were back and I was brimming with energy, my body wasn't fully recovered from the massive amount of healing Cynthia had done to me. Two days of rest and good food would go a long way to fixing that problem. Lastly, having Pierre and his minions being declared wanted fugitives took care of any legal issues that might result from us going after them.

I agreed to give him the time and hoped that I'd made the right decision.

Chapter 14

Wednesday, November 23

After I got Cynthia settled into Bree's room, the two of us joined Stella and Blue in the office. I smiled at the pictures and bright red string on the walls. Blue and Stella had already gotten a mini version of Detective Grissom's Misfit Mafia organization chart up in the short period we'd been gone.

It was times like these that I appreciated how damn good my teammates really were.

To get all of us on the same page, I went over the entire discussion I had with Detective Grissom and my agreement to give him forty-eight hours to apprehend Pierre, Logan, and company.

Blue was less than amused with the last part. "I fail to understand why you allowed this. If he arrests them, we don't see a penny in bounty money."

"Bounties aren't my priority here. Keeping everyone safe is." By the look I got from her, I knew I hadn't made my case. "Also, if you recall, we were supposed to be on hiatus until Liv and Bree return." I got a slight grudging nod of acknowledgment at that and said, "The other factor in my decision was my physical condition and my powers. I just got my powers back, but what if that is temporary? I am still feeling the effects of the healing Cynthia did to keep me alive. I need a couple of days of recovery time to get back to full health."

I half expected Blue to lecture me about being in better shape, but to my surprise her stern expression softened, and she said, "Having extra time to recover and assess your abilities was a prudent decision."

I was taken aback by that, but the important thing was Blue now seemed okay with my choice. It was my turn to meet her halfway. "That said, EIRT's record with the Misfit Mafia hasn't been good, and we may get our shot at Pierre and company soon enough." Blue gave me a satisfied pointy-toothed grin at that. "We need to prepare as if that might happen. The two days will give us more time to research the Misfit Mafia and allow us to plan our next move. Whether EIRT is successful or not, Alex Gray doesn't strike me as a man who will let valued members of his organization be taken without a fight. He has a history of eliminating witnesses and evidence, and Cynthia and I are key witnesses."

Stella piped up and said, "Blue and I have got some information on them, but the details so far are limited. For such a large organization, they do a surprisingly good job of maintaining a low profile. Most of the things we've found on Alex Gray are about his charitable work and donations to the Toronto community. On the surface, he looks like a valued member of Toronto society." She paused for a moment and then her youthful-looking face lit up. "I haven't checked the English Vampire Court's files about him yet; they should have more details on him."

"How do we have access to those files?"

Stella smiled. "Sarah hasn't yet revoked our access from our last case."

Our last case involved taking down a lich that was using vampires to do his bidding. After the vampires went on a murder spree, we ended up being the English Vampire Court's official representatives, working with law enforcement to stop the deaths. "That's odd. Sarah isn't the type to make security lapses like that."

Sarah was the court's champion and the one who granted us access to the files in the first place. She was also acting as Olivia's mentor while she was at the court.

Stella shrugged as she started working on the computer. Over her shoulder, she said, "Sarah does have a soft spot for me. This also wasn't the first time we've been their official representatives and probably won't be the last."

Sarah's soft spot was a massive understatement. Stella and Blue had spent a lot of time at the English Court after Stella came out of stasis and Blue first arrived in our world. Stella's youthful looks had not just endeared her to Sarah but to most of the English Vampire Court, including Elizabeth who ruled it. She was also correct that we'd probably end up being their representatives in the future, as that duty wasn't popular with vampires who lived here in Canada. On a more practical level, we weren't stupid enough to disclose anything we learned from those files to law enforcement, as we didn't have a death wish. I thought about the criminal side of the English Vampire Court's operations and my stomach knotted up in fear as a thought hit me.

"Zack, are you okay? You look like you just saw a ghost," said Cynthia, rapidly closing the distance between us. Stella spun around in concern and Blue narrowed her gaze at me as well.

I waved Cynthia off and said, "I'm fine. I just had a worrying thought. The English Vampire Court, like all vampire courts, have their hands deep in any criminal activity happening in their territory, right?" Stella nodded and I said, "If the Misfit Mafia, the largest criminal organization in Canada, is paying protection money to the English Vampire Court, it must be a substantial sum. They may not approve of us cutting off that revenue if we go after the Misfits."

The idea of taking on the English Vampire Court and the Misfit Mafia at the same time was more than just daunting; it was suicidal.

Stella tugged on her braid for a moment, which was a tell that indicated when she was thinking deeply about something, and then shook her head. "I don't think it works that way. It's less a protection fee and more of a franchise fee."

"Huh?"

"The Misfits aren't paying for protection; they are paying for the right to do business in their territory. If we wiped out the Misfit Mafia, other gangs and criminal organizations would quickly fill that void and they too would pay the Court, which means they still get their revenue no matter what happens."

Relief filled me at Stella's words. If that was the case, they wouldn't care if we took down the Misfits. "Just to be safe, can you please call Sarah and confirm that?"

Stella nodded and hopped out of her chair and left the room with her phone in hand.

While we waited for Stella to return, Blue went over what they'd found out so far and went into detail about some of the pictures on the wall.

Just as Blue was wrapping up, Stella returned with a big grin on her face. "Good news. I was right. If we have to go after the Misfit Mafia, the English Vampire Court will not get involved."

"Nice. Any news about Liv?"

Stella shook her head. "Nothing new, other than she is doing okay."

While it was great to hear that we didn't have to take on the English Vampire Court in order to get the Misfit Mafia, another part of me wondered if we might have to in the end anyways. If Liv had gotten herself into big trouble with them, we might have to rescue her and risk the Court's wrath in any event. I pushed that thought aside. Olivia's hearing was more than two weeks away, and we had more pressing matters to deal with.

***

Less than an hour later, Cynthia and I found ourselves at our secret lab below London. The two of us had been trying to help with the research but mostly just ended up in the way. Blue was only too happy to shadow travel us to the lab when I mentioned I was hungry.

Cynthia was currently in a state of shock. "So you're saying that in less than a second, we traveled from Hamilton to London, England?" I nodded and she said, "And this underground lair was built more than one hundred years ago under one of the world's major cities, and no one even knows it is here?"

An image of us staging here with our allies before the final battle with the Master a few months ago popped into my head. As I pictured the Weres, pixies, vampires, and various Enhanceds that had been a part of that, I realized that the lab was certainly less secret than it had been. "Well, very few people know it is here. Over the last year, we've had several guests."

Cynthia shook her head in amazement as she glanced around. Her reaction was a good reminder of how special Blue's powers and this lab were. I'd used both frequently over the last year and had started taking it all for granted.

I gently led her over to the Food-O-Tron, and upon seeing it she asked, "Is this some sort of early computer?"

That wasn't a bad guess, as with its various dials and levers, it did sort of look like one. "Better. I know you watched *Star Wars*, but didn't you ever watch *Star Trek*?"

"Some. It was more of my dad's thing than mine, why?"

"The Food-O-Tron is like the food replicators on the show. What is your favorite food dish?"

Cynthia didn't hesitate and said, "Lobster rolls."

I laughed and shook my head.

Figures, she had to find the one item that isn't on the Food-O-Tron's menu, I thought to myself.

She frowned at me, and I explained the reason for my mirth. "I'm sure you have a favorite spot back on PEI that does lobster rolls." I got a nod and warm smile from her. "When all this craziness is over, I'll have Blue take us out there and we'll add one those rolls to the Food-O-Tron." Her smile grew and I asked, "What is your next favorite food?"

Cynthia got a thoughtful look on her face and said, "How about a Philly cheesesteak with fries?"

"Now you're talking. Fresh lemonade to go with it?"

"Please."

I knew the code for both items, as they were a personal favorite of mine. I changed the levers to the setting for lemonade and pulled the main one to start the process. Lights flashed on the Food-O-Tron and various whirls and clicks filled the air as it did its thing.

After about thirty seconds, it dinged, and I opened the hatch and extracted a glass pint mug of ice-cold lemonade and handed it to Cynthia. I pulled the main lever again to make another.

Cynthia took a small sip and smiled. "That's really good."

A few minutes later, we were both seated at one of the tables in the main room of the lab eating our food. Cynthia let out a deep moan of approval as she took her first bite. I may have matched it with one of my own.

I found my first Cynthia quirk while we ate, noticing she put both malt vinegar and ketchup on her fries. Malt vinegar on fries was cool, and ketchup on fries was also good, but both was just odd to me. As flaws go, this was a very livable one, though.

Cynthia paused between bites and said, "Stella and Blue seem a bit, um, intense . . ."

"Normally they aren't that bad, or at least Stella isn't. They both take research very seriously. If you really want to see intense, you should see Bree around a box of donuts or Liv talking about fashion."

She smiled at that. "You really care for them, don't you?" I nodded, as she'd caught me with my mouth full and she said, "How did you and your team come together?"

I went over how we'd met and some of the adventures we'd had together in the past year. Cynthia was shocked that we'd only been a team for less than a year. I couldn't blame her. While it had been under a year, it had certainly been eventful, and that made it seem like we'd been together for longer.

I imagined it was probably the same for combat troops on a one-year tour in an active combat zone. You spend your time in the shit and seeing things that normal people never will and you're going develop friendships and a brotherhood that would have never been created under any other circumstances. My team and I had certainly seen some things over the last year that still haunted my dreams.

After dinner, I gave Cynthia the ten-cent tour of the lab. She seemed a little nervous when I pointed out that the three exits were all booby-trapped and none of us knew the codes to disarm them. That nervousness grew when I helpfully pointed out that even if we did know the codes, at least two of the exits had been blocked from the surface for decades if not longer.

"So, if something, um, happens to Blue, we'd be trapped here?"

I gave her a lurid glance and said, "I can think of worse fates."

She rolled her eyes at me, but a small smile peeked through, and a bit of heat filled her cheeks.

"Sorry. It's not that big of a deal. If Blue's services weren't available, then yes, we'd be trapped, but we have unlimited air and food. There are also some tools in the storage room, and we'd probably be able to dig ourselves out eventually."

She seemed mollified at that, and we continued the tour.

We finished up in the main hangar, and I explained how we used it for mainly training and occasionally practice runs with the modular buildings to prepare for bounty takedowns.

Her grey eyes twinkled as she glanced around and she asked, "So, other than being able to fly and shoot lightning and big gusts of air, what else can you do?"

"You forgot being a world-class ladies' man in that list of achievements." The snort of laughter I got in response certainly took me down a peg. "There are more subtle things I can do with my powers. For instance, I can manipulate the air around you and remove oxygen from it, leaving nothing but nitrogen and CO_2."

Her eyes widened a bit and she said, "You've done that before?"

I nodded. "I did it to a Super that could mentally control people in a restaurant in Vegas. She was using her power to get one of the security team we were a part of to shoot his boss. I didn't want to make a scene, so cutting off her air was enough to stop her attempt and make her flee the restaurant."

"What else?"

I smiled and called on my powers to mess with the air around Cynthia and said, "I can also silence people like I'm currently doing with you."

She frowned and then tried to talk. Her mouth moved but no sound came out. I released my power and said, "You can talk again."

"That was a cool trick. Anything else?"

I thought about my abilities for a moment. "Come closer."

Once she got a couple of feet in front of me, I used my powers to thicken the air between us. "Punch me as hard as you can." Cynthia lifted a questioning eyebrow and I said, "Trust me. Neither of us will get hurt."

She shrugged and threw a wild right hook at me. The moment her fist encountered the air shield, it slowed like she was trying to punch through a wall of Jell-O.

Cynthia laughed and pulled her arm back and I dropped the shield.

"Can you make me fly?"

I nodded and began calling on my powers. The ceiling in here was a good twenty feet high or more, and I was about to lift Cynthia up close to it but stopped. A small part of me still wasn't convinced my powers were permanently back, and having them cut out while Cynthia was up that high would be dangerous. I told her my concerns and revised my demonstration plan.

I lifted Cynthia off the metal floor of the hangar, using my Air powers to float her up a few feet. I then pushed a bit of air behind her to slowly start moving her around.

At first she was a bit nervous, but soon her laughter was echoing off the walls. Hearing that carefree laughter healed my soul and brought a warm smile to my face.

I didn't engage in frivolous displays of my powers like this very often, as I could almost sense my departed mother admonishing me. A memory of her catching me doing this with my grade seven classmate and next-door neighbor, Susie Derkins, came rushing back. My mother had been furious, and at the time I thought she had overreacted.

Looking back on that now, she'd been right. I'd only had my powers for a few months then, and my control was less than optimal. I could have seriously hurt Susie.

Today, though, was a different story. I could have been blindfolded and still floated Cynthia with ease, as this exercise was almost effortless. The difference now was that I had more than two decades of experience with my Air powers. I'd also only had them back for less than a day and running through the different abilities of my powers was a good test to make sure everything was back to normal.

Cynthia let out a playful scream as I moved the air around her. She was now floating face down, horizontal to the floor, like Superwoman. I kept her just a few feet high in the air, and she soon relaxed and enjoyed the ride. I laughed as she mimed like she was swimming and then switched to sticking her arms and legs out in different random directions.

In the back of my mind, I went over my list of abilities, seeing if there was something else I could try, but I dismissed those ideas, as they were either variants of things I'd already done or weren't suitable for use in this enclosed environment.

"How long can you keep this up?" asked Cynthia as she floated by me.

I shrugged. "You don't weigh much, so probably for hours. Why?"

"Just curious." She paused. "So, is this what it's like flying over the city?"

"Pretty much, but the view is better than just staring at a metal floor. I'll take you up with me some time and you can see for yourself."

"I'd love that, thank you."

I sent her on another lap of the hangar before floating her back, setting her gently just in front of me.

The moment I released my powers, she moved closer and hugged me tightly. "Thank you. That was fun."

"My pleasure," I said as I enjoyed the feeling of her warmth against me.

After a bit, she broke the hug and stepped slightly back from me. To my surprise, she tilted her head slightly and closed her eyes. I took that as a sign and leaned in and kissed her. It started hesitantly but quickly grew to have some heat, and we moved tighter together as it continued.

Cynthia broke the kiss after what felt like too short a time but was probably much longer than it felt. She blinked her eyes open and smiled. "So does that Food-O-thingie also have desserts?"

"Not as good as the one I just had," I quipped.

She laughed and playfully smacked my arm.

I nodded and offered her my hand. She took it and we left the hangar.

After our dessert break, we sat at the table in the main lab, enjoying coffee and conversation. It ended up being a more balanced discussion than the initial one we had on our first date at Tim Hortons, as Cynthia was much more open about her past now.

I was surprised at how much time had passed when Blue appeared from the shadows to bring us home.

I guess time really does fly when you're having fun, I thought as we got up from the table.

We emerged back into the living room, and Blue wished us a goodnight.

A part of me was tempted to invite Cynthia to sit on the couch and continue our conversation, but an ill-timed yawn from me had Cynthia suggesting we call it a night.

I walked her up to Bree's room and gave her a chaste kiss and wished her a good night.

"Thanks for everything. I had a really nice time today," she said with a warm smile.

She laughed as I smothered another yawn and nodded. I headed for my room tired and happy.

Chapter 15

Thursday, November 24

The broody overcast skies certainly didn't match my mood the next day when I got up. I had a solid night's sleep and felt almost back to normal with only the slightest hint of fatigue from my recent massive healing session.

The house was quiet, but I spotted Stella and Blue in the office as I headed down to get a cup of morning pick-me-up.

With coffee secured, I joined them. I was disappointed to find that Cynthia wasn't with them and assumed she must still be sleeping. I worried a bit about that but figured that maybe she had trouble getting to sleep in a strange bed. Or she might be nervous about being a key witness against a major criminal organization. On the other hand, she had used a ton of her powers to heal me in the past forty-eight hours, and she might be feeling that.

"Are you worried about something? If your concern is for Marion, I have checked on her hourly since you requested, and she is functioning normally," said Blue as she studied me intently.

"Thank you for that. I was just surprised that Cynthia isn't up yet."

Stella shrugged. "I'm sure she is fine. The wards would have gone off if someone had tried to grab her."

My attention was pulled to the organizational chart on the wall, which had grown significantly. There were now various news clippings and such pinned to the walls around the office as well. The display had become a much closer match to the one in Detective Grissom's office. "You two have been busy, I see."

Stella nodded and got out of her chair and wandered over to the organizational chart. "Shady Inc. has three main locations—"

"Shady Inc.?" I asked, cutting her off.

"That is the name of the main corporation the Misfit Mafia uses as a cover for their dealings."

"Is it a functioning entity or just a front?"

"Functioning. They are one of the largest importers of patio furniture, hot tubs, pools, and pool supplies in Canada. They started with deck umbrellas and the business grew from there."

I laughed and Stella gave me an odd look. "Oh, c'mon. Shady Inc. is a pretty funny and ballsy name as a front for an organized crime syndicate."

Stella gave me a small smile and nod of understanding. "They've recently added lawn mowers, riding mowers, and outdoor power tools like leaf blowers to their lineup."

"How big of a company are we talking about here?"

"About 800 employees."

I whistled at the number, as that wasn't insignificant and probably put it in the top 500 companies in Canada. "Public or private?"

"Private."

I cursed to myself at that. It made sense, though, as public companies with shareholders would be under a lot more scrutiny, which would be something Alex Gray wouldn't want. It would be much more difficult to find out more about a private company. "Any idea of how many of the employees are just normal employees and how many are part of the Misfit Mafia?"

Stella gave me an annoyed glance and said, "I was getting to that. We think more than half are just employees but can't confirm that. Of the 300 or so that we think are part of the Misfits, we also have no idea how many are Enhanced or not. Our best educated guess is that fifty to sixty of them may be Enhanced."

I was going to interrupt her to ask how they came to that conclusion, but as I'd bothered her already, I decided to keep quiet and just let her give her briefing.

"Shady Inc. has three locations across Canada. The main one is in Toronto where about 70 percent of the company is based. The other two locations are Halifax and Vancouver, both about the same size. Pierre LaPointe, as you may have guessed, is the head of the Halifax location." She paused and drew my attention to her organization chart, which backed up her size estimates of the three locations. On the right side of the chart, I recognized Logan's picture, and the shot of Pierre was the same as the one on Detective Grissom's wall that I'd seen earlier. I also spotted the two Weres that had been involved in the kidnapping and their last names were the same, so my guess about them being brothers or cousins was accurate.

Some of the photos also identified the individuals as vampires, Weres, fae, mages, and Supers, but the vast majority of them were labeled with a note that indicated their powers were unknown.

Stella continued going over various aspects of the Misfit Mafia's operations. She believed the ports in Halifax and Vancouver were where they smuggled in most of the drugs, weapons, human traffic, and counterfeit currency they dealt in. From there, they were sent around the country.

By the time she wrapped up, I was just a wee bit intimidated at the empire Alex Gray had built and wasn't anxious to take him on. "Well, hopefully EIRT can take down Pierre LaPointe, Logan, and company in the next day or so and we won't have to use any of this information."

Blue shook her head. "Unless they are killed during the arrest, then nothing changes." When I frowned at this, Blue explained, "If they are killed then they pose no threat to Alex Gray. If they are taken alive, he will be concerned that Pierre will betray him. Pierre is the second or third highest member of the Misfits. It stands to reason that he could be utilized by police to bring down the entire Misfit organization. If Alex Gray eliminates you and Cynthia, then EIRT has no leverage or case against Pierre."

My stomach clenched as I realized that Blue was right. We might have to go against Alex Gray and the Misfits whether we wanted to or not.

***

Just as we were wrapping up our briefing, I spied Cynthia scoot by the doorway and disappear into the main bathroom. My stomach rumbled and I decided to slip downstairs and cook up some breakfast. It would just be Cynthia and I, as Stella and Blue had already eaten.

Twenty minutes later, I lifted my gaze from the scrambled eggs I was making when Cynthia said, "Do I smell bacon?"

I nodded and told her to help herself to coffee on the counter. Her hair was still damp from her shower, and she wasn't wearing any makeup but looked stunning to me.

I really could get used to this, I thought with a smile as I lifted the fry pan of eggs from the element.

I laid out the food on the counter so we could build plates and Cynthia laughed and asked if Bree was coming home.

It took me a second, but I realized she was commenting on the spread I'd put out. I probably had gone a bit overboard. We built heaping plates and retired to the table.

"So, what is the plan for today?" asked Cynthia.

I shrugged because I had a mouthful of hash brown and pondered her question. I swallowed and said, "Stay close to home and take things easy."

As we were finishing breakfast, there was a knock at the door, and I got up to answer it. I looked out the glass and spotted a red, white, and blue courier van parked on the street. I guessed it was here to deliver our phones, and I was about to open the door when a memory came back to me. The last time I had a courier at the door, the Master had sent a robot dressed as a delivery man. The robot had machine guns for arms and tried its best to ventilate me. I thickened the air around me in case history was trying to repeat itself.

I opened the door and was relieved that it was just a normal courier who smiled and held out his electronic device for me to sign. I dropped the air shield, gave my signature, and he handed over my package.

Back in the kitchen, I used a knife to carefully open the plastic envelope and found two iPhone boxes inside. There was a sticky note on each with our names on them. I handed Cynthia's to her and we spent the next hour getting them set up. I was happy that I'd backed up my old one less than a week ago. Once I restored it, I was overjoyed to see my contact list was intact and felt complete again.

We tried to join Stella and Blue after that and help with research, but they shooed us out of the office after less than ten minutes.

The overcast skies had turned to rain, and with possible targets on our backs, going out somewhere wasn't a good plan, so Cynthia and I ended up on the couch in the living room watching movies. The movies were ones we'd both seen before, so it wasn't uncommon for us to talk during the slower parts.

Cynthia and I exchanged lines from classic movies—references that usually went over my teammates' heads. Being close in age meant we had a lot more cultural references in common, and I realized how comfortable I'd become with her. My nervousness about being around someone I found attractive had vanished.

I was a bit taken aback by that. I still found her very attractive but, more importantly, I found just being around her was fun. It was more like hanging out with a friend than a potential mate. I smiled to myself, as building a friendship sounded like a wonderful foundation for a long-term relationship.

The only awkward part of the afternoon was when Blue caught us making out like lovesick teenagers on the couch. We broke apart when Blue cleared her throat and said, "I was going to retrieve dinner from the lab, but if you wish to continue your human mating rituals, I can delay my departure until you're ready."

Cynthia's cheeks reddened, which probably matched the heat that had come to mine as well, but she turned her head away from Blue and laughed into her hand. I tried to casually tuck my T-shirt back into my jeans and said, "No, dinner sounds good. Thanks."

Blue nodded and then wandered past us and made a sharp gesture in front of the shadows deeper in the room. I got Cynthia's order and then hastily got to my feet to follow Blue through the shadows.

Dinner was a subdued affair. Stella used the time to bring us up to speed on what she and Blue had been working on this afternoon, which had mostly consisted of digging into the numbered companies and shell corporations owned by Shady Inc. and Alex Gray. It was a fairly dry topic, but I knew Stella was doing this to get a better picture of what assets and properties the Misfit Mafia had at their disposal.

After dinner, we offered to help once more but Stella and Blue declined our offer, so we retired to the couch again. This time we mostly just watched movies and managed to keep our hands off each other.

Blue came down to announce that she and Stella were turning in. Our movie was just finishing up, and I wished Blue a goodnight and said we wouldn't be too far behind them.

I had intended to walk Cynthia to her room again, but we didn't make it that far. When we reached the top of the stairs, Cynthia led me with a smile to my room and said, "It seems a bit cool in the house tonight. Can I stay with you for some extra warmth?"

I leaned in and kissed her and said, "Extra warmth sounds good." I closed my bedroom door behind us.

Chapter 16

Friday, November 25

I smiled when I woke up and found Cynthia snuggled peacefully beside me. I never got to do this with Liv when we were dating, as waking up with a corpse beside me wasn't something I'd ever wanted to experience.

My smile grew as I took everything in. The morning sun was peeking in along the edges of the window blinds. There were birds cheerfully tweeting out in the backyard. The faint tingle I could feel along my skin meant my Air powers were still strong and available to me. I felt no fatigue or itchiness, which meant all side effects from Cynthia's healing were gone and I was back to full health. In short, I'd found a slice of heaven on earth and hadn't been this happy in a long time.

I wanted to savor the moment for as long as I possibly could.

Stella pounded on the door and yelled, "Zack, get up. You need to see what's on TV."

And it's gone, I thought with a mental sigh as Cynthia stirred beside me.

I gave her a chaste kiss on the forehead and said, "Good morning."

She gazed over at me and was about to say something when another round of Stella hammering on my bedroom door interrupted her.

"Alright, I'm up. We'll be down in a minute."

The shadows of Stella's feet under the bottom crack of the door disappeared and I heard her going down the stairs.

Cynthia's lovely nude form rolled out of bed, and she began searching for her clothes on the floor. I mentally cursed Stella for her timing but knew she wouldn't have interrupted us for something trivial. I got out of bed and joined Cynthia in her hunt for clothing. I laughed to myself as I spotted her bra draped over top of the floor lamp and tried to remember how it ended up there. A flash of us tearing off clothing came back to me, and I figured one of us must have just been a bit overzealous in our throw.

A few minutes later, after a quick stop for coffee in the kitchen, we joined Blue and Stella in the living room. Stella had the remote in her hand, and there was an image paused on the TV. I recognized the news network logo as belonging to Canada's national news, and my stomach knotted up at the chyron on the bottom of the screen which read, *GRC13 raid results in five dead, including a police officer.*

The moment we sat on the couch with Blue, Stella hit play on the remote. The reporter's voice explained how GRC13 arrived at a warehouse in Halifax just after nine in the morning local time to serve an arrest warrant on four suspects wanted for kidnapping and attempted murder. GRC13 had barely entered the building when gunfire broke out and Enhanced Individuals inside the warehouse used their powers against the officers. GRC13 responded in kind and a battle between the two groups broke out and lasted for about ten minutes. When it ended, five people were dead including a GRC13 officer, two of the four suspects listed in the warrant, and two other warehouse employees.

I wondered if it was Dmitri's team that executed the warrant or if it was the other GRC13 team led by Jack the mage.

That thought was pushed to the side as both Logan's and Pierre's mugshots came up on the screen. The reporter announced that the two suspects shown were at large and considered armed and dangerous and should not be approached.

The image panned and an aerial shot of the warehouse appeared on the screen. There were emergency vehicles all around it, including fire crews that were actively hosing down the rear area of the building which was engulfed in smoke.

The footage ended with the reporter saying that Acting Director Cooper would be holding a press conference later today, and then the news program cut to commercial.

Stella paused it and said, "The coverage just repeats once they return from commercials."

She was about to add something else when her phone chimed. Stella checked her iPhone and smiled. "Bounties for both Logan and Pierre have just gone up on the UN bounty website. Each has a half a million-dollar price on their head."

I nodded at that. "Well, EIRT had their shot. Now it's our turn."

***

A couple of hours later, I found myself outside the main entrance of EIRT headquarters in Toronto. The Canadian news stations continued covering the botched raid, but they were all reporting the same things. I wanted more details, but Detective Grissom was ducking my calls which pissed me off. One way or another, he was going to explain what happened.

I entered the building and approached a uniformed sergeant sitting at the front desk. He looked up as I got closer. "Can I help you?"

"I need to see Detective Grissom."

He nodded and checked his computer screen for a moment and said, "He is listed as unavailable. Can someone else be of assistance?"

"Tell him Zack Stevens is here. I suspect he will want to talk to me."

The sergeant frowned. "Can I see some ID first?"

I pulled out my green hero ID and put it on the counter between us. His eyebrows lifted as he read it and he said, "Give me one moment, Mr. Stevens," and glanced pointedly at the empty seating area to my right.

The sergeant's reaction was probably from seeing my Hamilton Hurricane alias, which could be a good or a bad thing. Generally, my Hurricane persona was well respected by law enforcement, but robbing the Royal Canadian Mint earlier in the year, had hurt my reputation. The robbery was done under duress, as the Acolytes had kidnapped Bree and threatened to kill her unless we did the job. We pulled off the heist, but afterward, we took down the Acolytes, recovered all the gold, and were cleared of all charges. The robbery made front page news and got a lot of media attention. Unfortunately, the part where we'd been exonerated didn't get the same sort of coverage, and for most papers, it was buried inside.

I stared at the sergeant, trying to get a read on whether he was hostile or friendly towards me, but his expression was professionally neutral, which made it impossible to tell. I broke eye contact and shuffled over to one of the empty seats.

I watched him pick up the phone and make a call. I was tempted to use my Air powers to amplify the sound around the sergeant to hear what he was saying but decided to behave myself. There was an armed checkpoint to enter the building proper with scanners about fifty feet farther down, and I wasn't sure if using my powers here would trip an alarm or not.

I also found myself missing Alteea's services at times like this. Her small size and glamor made her ideal for snooping and overhearing things.

To my surprise, the sergeant, after hanging up the phone, said, "Detective Grissom will be with you shortly."

I thanked him and killed time, idly checking email on my phone. I was still ticked at Grissom for ducking my calls and at how the botched arrest went down. The bounties on Logan and Pierre were nice, but I would have been happier if both were in custody at this moment, as Cynthia would be safer.

I lifted my head from my phone as Detective Grissom said, "Mr. Stevens, right this way please."

My anger dissipated the moment I laid eyes on him. The man looked like he'd aged years in the few days since I'd last seen him and had the weight of the world on his shoulders. I kicked myself for not thinking about how this would have affected him. An officer died this morning, which meant he had another life on his conscience. Also, his best shot at taking down the Misfits was in the wind. I doubted that Pierre would surrender peacefully and if found by authorities after they lost an officer, they were probably more apt to shoot first and ask questions later. Bounty hunters, too, wouldn't be overly concerned about bringing him in alive either, as the bounty paid the same either way. Laying into him now would be like kicking a wounded puppy.

I got up. "Sorry for your loss," I said.

He nodded. "Thank you. Let's continue this conversation in my office."

I followed silently down to his office in the basement. I was relieved to see that he still took the time to check for the hair at the base of the door. At least that meant he hadn't given up.

We entered the office, and I took a seat in front of his desk. He slumped down hard in the seat and pulled a bottle of bourbon from a drawer. He lifted the bottle at me, and I shook my head; it was just coming up on noon, and I'd decided to continue my sobriety even though my powers were back. I'd have a drink once this case was behind us.

"I thought you were going to make sure this didn't leak," I said as he poured a healthy amount of the amber liquid into a stained coffee mug.

"It didn't leak."

I frowned at that. "Then why do we have a dead GRC13 officer?"

Grissom shrugged and said, "Unfortunately, even the best planned operations can fall victim to plain old bad luck."

I lifted a questioning eyebrow at that.

He took a deep breath and said, "I was talking to Director Cooper before you got here. He will be conducting an investigation to make sure, but we believe the operation didn't get leaked. We found a substantial number of illegal guns and drugs at the warehouse, and both Pierre and Logan were on site when GRC13 arrived. If the operation had been leaked, they'd have cleared out the warehouse, and Pierre and Logan would have been gone.

"On top of that, every precaution was taken to avoid leaks. After you and Miss Ryerson came in and gave your statements, I called Acting Director Cooper from home. He took the case out of my hands, and everything was done by people at GRC13 in Ottawa. The group putting together the case was small, and hand selected by the director. The crown attorney and the judge are used to dealing with highly sensitive cases and have the highest security clearances. The GRC13 team that made the assault were required to surrender their phones before they boarded the transport aircraft for Halifax and were briefed on the plane after it took off. I wasn't even aware of the raid until it hit the news."

I kicked that around in my head. It sounded like Ben Cooper did everything he could to keep things under wraps. "How did the officer die then? GRC13 aren't lightweights; it's not like them to make mistakes."

"Did you see any of the news footage?"

"Yeah, hard not to. Every Canadian channel was covering it this morning."

"So, you saw how large the warehouse was?" I nodded and he continued. "The warehouse had three entrances. The team split up into three groups of four to hit all of them at once. After breaching the entrances, due to the size of the place, those groups of four spilt into pairs to cover more of the warehouse. One of the pairs spotted Logan making a break for the basement stairs but came under fire from above. One of the pair was pinned down by suppressing fire from above and returned fire. The other went after Logan on his own. Logan ambushed that officer in a narrow corridor below the warehouse and snapped his neck."

The officer that was killed broke protocol, as he should have either assisted his partner with the gunman above or waited until another officer could join him in pursuit. I knew that from training with Dmitri's team. It sounded like a rookie mistake, but while someone might be new to GRC13, they would have had years of EIRT experience, and the protocols were the same. "Why did the officer break protocol?"

"Do you know about GRC13's grading system?" I shook my head. "GRC13 team members are graded from A to D, and there are six of each grade. The officer in question was a D and in the lower part of that group. My guess is he was trying to save his spot on the team by arresting Logan."

He gambled and that cost him his life, I thought shaking my head. The more I thought about it, the dumber the officer's gamble was. Even if he did manage to arrest Logan on his own, he still risked being reprimanded for breaking protocol. Desperate people do desperate things.

I sighed. "What I don't understand, though, is if there was no leak, how did Pierre and Logan get away?"

"There was a secret tunnel that runs from the warehouse to a diner two blocks away. Witnesses reported seeing Pierre and two unknown men emerge from a storage room at the back area of the diner and leave the scene. Logan appeared the same way a few minutes later."

I shook my head but had to admire Pierre's forethought. Two blocks away would put him outside the police perimeter, and he would be able to get away easily. "Any thoughts on where they might be now?"

Grissom took another long pull from his mug and then said, "Not in Halifax because that city is going to have local and federal officers looking in every nook and cranny. I also doubt that Pierre is heading for Toronto or Vancouver because I can't see Alex Gray being happy with him at the moment. Pierre is a smart man and has substantial wealth. My guess is he gets a new ID and disappears out of Canada. As for Logan, with his temper and his beast, I'd guess that he'll come after you and Miss Ryerson, so watch yourselves."

I smiled at that last part. "He's welcome to try. I'm not the same person he kidnapped before, and my teammates aren't to be trifled with either."

Grissom nodded. "I don't care what happens with Logan, but please try to take Pierre alive. If we get him into custody, I have a real shot at taking down the entire Misfit organization."

"Surely with the guns and drugs found at the warehouse today and the employees that were arrested on scene, you have enough to go after Alex Gray?"

He shook his head. "No. Alex Gray has some of the best lawyers in the country at his disposal. This will be framed as Pierre being a rogue employee that was running a criminal enterprise without the company's knowledge. I'm willing to bet that Shady Inc. will be issuing a press release along those lines any minute. Pierre and maybe Logan are probably the only ones with direct ties to Alex Gray. The rest of the Halifax employees will all say that Pierre was in charge and that was all they knew. If you saw the news footage, then you saw the fire trucks on scene?"

I nodded. "They were mainly there to deal with a fire in the administration office; all computers and records were torched and destroyed. That means we have no paper trail to tie Alex Gray to any of this. The Misfits have probably already cleared any illicit goods from their Toronto and Vancouver warehouses. They will go dark for a bit until the heat blows over, but then they'll be back in business in a few weeks. The only way we get Alex Gray is to get Pierre."

I thought about it and said, "I'm not promising anything, but I'll try to take Pierre alive."

Grissom sat a bit straighter at that. My comment seemed to lift a bit of the burden on his shoulders. I just hoped I could deliver.

Chapter 17

Friday, November 25

After a quick lunch, Cynthia, Blue, Stella, and I retired to the office upstairs to discuss our next steps. I went over my conversation with Detective Grissom to get them up to speed on where everything stood.

"EIRT had their shot at Pierre and company and whiffed. Now it's our turn. We have two fugitives that are on the run. Logan could be anywhere in the country and if Grissom's correct, Pierre might not even be in Canada anymore. Any thoughts on how we find them?"

"While you were gleaning information from law enforcement, Stella and I used that time to question your mate due to her prior relationship with Logan," Blue replied.

Stella giggled. Cynthia blushed lightly, and I felt the heat in my own cheeks.

Blue glanced at all of us with a confused look on her face and I explained, "Mate is not the appropriate term."

"Why? Are you not engaged in sexual relations with Cynthia? I assumed that by your exuberant noises and multiple cries to various deities late last night that that was indeed the case."

Cynthia's blush deepened and I was pretty sure my own cheeks mirrored her crimson coloring. Stella spun her office chair so her back was to us, her head bobbing with smothered laughter. I knew answering that question would take me down a deeper rabbit hole with Blue. I frantically tried to think of a way out of this that wouldn't lead to further embarrassing questions. "Cynthia is her own person and referring to her as my mate diminishes her individuality."

Blue nodded and turned to Cynthia. "My deepest apologies if I violated any social norms and caused you any offense. I am still learning about human customs and mating rituals and have not fully grasped all the nuances they entail."

Cynthia smiled. "It's fine. Thank you for your apology."

Stella turned back around and wiped the tears from her eyes as Blue went on. "As I was saying, we questioned Cynthia to get better insight into Logan's personality and habits. Based on that conversation and the fact he murdered a police officer, I suspect we will not need to find him because he will come to us."

I blinked at that and said, "Okay, I'll bite. How do you figure that?"

"Simple. His personality is incapable of accepting accountability for his actions. He will deflect that blame to you and Cynthia and then will seek vengeance for this perceived misdeed."

All the previous color left Cynthia's cheeks and she looked visibly shaken at Blue's words. Her reaction convinced me that Blue might be on to something. I moved to her and embraced her in a hug and said, "Cynthia, relax; he can't hurt you now. If Logan comes here, he will regret it. Any one of us is more than capable of taking him down. Against the three of us, he has no chance."

Blue's tail went still, and she said, "You are not looking at the big picture. Logan and Pierre are a concern but as wanted criminals, their resources are limited. The larger issue is Alex Gray. As long as Logan and Pierre are alive, it is in his interest to eliminate you and Cynthia. If you two are dead, then the case against Pierre weakens considerably."

I frowned at that and was about to point out that even if we were dead, Pierre would still be on the hook for the guns and drugs found at his warehouse. Blue was correct, though, that the kidnapping and attempted murder charges were more serious charges than those and gave police more leverage to flip him against Alex Gray. It would also be in his interest to eliminate us just to send a message to anyone who thought about interfering with the business. "What do you suggest we do about Alex Gray then?"

Blue's tail began moving in happy motions again and she glanced pointedly at Cynthia. "It would be prudent to have this conversation in private."

My stomach knotted up, as I was pretty sure what Blue's solution was and why she didn't want Cynthia to hear it. "We aren't killing Alex Gray."

Cynthia gasped in shock but I ignored her for the moment as I tried to figure out what we could do about him instead. Blue was right that he'd be gunning for us, and with his considerable resources, he was a bigger threat than Logan or Pierre at the moment. A defiant part of me thought that if Alex Gray wanted a war, we'd give him one. We had a lot of allies, like the Barrie pack, the two swarms of pixies we'd saved, my own foundation members, and members of the English Vampire Court, just to name a few, and we could make a war very costly for him. I suddenly had an idea. "Stella, do you think the English Vampire Court could arrange a meeting between Alex Gray and me?"

Stella frowned and said, "Probably, but why? That's like walking into the lion's den."

"If the English Vampire Court arranges it, he will be hesitant to do anything to me during the meeting for fear of upsetting them. By showing up to meet at his office, I can lay out why it would be a very bad idea for him to come after us. He may have more resources than us, but we can strike anywhere. And unless he wants to spend the rest of his life glancing sideways at shadows, he'd be apt to let this one go."

Blue nodded and smiled a pointy-toothed grin at that. "I approve of this course of action."

Stella shook her head. "Won't warning him just make him up his security?"

I shrugged. "Does that even matter? If Blue was hunting you, do you really think you could do much to stop her?"

Stella made a sideways glance at Blue and then she just slowly nodded. "I'll call Sarah and see if she'll arrange a meeting for you. You really want to meet him in his office and not on neutral ground?"

I nodded and Stella mumbled something about "your funeral" under her breath as she walked out of the office. I turned to Blue and asked, "While we wait for Stella to return, do you have any thoughts about how we might find Pierre?"

"In our earlier conversation with Cynthia, she mentioned an individual named TJ Harris. He manages a club in Halifax owned by Shady Inc. It seems that this person was close to both Logan and Pierre, as they spent a significant amount of time at the club. He may be able to provide us insight into their whereabouts."

At first, I wasn't overly excited about this lead, but if Pierre had spent a lot of time drinking at the club, this TJ person might have decent intel about him. People say things when drunk that they normally wouldn't while sober. Pierre might have let something slip. I shifted my attention to Cynthia. "Do you think TJ would be a good person to talk to?"

She nodded. "Pierre was close to him, and TJ always seems to be in the know with everything going on around the city."

"Any idea of his schedule?"

Cynthia laughed. "TJ almost lives at Club HX. It's Friday, so he'll be working tonight. He's usually there by five."

I checked my phone and saw it was coming up on two. Halifax was an hour ahead of us, so it was three there currently. "What does TJ look like?"

Cynthia smiled again. "He isn't hard to spot. Look for a guy covered in tats and enough piercings to set off a metal detector from a mile away. Two weeks ago, he had bright green hair. He changes the color often, but it's always some loud, unnatural color."

"Should be easy enough to spot. Blue, find this Club HX via the shadows and let me know when TJ arrives."

Blue nodded just as Stella came back. "Sarah will arrange the meeting and will call me back shortly."

"TJ and this meeting with Alex Gray are a good start but we need more," I said. "Do Logan or Pierre have any known family? Or are either active on social media? Have we got any credit card information on either of them?"

Cynthia piped up. "Logan never talked about his family. Any time I brought it up, he got angry or withdrawn and changed the conversation. I got the feeling that either he doesn't have any living family or, if they are alive, he wasn't close and never speaks to them."

Stella said, "We haven't found any family for Pierre, but with him being a mage, that is not surprising."

Cynthia frowned in confusion, and I said, "Pierre might look like he is in his thirties, but mages have long life spans, and he could be much older than he appears."

Stella jumped in and said, "By his birth certificate, he is ninety-eight years old."

Cynthia's face lit up in understanding and then she got a look like she'd bitten into something rotten.

"What?" I asked.

"Pierre liked to date girls in their early twenties. I found it a bit creepy when I thought he was mid-thirties but the 'ick' factor on that just went up dramatically."

I was about to agree and make a comment, but then I remembered that I had dated Olivia and I decided to quickly change the topic. "Family seems like a dead end. How about credit cards and social media?"

Stella pulled up a file on the computer and said, "Pierre doesn't exist online, but Logan was active on social media. The last thing he posted was last night but nothing since the raid this morning."

Pierre's lack of social media presence wasn't a surprise. Mages, wizards, and other magic users were generally a secretive bunch, which usually kept them far away from social media.

"As for credit cards, we have numbers for both, but they aren't showing any activity since the raid," finished Stella.

I mentally sighed at that but shouldn't have been surprised. Logan and Pierre were career criminals and wanted fugitives, so neither was likely to tip off authorities by using social media or credit cards. I was willing to bet that both were now using an alias, which gave me an idea. "Cynthia, you mentioned that girl who you fixed up before you left was using a fake ID. Do you have any idea who would have created it?"

Cynthia shook her head. "No clue. I knew from Logan that they could get fake IDs, but I never asked more about it."

Stella perked up. "You're betting that Logan and Pierre are using aliases now and if we could find who created them, we might be able to find out what aliases they are using?"

"That was my hope."

Cynthia said, "Ask TJ when you talk to him. If anyone will know, it will be him."

With that, I was getting more enthusiastic about my upcoming meeting with TJ.

Stella's phone rang and she quickly answered. I assumed it must be Sarah calling her back. We all went quiet, but Stella's side of the conversation didn't give us much information, only the occasional "yes," or "okay," and "thanks." She wrapped up the call with a "Thanks again, Sarah. I owe you one."

Stella gave a half-hearted smile and said, "The meeting is set for tonight at seven in Alex Gray's office in Toronto."

"Good work, Stella."

Tonight looked to be a busy night, but hopefully these meetings would get us closer to taking down Logan and Pierre once and for all.

***

I popped out of the shadows and into a brightly lit but deserted nightclub. By the furnishings and fixtures, the place looked to be high end, but the current lighting showed the flaws that wouldn't be revealed when the strobe and laser lights were going. The place seriously needed a good cleaning and a touch of paint here and there.

A man with bright purple hair came out of the back area carrying a case of booze. By the neck and face tattoos and the metal piercings around every orifice, I assumed this must be TJ. I wasn't a fan of tattoos but had to admit that the artwork of his neck tattoos was well done. Back in the day, tattoos were the sole province of bikers, sailors, and inmates, which made me dislike them. Now with every soccer mom on the planet sporting ink, they didn't seem as special. I couldn't count how many times a suspect was spotted due to their ink. While I planned on staying on the right side of the law, I'd still avoid tats just because of their ability to broadcast your identity to the world.

"TJ Harris?" I said in a commanding voice.

TJ's green eyes locked with mine and he dropped the case with a crash and bolted.

Why do people always run? I thought with a sigh.

I chased after him and was glad I'd left my armor at home. I used my Air powers to lift me over the bar and thickened the air in front of me as a precaution in case TJ was waiting with a weapon in the back area. I slammed through the swinging door he disappeared through and entered the club's kitchen.

There was a burly guy chopping lettuce with a knife almost big enough to be considered a machete off to my right. He looked up and frowned as I entered. He raised the knife and started to walk in my direction.

I called some showy blue sparks to my hands and said, "You really want to do this?"

The whites of his eyes became huge as he gazed at the electricity dripping from my hands. He shook his head and pointedly stepped back to the prep area he'd been working at.

I was about to ask him where TJ was when I heard the thunk of a door's locking bar come from deeper in the kitchen and sprinted in that direction. I turned a corner and spotted a lit exit sign at the end of the corridor. In my haste, I barely managed to avoid boxes of produce as I went down the hall. I crashed into the door before emerging outside to an overcast day in Halifax.

I frantically looked around and then smiled as I spotted the bright purple hair hightailing it down the alleyway to my right. With no ceilings to worry about, I lifted myself into the air and shot off after him.

This is so much better than running. I rapidly closed the distance between us.

TJ was just about exit the alley, so I sent a blast of wind under him and lifted him into the air. He screamed in panic as he climbed higher and higher into the dreary sky.

When we reached about a thousand feet from the ground, I stopped. This was a nice height for what I had in mind. People looked like ants from this high up. I flew up from under him until we were at the same height.

"Please let me down!" said TJ as he avoided looking down.

I stayed quiet and just let him stew. People don't realize how effective silence can be in an interrogation. I used the opportunity to take in the spectacular view of the city and the ocean. There were a couple of cargo ships coming in to dock off in the distance as well as some smaller boats. Seagulls followed a fishing trawler, probably hoping to score a free meal. I'd never been to Halifax before and by the amazing scenery, I was regretting that choice. I figured maybe after this case was wrapped up, I'd have Blue travel Cynthia and me out here and she could show me the town.

"I'll pay whatever I owe and more. Please let me down," pleaded TJ, bringing my attention back to him.

"I don't want your money; I just need you to answer a few questions. First, why did you run?"

"I owe a lot of people money. I assumed you were coming to collect."

I guessed that the people that TJ owed money to had probably been hesitant to enforce payment due to his close relationship with Pierre. With Pierre in the wind, some of those people would now try to collect.

"I'm looking for information on Logan Reeves and Pierre LaPointe."

"They're gone, man, no idea where they went."

"Wrong answer," I said and cut the flow of wind I'd been using to keep him in the air.

"WAIT!" he screamed as he began freefalling back to Earth.

I pushed some wind under him and lifted him back up to my level again.

I felt a little bad, as TJ was shaking so much it almost looked like he was having a seizure. I wasn't sure if that was from fear of becoming a splotch on the pavement or due to the cold, as it was a bit nippy at this altitude. I figured it was probably a bit of both.

The moment he was eye-level again, he said, "Logan is probably either going to PEI or Hamilton. He has a beef with his ex and is looking for payback. Pierre has a cabin on a lake in Quebec. He loves that place and how isolated it is. He's probably going to hide out there."

I perked up at mention of the cabin. If that was where he was going, it would be easy enough to check. It certainly gave us a better starting point. "What aliases are Logan and Pierre using?"

"I don't know, man. I swear. Please don't drop me."

I eyed him critically for a moment but decided he was telling the truth. "Who makes fake IDs here in Halifax?"

"The Misfits use Max at CopyMart. Max makes fake Nova Scotia drivers licenses in the back area of the store."

I sensed that he had more to say, so I prompted him. "It takes some effort to keep both of us up here . . ."

TJ gulped and shook harder. "Logan and Pierre wouldn't use Max for themselves. There is a guy in Ottawa called the Fixer. He makes top-notch fake IDs. SIN numbers, driver's licenses, passports, credit cards, online histories, the works. All of it as good as the real thing."

That sounded more promising. A fake driver's license wouldn't get either of them far. They'd need solid aliases, with all documentation, especially if either wanted to leave the country. I kicked around asking TJ more questions, but none came to mind. The cabin and this Fixer were two good leads, and I figured that was enough for now. "Okay, TJ, you've been very helpful. Let's get you back on solid ground. And the next time you see me, don't run."

He nodded rapidly in agreement, and I lowered us back down. TJ stumbled as he took his first steps back towards the club but managed to stay upright. I felt a little guilty for rattling the guy like that, but by his associations, I doubted that TJ was an innocent shrinking violet. A small part of me worried that he could report me to law enforcement and that there might be consequences for my actions. I dismissed that, though, as TJ probably wasn't the type to go running to the police with an issue. I watched him disappear back inside the club and then called Blue for a lift home.

Chapter 18

Friday, November 25

We'd spent the last couple of hours since I'd gotten back from questioning TJ going over the plan for the meeting with Alex Gray this evening.

Blue had been spying on Shady Inc. and Alex Gray during the time I'd been away and would continue to until the meeting. So far, it didn't look like I'd be walking into a trap.

The biggest debate we had about this meeting was whether I should wear my armor or not. I wanted this meeting to be a show of strength on our part and walking in wearing armor could be taken as a sign of weakness. Stella argued that it was part of my Hamilton Hurricane persona now and that I should wear it to reflect that status. Neither Blue nor Cynthia had an opinion one way or the other. In the end, I decided to forgo the armor and opted to go with the formal wear I usually wore to the English Vampire Court. The vampire mob boss we'd dealt with in Vegas seemed to appreciate that I dressed up to meet him and I hoped Alex Gray would too.

Fifteen minutes before the meeting, Cynthia's phone rang, and she announced it was her mom calling. She moved to the far corner of the room as she answered it.

As Blue put the final adjustment on my tie, I kept an eye on Cynthia and noticed her body stiffen, and I grew concerned. She had her back to me, which meant I couldn't read her facial expression to get a better read on what was going on. She was also keeping her voice low.

Blue stepped back and nodded in approval at her work and then frowned as she noticed my demeanor. She turned her attention to Cynthia and we both waited for her to end the call.

Cynthia hung up and was clutching her phone so hard her knuckles were white. "Logan was spotted in my hometown."

"Is your family okay?" I asked. Cynthia nodded. "Where and how long ago was this sighting?"

"The bastard actually stopped for dinner at Betsy's diner in town. He was just finishing up his food when a news report came on the TV and his picture was displayed. Mom said this happened an hour ago. An alert to law enforcement went out, and police have blocked outbound lanes of the Confederation Bridge and are searching vehicles before allowing them to cross. That is probably a waste of time; I'd bet Logan used a boat to get there."

I hadn't known the name of the bridge, but I knew there was just one roadway that connected PEI to the rest of Canada. "Why do you think he used a boat?"

"He fled from the diner on foot."

The lack of a vehicle outside the diner certainly added weight to Cynthia's theory.

"Do we go search for him?" asked Blue.

I glanced at my phone and weighed our options. It was coming up on seven and I needed to make that meeting with Alex Gray. Another part of me really longed to have Blue open a portal so I could see if I could spot Logan from the air. It would be dark out there now, but his aura would show up like a beacon. With an hour gone, though, he could be back on the boat. Whoever was smuggling him on and off the Island wouldn't have him up on deck, which meant his aura wouldn't be visible from above. I was also dressed like James-freaking-Bond at this moment, which really wasn't practical for that kind of outing, and getting into my armor would add even more time to the clock. I shook my head, "No. Too much time has passed. We have to assume he is in the wind. Just to be safe, use the shadows to check on Cynthia's parents every five minutes or so."

Blue nodded.

"Why would Logan flee the diner?" The way his beast was riding him, I'd have assumed he would have happily fought anyone who got in his way. The diner probably held thirty people max, but some of those would be elderly and children and most would try to get away if Logan got aggressive. The impression I got from Cynthia was that her hometown was tiny, which meant either little or no local law enforcement.

To my surprise, Cynthia laughed and said, "Betsy, the owner, and all her family that work there are orcs."

Now Logan's hasty departure made sense. Orcs were dark fae and were known to be tough, vicious fighters. Like all fae, they usually carried silver weapons, and that would be a fight even a Were wouldn't want. They probably used glamor to hide their real appearances, but Logan's nose would have detected they weren't human. He probably would have sensed the silver on them as well. "Orcs are dark fae and have bounties on them . . ."

Cynthia put her hands on her hips and glared at me. "Don't you dare! Betsy and her clan are beloved community members. They have been there since my Grandma was a little girl and never caused a hint of trouble!"

I raised my hands in surrender. "Sorry, I've had bad experiences with dark fae in the past, but it sounds like these orcs aren't a threat to anyone."

Cynthia gave me a nod. "Besides, if you tried to take them down, the whole town would lynch you. Betsy makes the best apple pie on the Island."

"How did you know they were orcs?" I asked out of curiosity.

"It's an open secret around town, but back when I was a teenager, one of Betsy's grandchildren got into a bad farming accident. Mom saved him and I was brought along to learn. The young orc was hurt badly enough that he couldn't use his glamor to disguise his real form. Betsy's clan swore a blood debt to my mom for saving him. Mom said that there are now two orc warriors camped on their front lawn to keep them safe."

That last part made me smile and feel better about a clan of orcs on the loose. If they were protecting Cynthia's family, it showed that they'd forsaken their dark ways. The part about them being an open secret was also another strong indicator that they were good people. Their neighbor, the retired EIRT officer, would have to know, but if she wasn't willing to turn them in, then they must have earned her trust too. "Orcs and healers all in the same town. Your humble home sure has more than its share of Enhanced."

Cynthia grinned. "There is also a family of witches and Mr. Johnson. No one knows what he is, but he's definitely more than just human. Rumors about him range from demi-god to fae to being a member of the Super class."

Fascinating, I thought. Enhanced Individuals were fairly rare, but I had read about small villages where there were clusters of them living together. This was the first time, though, that I'd personally come across one of these clusters. The academic in me longed to pester Cynthia with more questions but duty called; it was time to visit Alex Gray.

Blue opened a portal and said, "I will observe everything from the shadows. The first sign of betrayal or trouble, Stella and I will be there. Use the standard code word if you need us."

The code word was *Lincoln*, and it was one we'd used before on other cases. I nodded and stepped into the shadows.

I popped out to a cool night in Toronto by a bus shelter on Bloor Street. Blue had put me just outside of a modern forty-story mirrored glass office building. I was pleased to see that the sidewalks were pretty quiet without much pedestrian traffic. Not really a surprise, as it was seven at night on a Friday and most office workers had fled for the weekend. The light public presence was a blessing; if this meeting went bad, there was a good chance that glass and other debris might be raining down on this area shortly.

My stomach knotted up as I walked into the marbled foyer of the building. Stella's earlier words about walking into the lion's den came rushing back. I pushed those doubts aside and approached the security desk in the lobby. The guard behind the desk had been warily eying me since I walked through the door.

"ID and reason for your visit?" he asked as I stepped up to the desk.

So far this was going to plan. Stella and Blue had checked into the security service the building used and could find no connection to Shady Inc. If the worst happened, at least there'd be a record of me entering the building for the authorities to investigate. "I'm here to see Alex Gray of Shady Inc.," I said as I handed over my Hero ID.

The guard's expression changed to one of confusion for a moment as he took my ID. I assumed he expected a driver's license and not a bright green hero ID. I really needed to get my driver's license, as it would be much more discreet in cases like this. I'd actually picked up an Ontario driver's test handbook a couple of weeks ago due to my loss of power, but it was still unopened on my bedside table. Now, with my Air powers back, I doubted it would be opened anytime soon.

"Please sign in here, Mr. Stevens," said the guard as he pushed a clipboard towards me with my ID resting on it.

I picked up my ID and signed the sheet and handed it back to him.

"The bank of elevators on your right," said the guard as he took the board back.

I nodded and headed that way. My leather-soled shoes echoed off the cream marble as I walked through the quiet lobby.

One of the three elevators opened the moment I hit the button. I got on and pressed thirty-seven. Shady Inc. occupied the thirty-sixth and thirty-seventh floors. According to Blue, Alex Gray's office was just to the right of reception on the upper floor.

I was caught off guard by the music playing in the elevator. It was a song from my childhood that was upbeat and controversial. My mom wouldn't let me listen to it when it came on, so I only got to hear it at friends' houses or during breaks at school. Now that hardcore song was elevator music. I shook my head, as that made me feel a bit old. I tried to reassure myself that it was technically the weekend, so maybe they modernized the playlist during this time.

The elevator dinged and opened. I stepped out into a ceramic-tiled hallway. In front of me was a large TV screen behind protective glass with the name of the company and their umbrella and lawn chair logo. There was an arrow at the bottom pointing in the direction of the lobby. A slight tingling sensation ran up and down my body as I sensed Alex Gray's Ice Elemental powers. A slight smile appeared on my face. By how faintly I sensed his power, I suspected his abilities fell in the medium range, which was less than I'd been expecting.

I turned and spotted the glass doors of the main entrance. As I got closer to the doors, I noticed a doorbell discreetly tucked to the right. I reached for the chrome handle first and was surprised as the door opened. I figured with it being after hours, the door would be locked. Though I guess if I thought about it, who would be dumb enough to break into the main office of the most powerful organized crime group in Canada?

The lobby was spacious and tastefully decorated. To my left was another TV mounted on a cherry wood wall displaying a news station, the sound off. There were dark grey leather chairs and a couch around the TV. I jumped slightly. To my right was a reception desk with a stunning blonde with glasses. She sat unnaturally still and that was why

I didn't notice her right away. The bloodred and black aura around her meant she was a vampire, which explained the lack of motion.

She smiled in amusement at my reaction. "Good evening. You must be Mr. Stevens. Mr. Gray is expecting you. I will let him know you are here."

Her voice was rich and deep and almost curled my toes at how sexy it sounded. The glasses and her conservative attire was a look I found very appealing. An image of Liv dressed in a similar fashion came rushing back to me. I called that outfit *sexy librarian*. Some guys liked cheerleader costumes, or women in a short formfitting black dress, but for me sexy librarian was my absolute favorite look.

An image of Cynthia popped into my head and broke the spell I was under.

Focus, Zack focus. The receptionist is much closer to a nightmare than a fantasy, especially if this meeting goes badly.

By the size of her aura, she had been a vampire for a good sixty years. She appeared to be in her mid-twenties, which meant she was actually closer to her mid-eighties.

Damn, Grandma's hot.

I pushed the thought aside and brought myself back to reality. A vampire of that age could come across that desk and snap my neck before I even realized what was going on. That last thought tempered my sudden lust.

The vampire hung up the phone and said, "Mr. Gray's office is just over there to the right."

I blinked in surprise, as I'd expected Alex Gray to play the usual power game and make me wait in the lobby for a few minutes before seeing me. I wasn't sure if this was a good or bad thing. I took a deep breath and headed for his office.

Just as I passed the reception area, the executive's corner office door came into view. There were two men in suits that looked like they could be NFL linebackers standing guard outside the doors. The tingling sensation I had felt earlier grew as I got closer.

As I approached, the goon on the left pulled out a yellow electronic wand from the inside of his suit jacket. The open flap of the jacket also exposed a pistol he had holstered there. My eyes went to his partner, and I spotted a slight bulge in his jacket, which meant he was packing too. The upside was that neither had an aura, which meant they were just humans. Their size and the fact that they were armed meant they were a threat I couldn't take lightly, however.

The guard held up his free hand to indicate I should stop. I complied and he turned on the wand and began scanning me for weapons and listening devices. The wand chirped as he ran it over my chest. I slowly opened my jacket and showed it was just my phone. He made a gimme motion with his hand and eyed my phone. I sighed and handed it over to him. He took it and continued scanning.

When he turned off the scanner, I thought we were done. I went to move, but he held out his hand in a stop motion. The guard put away the scanner and began patting down my arms. "Hey! At least buy me dinner first," I quipped.

I got no reaction. He crouched down and worked his way up my legs. As his hands got higher up my inner thigh, I said, "Another inch or two and I might have to buy *you* dinner."

I thought that was funny but neither of the guards reacted in the slightest. He stood back up and nodded and the other guard opened the door. The office was large and spacious, but my attention was drawn to the spectacular view of the Toronto night skyline.

A soft clunk behind me pulled my attention back to the here and now. The guards followed me into the room and closed the doors behind them. They each took up a position in front of the doors.

I glanced around the large office and quickly assessed things. I suppressed a smile due to the large bookshelves that lined the wall to the right that created a big enough shadow for Blue and Stella to use. In front of me and just in front of the floor-to-ceiling windows sat Alex Gray behind a solid oak desk. His six-inch pure blue aura confirmed my earlier theory that he was an Ice Elemental with medium power. Off to his left stood a pale thin woman who studied me intently with sharp blue eyes. She had a four-inch pale green aura around her, which meant she was a telepath with decent abilities.

A movement to my right shifted my attention to the mage sitting on a couch in the corner. His aura was about five inches in size with blue making up the largest part, a sizable brown segment, and two tiny slivers of yellow and red. This meant his primary casting abilities were water and ice with a secondary skill in earth magic. The two slivers of yellow and red represented air and fire, but it was barely enough ability to light a candle and just enough air magic to blow out said candle.

I mentally worked out a plan of action if things went south. Alex Gray was the most dangerous person in the room, as he could access his Ice elemental powers almost instantly. If things went bad, I would thicken the air around me to shield me from any of his attacks, which would also prevent the goons from behind shooting me in the back. The next move would be to hit Alex Gray and his desk with a blast of air strong enough to send both out through the glass window behind him. There was a good chance the huge gust of wind would also take out the telepath. A quick lightning strike to finish the mage and then I'd turn and deal with the goons. The dicey part was whether the mage would be fast enough to get off a spell before I got to him, but I felt pretty confident about my chances.

With that settled, I put on a false smile and approached the desk where Mr. Gray was sitting. The intensity of the tingling across my skin suddenly jumped by a factor of three as Alex Gray must have been accessing his powers, and on reflex, I thickened the air around me. "You really want to try ice versus lightning, Mr. Gray?"

He gave me a smile that didn't reach his cold green eyes and nodded. The tingling sensation dropped back to normal levels. That had been a dick-measuring contest and a way of sizing up how strong my powers were. Lesser elementals couldn't sense when another elemental was accessing their powers. As I could tell how powerful someone was by my aura abilities, it made no sense for me to play elemental power-sensing games.

Alex Gray gestured to the chair in front of his desk. I took the offered seat and the two of us locked eyes in silence.

I was a bit disappointed with his presence, as I'd been expecting more of an intimidating appearance. He was probably about my height and weight, though with his tailored suit it was hard to get an exact read on his weight and he could be ten pounds lighter or heavier than I was. I spotted his manicured nails and what looked to be an expensive gold watch on his wrist. His face was remarkably average and unmemorable. The two exceptions were the small but noticeable scar above his right eyebrow and his green eyes. The intense green eyes were like a hawk's in that they seemed to miss nothing. His light brown hair was a bit too uniform in color, and I suspected there was some help from a bottle to hide the grey that his fifty-seven years of life would have brought.

"I was a bit surprised to hear that you wanted to meet, Mr. Stevens. I don't receive calls from the English Vampire Court's champion very often," he said in a coolly measured tone.

I smiled to myself that he was the one to break the silence and took that as a point for me. "I felt it would be a good idea to talk to you and save you from making a big mistake."

"And that would be?"

"Coming after Cynthia and me."

He nodded and reached over and hit the button on a small metallic cube on his desk. The cube lit up with red lights that started one by one changing to green. He held up his hand to indicate that I should wait and once all the lights went green, he said, "Mad Scientist tech; it prevents anyone from listening in on our conversations electronically." He paused and then added, "Tell me why I shouldn't just kill you right now."

I got a bit nervous when he said it would prevent anyone from listening in, but Blue didn't use electronics to spy. She would still be able to listen in. If he'd blocked her as well, then things would have gotten ugly fast, as Blue and Stella would have stormed this place as if it were the beaches of Normandy on D-Day. "Because it would be the last thing you do. You might be able to kill me, but I promise I'll take you with me." A look of disbelief crossed his face. "Check with your telepath to see if I'm telling the truth or not."

His eyebrows lifted and he turned his head towards her. She gave him a slow nod.

I caught movement out of the corner of my eye. "Also, if your mage keeps reaching for that wand in front of him, I will fry him where he sits."

I smiled as the mage froze. He lifted his palms up in surrender and sat back away from the wand. "Lastly, if either of your goons by the door attempts to draw their weapons, my shadow traveler will put them down."

Alex Gray looked beyond me to the guards and shook his head at them. He turned his attention back to me and was visibly angry, but there was a look of uncertainty there too. "State what you want."

"Leave us alone. If you come after us, it will be costly to you and bring a lot of unwanted attention your organization cannot afford at this time."

He smiled, looking like a lion about to devour a gazelle and said, "My intel tells me half your team is currently unavailable to you. Your Werepanther is currently in Alberta on Were Council business and your vampire is at the English Vampire Court. Do you really think that just you, your shadow traveler, and your Hyde are a threat to my operations?"

I hoped I managed to keep a neutral expression, as his statement rattled me. He'd obviously done his homework. "Impressive. Did your research also inform you about the allies we've made in the last year? We have established ties to the English Vampire Court, the Barrie Pack, the fae, and several Super class individuals. Many of those would be happy to fight with us. Imagine the damage a swarm of pixies could do to your Vancouver warehouse. Or how would you feel if your organization was constantly monitored from the shadows and all sorts of anonymous tips started getting fed to law enforcement?"

A look of concern briefly appeared on his face before he turned to look at the telepath again. She once again nodded to verify my statement.

I was relieved at that as I was stretching the truth a bit. We had established ties to all the groups I'd listed. And some of them would fight with us if things got ugly, but the English Vampire Court wouldn't officially get involved. A few members of the Court, though, would be happy to freelance their services for a fee. The same deal with the Barrie Pack. I'd just hoped that there was enough truth in my statement that the telepath would confirm that, and it seemed my gamble paid off.

Once he turned back to me, I said, "Neither of us wants or is looking for a war. I'm asking you to treat this incident as a businessman would. Your employees screwed up. Pierre shouldn't have gone after Cynthia, and Logan should have killed me when he had the chance. You don't strike me as someone who takes failure lightly, so write them off and move on. I'm sure you have an up-and-coming associate that would love to run your East Coast operations. You let this go, and a month from now once the heat has died down, it's back to business as usual."

The mage in the corner sat up straighter and became much more interested in the conversation. I was pretty sure he was looking to be Pierre's replacement.

Alex Gray's eyes flicked over to the mage for a moment and then he studied me quietly.

After a long, drawn-out silence, he said, "Very well, I will leave you and your companion alone. You and your team have had an impressive run this past year: a demon, the Master, the Rose, and a lich. The one thing they all have in common is that you brought none of them in alive. If that trend continues, we won't have an issue. Do we have an understanding?"

Shit! It dawned on me what he was implying. Logan being killed wasn't an issue, as there was no way he or his beast would allow themselves to be taken alive and spend the rest of their days locked in a small cell. Detective Grissom's weighted visage popped into my head, though, when I thought about Pierre. He was counting on me to take Pierre alive so he could build a case against Alex Gray, and I really wanted that to happen. On the other hand, Pierre was an experienced mage, and I might not have the luxury of taking him alive anyways.

I caught the telepath eying me intently out of the corner of my eye and realized that I needed to choose my words here very carefully. I wasn't going to promise to kill Pierre if I had a chance of bringing him alive. I smiled to myself as the perfect response came to mind. "Understood."

Alex Gray glanced at the telepath, and she nodded. He smiled and said, "It seems our business here is concluded. Hopefully, this meeting will be our first and last one."

Chapter 19

Friday, November 25

The moment I stepped out of the shadows, Stella held out her hand and said, "Your phone."

I fished my new iPhone out of my suit pocket and handed it to her. The goons had returned it to me on my way out of the building. "Why do you need my phone?"

"They might have tampered with it or bugged it," she said as she disappeared out of the living room.

Blue's tail was making happy circles behind her, probably in approval of Stella's caution. I glanced at her and said, "Your paranoia is rubbing off on Stella."

She flashed me a mouthful of pointed teeth and said, "It is only paranoia if someone is not trying to kill you."

Cynthia came over and hugged me and said, "It sounds like the meeting was a success and that Alex Gray and the Misfits won't be coming after us."

I broke the hug. "We'll see. I think I worried Alex Gray enough that he'll think twice before coming after us, but we still need to be on alert for the possibility." I turned to Blue and asked, "Anything interesting happen after I left?"

"The conversation in the office was about mundane and about non-related items that did not pertain to us. That was to be expected. Alex Gray is aware of my abilities and probably assumed we'd be monitoring him for the next while. I will continue to observe him from the shadows, but I cannot do that full time."

I pondered Blue's words. She was right; if he was planning on betraying us, he'd be careful about it. It wouldn't have surprised me if he had a contingency plan in place before this meeting took place. A code word to an associate and he could send people after us without us being the wiser. All I could do was hope that I'd made enough of an impression on him that he wouldn't make that decision without a reason.

Stella returned and handed me my phone and said, "It was clean."

"Thanks."

With Alex Gray dealt with for now, we could turn our attention to Logan and Pierre. It also meant it was time to give credit where credit was due. "Blue, it looks like you were right about Logan coming after Cynthia and me. He was obviously looking for Cynthia in PEI. If we assume he has fled, that means he is coming here next. Any thoughts about how we can prepare for this?"

Blue gave a nod of approval at my comment and Stella tugged on her braid in thought. Cynthia seemed nervous, so I said, "We're safe here. He isn't going to get by the wards without help. Even if he does hire someone or buy an object to get past them, at a minimum they will alert us to his presence, and he has no hope against the three of us."

I got a half smile and nod in response from her, and then Stella said, "I think we are too reliant on the wards."

"How so?"

"We are counting on them to keep him out, but we should add another layer of protection."

I rubbed my chin and said, "Like another set of wards on the house itself?"

Our current wards ran along the outside edges of the property rather than on the various entrances to the house like Marion's wards were.

Stella shook her head. "No. If someone can defeat the current wards, then they'll probably be able to bypass another set. I was thinking of technology rather than magic. A couple of wireless cameras monitoring the front and back of the house and contact sensors on all the doors and windows."

I kicked the idea around. It would be cheap enough to get an alarm system installed with the features Stella was looking for. She was right that it would provide another layer of security if Logan somehow managed to take down the wards without them giving us a warning. "The contact sensors make sense, but why the cameras?"

"If Logan approaches the house and sets off the wards, he'll probably flee. The cameras will give us an idea of what direction he went. They will also show us his current appearance. Lastly, if he drives up, we might get a license plate number to track."

All of those were solid reasons for the cameras. "I believe our Internet provider does alarm systems, should we call them?"

"No. If Logan drives nonstop, he could be here in less than a day. Besides, they'll charge us for monitoring, and we don't need that. There are lots of do-it-yourself options out there. Blue and I can go shopping this evening and install everything first thing tomorrow."

I glanced at my phone and saw it was coming up on eight. The stores would be closing by nine. "Sounds like a plan. You and Blue go shopping, and we'll resume this discussion first thing tomorrow."

***

I awoke the next morning to a deafening sound. *WHOOP, WHOOP, WHOOP* echoed through the house. Cynthia was startled and in a slight panic beside me, and I yelled, "Relax! Stella and Blue are probably testing their new alarm system." The noise stopped midway through my comment, and I felt like a total prat as I screamed the last part of my sentence several decibels louder than I needed to in the now quiet room.

Stella's crisp English accent broke the silence when she yelled, "SORRY!" from downstairs.

At least Cynthia seemed to find that amusing. I was taken aback for a moment at how beautiful she looked, though by the bedhead and the little bit of drool on her face, she'd probably not agree with my assessment. I leaned over and kissed her chastely on her forehead and said, "I promise, once all of this is over, I'll find us a nice—"

I was cut off as another *WHOOP, WHOOP, WHOOP* filled the air, and I mentally sighed.

The noise stopped. "—B and B where the loudest thing will be the birds happily chirping in the morning."

She leaned in and kissed me. "I'd like that," she replied.

I became very much aware of her naked form against me and deepened the kiss. Just as I was about to take things further, the alarm went off again. Cynthia broke the kiss, giggled again, and then said, "Coffee?"

I reluctantly nodded. I loved coffee but today that option was a distant second to what I had been hoping for. Between yesterday morning and today, Stella was just one more cockblocking incident from being removed from my Christmas card list.

A few minutes later, seated at the kitchen table with a coffee in hand, I felt my anger towards Stella disappear. She was smiling from ear to ear about the new system and excitedly going over all the different features of it. Only a monster would be able to stay mad at her.

"And there's an app for your phone that allows you to access the system and cameras. We'll also get an alert anytime something trips the motion sensor in the camera. I used the main PC in the office to store any recorded camera footage and it will keep all recordings for up to a month, but we can set it for longer if needed," said Stella as she showed the app on her phone to us.

After her quick demo, I was suitably impressed and thanked her and Blue for their work. Stella installed the security app on my phone and Cynthia's as we had our coffees.

Once she was done with our phones, she added, "I've also configured the alert system to notify us about any news regarding Logan, Pierre, or the Misfits in general."

Stella had designed a monitoring program that scanned police sources, social media, news outlets, and Odin only knew what else. That program had been essential during our hunt for the Master and the Acolytes. I kicked myself for not thinking of it, too, but that was the great thing about having smart teammates; I didn't have to think of everything myself. "Thanks."

Stella nodded and said, "We'll leave you both to have your breakfast. Join us upstairs in the office once you're done."

Blue and Stella left and the moment they did, Cynthia said, "I had trouble believing that cute little girl was over one hundred years old, but the more time I spend around her, the easier that is to believe."

I smiled in understanding. Stella certainly did not conduct herself like a little girl, and being around her certainly made you realize she was miles more mature than any ten-year-old had a right to be.

After some food, we joined Stella and Blue in the office. Neither of them even looked up from their screens as we entered, as they were both engrossed in their research. I hoped that meant they were finding good leads on Logan and Pierre. I was about to ask about what they'd found so far but another thought crossed my mind. "Blue, any news on the Alex Gray front?"

"I have been monitoring him and his various associates since your meeting last night and there has been little mention of us. It seems he is content to let us deal with the issue."

Other than waking up with a beautiful woman in my arms, that was the best part of this morning, and I hoped that meant Alex Gray would keep his word. I still didn't trust him, but it would be nice not to have to look over my shoulder as much. "Great. Any leads on Logan or Pierre?"

Stella spun around in her swivel chair and said, "Nothing new at the moment. We've been looking into their finances and trying to track down the Fixer that TJ mentioned. On the finances side, the progress is slow, as they have a slew of numbered and shell companies that make it hard to find out concrete information, but we are getting there." She paused and took a breath and added, "As for the Fixer, at first I couldn't find anything about him on the Internet or through any of our usual sources. It was like he didn't exist. I then remembered our access to the English Vampire Court's files and tried there. They have a full file on him and you're not going to like it."

I guess if I wanted things to be easy, I probably should have picked a different career, I thought. "How bad?"

"The Fixer is Alios Moonblade, an elven mage. According to the file, the penthouse condo he works out of in Ottawa has a portal to the fae realms and he spends most of his time there. He is a recluse and on the odd occasion when he is at the condo, he never leaves it."

I mentally cursed at the news. That condo would be warded and trapped to the nines, which meant visiting him unannounced would be a very bad idea. Even if we got past that, chances were that he wouldn't be there. Following him to the fae realm would be suicide and was not an option. "Does it state what type of elf?"

Stella spun around and tapped some keys and said, "Wood elf."

At least he isn't Drow, I thought. That made things slightly better, but all fae were tricky and dangerous to deal with. I had hoped the Fixer would just be some human with good forging and computer skills, someone that we could pressure for information. The Fixer being an elf took that option off the table. If we wanted the information, we'd have to make a deal. My fear was the cost of that deal might exceed the value of the information.

Stella swung back around and said, "Now for the interesting part. The file has a warning to not disturb or approach the Fixer without clearing it with the English Vampire Court first. It also states that any interaction with the Fixer is to be done via Manny."

Blue's tail started making happy motions behind her, and I knew why. Manny was a vampire that was the primary arms dealer to all the vampire courts. We'd come across him in Las Vegas when we'd been hired to keep Max, a legal arms dealer, safe for the week during a weapons convention. Manny had been delighted by Blue, which wasn't a reaction her blue alien appearance usually elicited. Blue had enjoyed his company that night, and I was pretty sure she'd kept in touch with him after that meeting.

Blue said, "Shall I arrange a meeting with Manny?"

I was about to ask Blue to make it happen but then remembered the meeting with Manny in more detail. Manny came across as flamboyant and harmless, but while we were having dinner with him, a vampire lieutenant from the West Coast Court spotted me and approached the table looking for blood. The moment he registered Manny's presence, his whole demeanor changed to one of fear and extreme respect. He deferred to Manny and apologized, which as the right-hand man of a powerful vampire court, he shouldn't have had to do unless ordered by his Master.

The incident at the time puzzled me. There were rumors of a secret vampire council made up of the oldest vampires on the planet. According to the rumors, this council kept the vampire courts in line and was the real power in the vampire world. Manny was nowhere near old enough to be on that council, but supposedly the council had representatives that enforced their will, and I speculated that Manny might be one of those mysterious enforcers. This warning on the Fixer's file just added to my concerns. If Manny was an agent for this powerful and mysterious council, we needed to be very cautious about how we dealt with him.

On the other hand, Manny may be able to get the information from this Fixer without much effort, but we'd owe him for that. Owing a favor to Manny, if he was what I thought he was, also might be too high of a price to pay.

In the end, I decided that it was at least worth having a meeting with Manny and seeing if he could help us. "Yeah, let's meet with Manny and see what he has to say."

Blue nodded and began texting on her phone.

Once she was done, Blue said, "I am unaware of where Manny currently is in the world, so the response may take some time."

I nodded at that. No matter how powerful Manny might be, he was still a vampire, and if he was somewhere where the sun was still up, he'd be unavailable until sunset.

***

As luck would have it, Manny was in New York on business and therefore in our time zone. He contacted Blue just after we'd finished dinner and we set up a meeting for twenty minutes later at his hotel suite, which gave me just enough time to change into my formal wear and have a quick discussion with Blue. Since only Blue and I had met Manny in Vegas, we decided that only we would go tonight. Stella and Cynthia would stay home.

I shared my concerns about Manny with Blue and asked for her input.

"Interesting theory. The other possibility is that this vampire council does not exist. The respect the vampire lieutenant showed might just be from Manny's position as the weapons dealer to all the vampire courts."

"That makes no sense. The West Coast Court would be paying customers and therefore it should be Manny showing respect, not the other way around."

Blue's purple eyes gleamed with triumph, and I instantly knew I was missing something.

"While you humans have your quaint 'the customer is always right' slogans, there are times when that relationship reverses. Such as when a product or service is in very high demand, or very exclusive."

She paused as if to let me consider that. The fact that Manny was the supplier for all the vampire courts was impressive. Usually, due to rivalries and past feuds, there were very few things all the courts agreed on. The vampire courts always dealt with the best, and if Manny was the exclusive supplier, a single court wouldn't be anxious to sever that relationship.

Blue then added, "You are not looking at the bigger picture. Someone like Manny who has contacts at all the courts is in a position of power. Think about how easy it would be for him to make life challenging for one of the courts..."

"I'm not sure I follow. If Manny stopped dealing with one of the courts, they'd still be able to get weapons from other sources. They might not be to the same standard or quality, but I can't see that being overly detrimental to their operations."

Blue tsked at me under her breath and said, "His power is his influence. Take the West Coast Court and that lieutenant who approached us. Imagine the scenario went differently and he attacked you, thereby insulting Manny. At his next meeting, he could casually mention to his contacts at the East Coast Court that the West Coast Court ordered four times as many weapons from him as usual. The East Coast Court would infer that those weapons might be used against them and go on alert. Or, he mentions to the South American Vampire Court that he heard a rumor that the West Coast Court is working with the DEA to prevent cocaine shipments from entering the US, as they have a new supplier in Asia. In his next meeting with the English Vampire Court, he lets slip that he heard that the West Coast Court is eying expansion into BC, and so on."

My eyebrows rose as what Blue was saying hit home. The vampire courts were always suspicious of their rivals, and a whisper campaign like that could very quickly have four or five courts ganging up on the West Coast Court. Maybe my whole secret vampire council theory was just my imagination and Manny was simply respected because he was the premier supplier with an impressive list of contacts around the world. "Yours is more of a logical explanation of events than mine."

Blue nodded. "To be fair to you, you might be correct about Manny's true role. The arms dealing might be a cover. In my previous occupation as an assassin, the common technique for infiltration of a target was to blend into the shadows and remain unseen. Another technique for doing the same thing is to hide in plain sight. Manny's charm and flippant mannerisms might be just that. I will observe him closely during our meeting to see if your concern has merit."

I rubbed my temples at Blue's sudden change. I swear that there were times Blue just liked to mess with me and wondered if this was one of those times.

Blue opened a portal, which ended any more discussion, and I stepped through. We came out of the shadows behind a large planter in an upscale hallway. I was still orienting myself when Blue began heading down the hall, and I had to run to catch up.

I'd just joined her when she stopped in front of a set of ornate white wooden doors and knocked.

After a short wait, the door opened and Manny stood there with a big smile on his face. He'd changed his hair color since I'd last seen him, and now it was the same shade of purple as Blue's. Purple seemed to be a theme for tonight's outfit, as he was wearing a velour suit in a similar shade with a pink dress shirt and bright purple cowboy boots. That sounded like the world's tackiest ensemble but somehow it worked and looked good on Manny. His blue eyes really popped against the purple.

"Blue! So good to see you again! I told you I loved your hair color," he said, pausing to lift a lock of his own hair. "Well, girlfriend, we could be like sisters now, though mine is just a pale imitation of your gorgeous locks."

Before Blue could even respond, Manny shot forward and wrapped her up in a warm hug. To my surprise, Blue returned the hug with affection and a pointy-toothed smile. Blue's usual demeanor was reserved and a bit standoffish. The one exception was when she was with Dmitri.

Manny broke the hug and Blue said, "It is wonderful to see you again too, Manny."

His smile widened at that and he turned his attention to me. "Be still my heart. RoboCop, you do clean up nicely."

He had given me the RoboCop pet name after our last meeting where I was wearing my armor. It was my turn for the full Manny experience, and I suddenly found myself wrapped in a hug. I awkwardly returned it and hoped it would end soon.

My wish was granted a moment later when he stepped back and said, "You do smell good. It is a shame that you've been marked. Nothing gets the juices flowing like tasty elemental blood."

Olivia had shared her blood with me a few months ago when I was bleeding out badly due to a vampire attack. Afterward, I hadn't been too happy about it, as the mark bound me to her. If she shared her blood with me again, the bond would be stronger, and if it happened a third time, I'd become her human servant and lose my free will. The act saved my life so I wasn't that mad about it. The one side benefit was that it made me hands off to other vampires. Not having to fear that I would become a tasty snack was a nice perk. "Um, thanks. I love your outfit."

Manny preened and posed in front of me for a few moments and said, "It's from an up-and-coming designer in Paris. She is young but so creative and unique; I look forward to watching her career. Her rates are very reasonable; I'll give you her contact information. Your wardrobe could use a little perk up."

I nodded but doubted I could pull off an outfit like that. Manny stepped back and made a grand gesture with his arms, indicating we should come in.

We entered the luxury suite, and my eyes were pulled to the full-length windows and the impressive view of the brightly lit New York skyline. The suite was huge and probably had the same square footage as our house. It was a nice balance between classic and modern with the glass and leather furnishings.

Manny sat down in a cream-colored leather easy chair and motioned at the couch in front of him. We took our spots on the couch and I almost moaned at how comfortable it was but managed to restrain myself.

Once we were settled, Manny went into an animated and amusing story about what he'd been up to since we'd last seen him. At one point, he had me laughing so hard, that I was having trouble catching my breath. He made Blue snort with laughter, which just made things even funnier. The man certainly had a lust for life and packed more into each day than most people did in a month.

". . .and how was I supposed to know the Sultan didn't like eels?" finished Manny.

I wiped the tears of laughter from my eyes and was grateful for the time to compose myself.

Manny broke the silence and said, "But I'm assuming you didn't come all this way just to hear little old me prattle on. What can Manny do for you?"

"Hardly prattle, Manny. Listening to you makes the trip here easily worthwhile," I said, and he smiled and nodded in acknowledgment. "But, you are correct. We came here hoping to get information about Alios Moonblade."

Manny straightened in his seat at the elf's name and said, "Surely the English Court can provide you or your teammates with adequate false IDs?"

I shook my head. "I wish it was that simple." I took a deep breath and went into the whole story about Logan and Pierre and why we needed to find out their current aliases.

When I was done, Manny rubbed his chin and said, "You've gotten yourself into quite a pickle. Alios Moonblade is not an easy man to deal with. He is prickly and prideful." He paused and grinned. "Though he is a completely different character in the bedroom. Elves are so tasty and open to so many things sexually."

Too much information, I thought.

"He will be very reluctant to give up the information you require, as he prides himself on his work. Fortunately for you, he owes me a favor." He let that hang in the air as his blue eyes studied me intently and added, "I'm reluctant to give up that leverage. Normally, I'd happily trade for a sip or two of your Air elemental blood, but as you've been marked, that is so icky and off the table."

He shifted his attention to Blue and with a smile said, "Your alien blood would also be something I'd normally be interested in, but my bloodlust doesn't stir around you at all. That is actually a refreshing change, but it also means that, at best, your blood will provide no sustenance and, at worst, may be harmful to me. No offense, my dear."

Blue nodded curtly and said, "None taken."

Manny looked back at me and said, "Your team has pulled off some impressive feats this past year. A favor from you and your team would be something I'd value more than a favor from Alios."

I was about to agree, but out of the corner of my eye, I spotted that Blue's tail had gone dead still and that gave me pause. The lack of motion usually meant danger or fear. I was puzzled as to what Blue was concerned about. Listening to Manny earlier, I'd decided that my fears about him being some secret operative of a mysterious and powerful vampire council had been unfounded. Blue's theory now seemed the more logical explanation.

I decided to play for time. "Thank you for your generous offer, but I've spent enough time around vampires and fae to realize that a favor isn't something I should enter into lightly. I also need to clear this with the rest of my team. Do you mind giving us some time to think about it?"

Manny smiled and made a magnanimous gesture with his manicured hands. "Of course, take your time. You have my contact information. Now, if you'll excuse me, I have a date with a hunky Werewolf I must prepare for."

Manny got up and walked us to the door. We exchanged goodbyes and hugs, and he closed the door behind us.

I was about to question Blue when she shook her head and marched with purpose back to the planter with the shadows. I shrugged and followed her.

We came out of the shadows in the living room of our house. Cynthia and Stella were nowhere to be seen, and I assumed they must be up in the office doing research.

"Care to tell me what is going on?" I asked.

"I believe your assumptions about Manny were correct; he is more than he appears to be."

I blinked at that and shook my head. I had just come over to Blue's theory, yet she now leaned towards mine. "How do figure that?"

"I believe his flamboyant nature is a ruse. I observed him closely while he was telling his tales. He uses the same five seemingly random hand gestures. Each of the movements is precise and identical. His arms, hands, and fingers finish in the same position to the millimeter. That leads me to conclude that much like my own routines with my sword work, these are done deliberately and have been practiced to a high degree."

If it had been anyone but Blue who'd decided something based on hand gestures, I would have dismissed their findings instantly. Also, only Blue would have been able to accurately map five different sets of hand gestures and know with certainty that they all finished in the same spot. If Blue was correct and Manny was much more than he appeared, then owing him a favor was something we shouldn't enter into lightly. "How do you advise we proceed then?"

"Making the deal should be our last resort. We have no deadline with Manny, so we should endeavor to explore other options first."

I nodded and said, "I'm sorry. I know that you liked Manny."

Blue's tail began moving in happy circles. "Your apologies are unnecessary; his new status just makes him even more interesting and intriguing to me."

Chapter 20

Monday, November 28

After our meeting Saturday night with Manny, the rest of the weekend was uneventful. Cynthia and I tried to help Stella and Blue with case research, but they kicked us out of the office in short order. Cynthia and I spent the rest of the weekend just hanging out and enjoying each other's company.

I canceled the Sunday night training for my foundation members as I felt we could all use a break. After last week's complaints about the continued defensive training, I decided it was time to get back to regular training. The week, though, had been so busy that Blue and I had not had time to prep.

On Monday morning, we joined Stella and Blue in the office to get an update on what they had found out.

Stella said, "Unfortunately, we have found no new clues that might help us find Logan's or Pierre's whereabouts. The one thing of interest we found after going through all the shell and numbered companies is that Pierre has spent a fortune on property around the lake where his cabin is located. That bodes well for TJ's theory about Pierre fleeing to the cabin."

I was about to ask Blue if there had been any activity around the cabin, but she had anticipated my question. "I have been monitoring the cabin, but there has not been any sign of Pierre."

"Keep checking. He might be stocking up on supplies or something before arriving and might eventually turn up."

My phone buzzed and I saw that it was Detective Grissom calling.

"*Zack, a car registered to Logan was found abandoned at a parking lot in Ottawa. A minivan was reported stolen from the same lot this weekend. We believe that Logan is in Ontario and might be heading your way.*"

"We'd assumed that he'd be coming for us, but it's nice to have confirmation. Any news or sightings of Pierre?"

"*No. We believe that Pierre has fled the country, but I'll keep you posted if I hear anything.*"

I thanked him and ended the call. I brought everyone up to speed on Grissom's update.

Stella tugged her braid and said, "Why steal a car if he had one already?"

"The Nova Scotia plates would stand out here like a sore thumb," Blue replied. A minivan with Ontario plates is much less likely to be noticed."

I couldn't fault Blue's reasoning. Minivans were so common on Ontario roads that no one would notice another one. The chances of a cop on patrol finding it were slim.

We talked about any other preparations we could make but nothing of note was suggested. The wards and the alarm system were our main lines of defense.

A part of me really wished we could get Olivia and Bree home. Their sensitive hearing would pick up Logan before he even got to the wards. They'd also be invaluable in tracking Logan if he did approach the house and fled. I could wish all I wanted, but that option was unavailable. I tried to reassure myself that with Blue's shadow abilities and my own power, we'd have a pretty good chance of catching Logan if he did show up.

The three teen Werewolves from my foundation came to mind. The main goal of the foundation was to support heroes financially so they could dedicate more of their time to patrolling and keeping the streets safe. The secondary goal was to provide us with more firepower when we needed it or to substitute for a team member who wasn't available. Having them fill in for Bree and Olivia now certainly fit that second goal. My stomach, though, knotted up at the thought of any of those three coming up against a psychopath like Logan. The death of Charlie, one of my young foundation members, was too fresh, and I couldn't bring myself to risk involving them.

Logan's imminent arrival also had me placing a call to my buddy Rob Quinn to get him to step up police patrols around Marion's apartment. I was pleased to find out that he already had done this. Hamilton Police had been alerted by EIRT that Logan might be in the area. His description and the stolen minivan's plate number had been included in today's briefing and they were all on alert.

In the end, I felt good about where everything stood. Now we just had to wait and see if Logan would show up.

***

I awoke out of a deep sleep to a repeated *cawing* echoing loudly in the previously quiet house. I rolled out of bed and scrambled to find my clothes.

"What the hell is that?" yelled Cynthia from my bed.

"It's the wards. The wizard who installed them is a bit of a nature freak," I said as I tossed on my jeans.

Her eyes went wide as the implications of that statement dawned on her; Logan was here. She grabbed for her phone as I got on my T-shirt. "I'll check the cameras."

I smiled at that. Hopefully Logan tripped the motion sensors on the cameras, and we'd have a clue whether he was waiting outside looking for a fight, or if he fled. If he fled, the cameras might show which way.

I debated skipping putting on my armor in favor of speed but decided it was worth the cost. Neither Cynthia nor my teammates had spotted him yet, so until they did, I had time. The armor had night and thermal vision as well as comms built in to allow me to communicate with Blue, and the physical protection it provided from a certain psychotic Werewolf didn't hurt.

There was a knock at my door. "Come in," I said.

Blue entered wearing her scale mail armor and her communication visor. Stella was in her normal dated dress. As I attached the right arm to my chest piece, I looked at Blue. "Do you sleep in that armor?"

"It seemed prudent," she said as she scanned her phone.

Stella handed me the left leg piece and I fitted it around my leg.

"Found him. There is a silver Werewolf in hybrid form on the rear camera at the 1:34:23 timeframe," said Cynthia.

It took me off guard that Logan was in hybrid form. Logan looked to be in his late twenties, and I assumed he was a younger Were. The hybrid form was only something a more powerful and experienced Were could do, and it usually took fifteen to twenty years for them to master. Bree was able to do it almost immediately, but she had been sired by the most powerful Werepanther alpha on the planet. I'd been in power-blocking cuffs the whole time when Logan kidnapped me, so I hadn't had access to my Aura-seeing ability, which would have told me that he was much more powerful than I'd assumed.

I suddenly felt better about my decision to put on armor. "Blue, start scanning the yard and the woods out back, see if you can spot him."

Blue shifted and crouched down beside my dresser. I assumed to use the shadows there.

"I'm checking the rear camera, but there is no sign of him there now," said Cynthia.

I was almost fully armored up when I turned to Stella and said, "Head to the living room and change into your Hyde form. I'll be there shortly."

Stella handed me my helmet and disappeared out the door.

I looked at Cynthia and said, "Stay here with Blue. Blue, call me on the comms if you spot him."

I attached the helmet and left the room. I sprinted down the stairs as fast as I could and made a beeline for the living room.

Stella was in all her Hyde glory when I entered. "If he jumps me as I leave, come help. Otherwise, once I'm in the air, change back and join Blue and Cynthia."

Her misshapen head bobbed in acknowledgment. I suspected my caution at having Stella here was unnecessary, as the wards had stopped sounding almost as quickly as they'd started, which meant Logan had probably fled and not breached them, but it was better to be safe than sorry.

I accessed my powers and then unlocked the glass sliding door to the backyard. I jumped as the electronic alarm went off when I opened the door; in our haste, we'd forgotten to disable them. I stepped out onto the back porch, looked around, and then took to the Air.

I shot up to about fifty feet and did a slow circle in the air, frantically scanning the ground below for any sign of a purple, brown, and silver aura. I wanted to make sure the area directly around the house was safe and free of Logan before going off looking for him. Thankfully, it was a clear night, which made things easier. I didn't spot him, but I switched to thermals on my visor and did another scan to make sure.

The area looked quiet and benign, so I turned towards the woods behind our house and flew in that direction.

I opened the comms and said, *"Blue, do you have anything?"*

"Negative, I have scanned the woods and found no sign of him. I am expanding my search out from there."

"Roger that."

The small woods behind our house weren't much bigger than a city block. This time of year they were easier to search from the air, as most of the leaves had dropped by now. I scanned them as I flew over but didn't see any sign of Logan. The woods were surrounded by other houses and roads, and I started flying in a widening circle pattern, hoping to catch sight of him.

Traffic was light at this time of night but there were still enough vehicles on the roads around me that I couldn't chase after all of them. Logan might not even be in a vehicle and might just be hopping through backyards at top speed on foot.

I checked the time on my visor and saw it was 1:39 a.m., which meant close to five minutes had passed since he tripped the alarm. Weres didn't have vampire-like speed, but they were no slouches in the speed department either. They could easily outrun the fastest human, and I realized he could already be blocks away.

I hovered in the air and surveyed the area in front of me. It was mostly housing as far as the eye could see. If he took off from the back of the house, there were three directions he could go: north, east, and west. North and east took him back deeper into the city itself. West took him towards Dundas, but there were many more trees and natural cover that way.

I guessed that his beast would prefer the more natural areas so I turned west and flew off. I flew in a zigzag pattern, trying to cover as much ground to the west as quickly as possible. I got excited when I heard dogs barking off in the distance to my right and poured on the speed.

I cursed as I spotted a cat making a beeline across the fence line with dogs yapping excitedly below.

I heard sirens starting to go off all over the area and spotted sets of blue and red flashing lights heading towards our house.

I opened the comms and asked, *"Everything okay at the house?"*

"Everything is fine. Stella called the police to alert them that Logan had been sighted here," said Blue.

There were times I was too fixed in my bounty mentality, and this had been one of them. Calling law enforcement when in pursuit of a bounty suspect was a no-no; if the police officers apprehended the target, there was no bounty. In this case, though, the bounty on Logan was secondary. Our priority was to get him off the streets and to keep Cynthia and Marion safe. Once again, I was grateful for teammates that thought outside the box.

The responding police officers would be on the lookout for Logan's stolen minivan and added multiple sets of eyes to our search. Even better, I knew that Stella would be monitoring the police radio for any mention that he'd been spotted. If an officer did see him, they would call for backup and maintain visual contact. That meant if we were quick enough, we could take Logan down and get the bounty. The bounty was not our priority, but half a million dollars was still a half million dollars. There was also a part of me just itching to get some payback on Logan.

I continued my westward flight, feeling that if I'd guessed wrong, at least there was a chance Logan might be spotted if he went north or east. Logan was a fugitive, and he was in my city. He wasn't getting away.

At the thought of Logan being a fugitive, I opened the comms and said, *"What I want from each and every one of you is a hard-target search of every gas station, residence, warehouse, farmhouse, henhouse, outhouse, and doghouse in that area."*

"I do not understand."

"Blue, just repeat that to Cynthia for me."

"Is this one of your obscure pop culture references?"

I loved my teammates dearly but there were times I wished they were bigger film buffs. I took issue with the obscure part of Blue's statement. *The Fugitive* with Tommy Lee Jones had to be one of the top one hundred films of all time, so it wasn't obscure. *"Yes, it is."*

"I would suggest that you focus on the task at hand and keep the comms clear then."

I rolled my eyes at that but Blue probably had a point. I continued my search for Logan.

A few minutes later, I had reached Dundas and still hadn't spotted him. Even if he'd been running at top speed, there was no way he could have made it this far, so I turned around and went back over the area between the house and Dundas again.

I mentally sighed when I spotted our house in the distance. I hadn't seen a trace of Logan while I backtracked and with the amount of time that had now passed, the search radius was now too big to be practical. I headed home.

I landed in the front yard and a German shepherd from the canine unit barked at my presence. Rob Quinn was there with three other officers—four if I included the dog.

I lifted the visor to my helmet and exchanged greetings with Rob and he introduced me to the other officers. "According to Stella, Logan approached from the woods and then fled the same way. We were going to search the woods in case he is hiding there. Care to join us?" he said.

I nodded. "I think he's long gone but better safe than sorry. Lead on."

The canine handler, who Rob introduced as Bill, took point and we proceeded to the backyard. The dog whimpered in fear as we entered the back area and he caught the Were's scent. Bill crouched down and rubbed the dog's head reassuringly and said something softly in the dog's ear. The dog barked excitedly and pulled at the lead. He darted across the yard to the back fence and stopped near the right corner area.

Bill said, "The suspect approached the house from here. We'll have to go around to pick up his scent again."

Rob grinned and looked at me. I knew what he was thinking.

"No need. Brace yourselves," he said.

I closed my visor and I called on my Air powers and used them to lift all of us, including the dog, into the air. It was a mercifully short trip, as I just lifted us up and over the fence. Lifting five grown men and a dog wasn't something I wanted to do for long.

The small, darkened woods lay before us. The dense skeleton-like trees looked foreboding in the pale moonlight. I was pretty sure this trip was a waste as Blue and I had scanned it earlier, and a practical part of me hoped it would be futile. Taking on an enraged Werewolf in the confines of these woods wouldn't be fun, and with the cops here, I couldn't take to the sky and fight from there.

The dog tugged at his leash as he found the scent again. I followed right behind Bill the handler and Rob, the two other officers behind me. I scanned the woods anxiously for any sign of an aura but couldn't spot anything.

The trail ended up being a straight line through the woods to the opposite side and we were clear of the trees in almost no time. The open residential street relieved the tension that had been building in me during our short trip through the spooky woods.

The German shepherd led us across the quiet street. The dog passed five or six vehicles that were parked on the street and then stopped at an empty spot in the road. He went in tight circles for a bit and then sat down and looked up at Bill as if to say, *"This is where it ends; my work is done."*

I glanced down the street and saw more parked vehicles just in front of us. The space we were standing in was just big enough to park a car.

Bill said, "Trail ends here. Looks like he got into a vehicle and drove off."

The two younger officers and Rob used their flashlights to search the front lawn and bushes of the nearby house, but not seeing an aura hiding there, I ignored them. "Remind all officers on patrol about the details of Logan's stolen minivan."

Rob shook his head. "They were reminded again when we got the call from Stella."

"Nice."

Rob glanced at his watch and frowned. "It would have been nicer if we'd caught him. There is still a chance the vehicle will be spotted but . . ."

He let that hang to express his doubts that that would happen after this amount of time.

I pondered his words and had to agree that Logan was long gone and we'd missed our shot at taking him down. I doubted, though, that this would be the last we'd see of him and prayed we had better luck next time.

Chapter 21

Tuesday, November 29

Cynthia and I slept in a bit later than usual due to the interruption of our slumber by Logan's visit. After the search, Rob wrote up a brief incident report and mentioned that he'd keep the increased patrols going around Marion's apartment building. After he and the rest of Hamilton's finest left, we'd stayed up for another hour monitoring police bands, hoping to hear that Logan had been spotted, but that turned out to be a fruitless endeavor.

After a late breakfast, we joined Stella and Blue in the office. Stella had finished mapping out Pierre's finances from all the numbered and shell companies, but other than showing he'd made a ton of money during his time with the Misfits, it didn't give us any new clues about his current location.

"The cabin remains undisturbed," said Blue.

I frowned at that news, as it looked like TJ's tip was a bust. If the cabin had been Pierre's destination, surely, he should have arrived by now. Detective Grissom's theory that Pierre had fled the country seemed more and more likely. The world was a big place, and if Grissom was right, that made our search a whole bunch more difficult.

Finding Pierre was our secondary objective. Stopping Logan was more pressing at the moment. I asked if there'd been any more news on him since last night.

"The Hamilton morning news put up his picture during their broadcast and the local papers also put his picture on the front page," Stella said.

I cheered up at that piece of information. There would be a lot more eyes out there looking for him now. All we needed was for a good citizen to get lucky, spot him, and call it in. An ugly thought occurred to me. "I hope the pictures were accompanied by a danger warning advising people not to approach him?"

Stella nodded and relief filled me. The last thing I wanted was some Good Samaritan trying to apprehend Logan, as that wouldn't end well.

My phone buzzed in my pocket, and I fished it out and saw Dave Collins's name on the display. Dave was a Hamilton cop and a good friend of Rob's.

"Hey, Zack, we found the stolen minivan. It was abandoned near Juravinski."

The Juravinski Hospital was located on the edge of the mountain brow. It was a bad place to dump a vehicle, as parking in that area was tight and city bylaw officers patrolled it nonstop, which was probably why it had been found so quickly. *"Any sign of Logan?"*

"No. We've been on scene for over an hour. Canine tracked the scent to the Bruce Trail but lost it there."

The Bruce Trail was a wooded area that bisected the city and ran the length below the mountain brow.

"The minivan contain anything interesting?"

"Nah, just a shitload of empty fast-food bags and beef jerky wrappers. We're towing it downtown and the techs will go over it. I'll let you know if they find anything."

Given Were appetites, the news about food wrappers wasn't a shock. *"Great, thanks for the call."*

If Liv and Bree were here, they would have filled everyone in before I'd even hung up the phone. I felt a pang of sadness at their absence, but I had a job to do. I turned toward the rest of the team.

"Good news, Hamilton police found the minivan," I said, and I went over my call with Dave.

The moment I finished, Blue said, "I fail to see how this is good news. The minivan was our best chance at finding Logan."

Blue had a point, as Logan would probably just steal another car, and we'd be in the dark about what make or model it might be.

Or maybe not. "Monitor the crime reports for stolen vehicles. Only two or three vehicles a day are stolen in Hamilton, so we might get lucky and the next one might be Logan's new ride."

Blue nodded and another worry popped into my head. "Have you been monitoring Marion?"

"Yes, every twenty minutes. She is unharmed," said Blue.

Cynthia perked up at Marion's name and said, "Can we visit her today? I also need to stop by my apartment and grab a few more things. In my haste last time I forgot to grab my guitar."

"I didn't know you played guitar."

She smiled and said, "And I sing too. Music is like a family tradition. Jam sessions were a great way to get through those long winter months on the Island."

"I'm jealous; all my singing is good for is making the neighborhood dogs howl." Cynthia giggled at that, and I asked, "How long have you been playing?"

"Since I was a little kid. My grandfather taught me to play. He passed away about five years ago, and I miss him. He was always smiling and was one of those people that just made you feel good. There are times I'm strumming on the guitar when I can almost sense him nodding encouragingly when I get the chord right."

I initially thought about getting Blue to shadow travel us there, but another idea came to mind. "Give your aunt a call and see if she is free. Let me wrap up here and then we'll fly over and see her."

The beaming smile I got at that let me know I'd made the right call. Cynthia had been cooped up here for days. It was a sunny day out with mild temperatures for this time of year—a perfect day to fly.

"I'll call her and get changed," said Cynthia as she left the room.

"Is that course of action wise?" asked Stella.

I knew she was referring to me flying us there rather than having Blue shadow travel us directly into Marion's warded apartment. "I'll wear my armor and keep the comms open. We'll only be exposed during the part of the trip from the rooftop of Marion's apartment to her front door."

Blue's tail made quick circular motions behind her, and she said, "I would not have thought that you would use Miss Ryerson as bait."

I blinked at that. "That is *not* what I'm doing. She's been stuck here for days, and I just thought she'd enjoy getting out for a bit. The chances of us running into Logan are remote."

Blue gave me a shrug in response, and she and Stella went back to working on their computers.

I group texted my street contacts a picture of Logan and asked them to contact me immediately if they saw him, adding that spotting him would be well rewarded. Over the years, I had built up a pretty wide range of contacts in Hamilton. Most of them were usually on the wrong side of the law, but whether it was the money or trust, they seemed happy to deal with me. They also didn't miss much, and if Logan got near any of them, they'd spot him.

Twenty minutes later, Cynthia and I were in the backyard. She looked both nervous and excited. I held out my armored arm to her and she snuggled closer to me.

"Do you usually jump into a pool or enter slowly down the steps?"

Cynthia grinned and said, "I'm a cannonball type of girl, why?"

I didn't answer and just called on my Air power and waited for a moment until I had a strong amount built up.

"Hold on tight." It was the only warning I gave before I released a massive burst of air beneath us, and we shot into the air like a rocket.

Cynthia screamed as the ground fell away behind us. My armor hid the huge grin I had on my face.

I stopped us at about one thousand feet up and asked, "You okay?"

She blinked her eyes open and slowly nodded her head. She bravely looked down and then around at the view with an expression of pure awe on her lovely face. I slowly rotated us around so she could take in the view from all directions.

"I can see now why getting your powers back was so important to you. This is amazing. It's so peaceful up here," she said, taking all of it in. She turned her attention back to me and with a coy smile added, "Can we go higher?"

I eyed her outfit, which consisted of a spring jacket, sweatshirt, jeans, and running shoes, and asked, "How are you finding the temperature?"

"It's a bit cool, but the sun is nice."

"The higher we go, the cooler it gets... you still want to go higher?"

I watched the struggle on her face, as I could tell she really wanted to go higher but the cooler temperatures were weighing on her decision.

She sighed and said, "Maybe another day when it's warmer?"

I nodded. "Marion's then?"

"Sounds good."

I turned us towards downtown Hamilton and then began leisurely flying us in that direction. The flight was quiet, as Cynthia spent most of it checking things out below us.

When I reached Marion's building, I circled around it a few times to check out the roof and the area around the building for any signs of Logan's presence. I didn't spot him but noticed there was a police cruiser parked at the front entrance of the building. I mentally thanked Rob for that.

I gently landed us on the roof. I instantly thickened the air around us as a precaution and readied my Electrical powers. I opened a channel on the comms and said, *"We just landed on the roof. Everything seems clear so far."*

"Roger that. I have been monitoring the interior of the building from the shadows and have not detected any threats, but stay alert."

I turned my attention to Cynthia and said, "Stay behind me and yell if you spot anything."

We exited the roof and made our way to the bank of elevators. The floor was empty and quiet but that didn't relax me in the slightest.

Cynthia jumped as the sound of the elevator broke the silence, and then she laughed at her reaction. I wasn't the only one feeling the tension of the moment it seemed. The doors opened and I was relieved to find the elevator empty. We boarded the car and were on our way to Marion's floor.

The elevator opened again, and I spotted an older lady entering her apartment at the end of the hall. She had a white poodle with her, and it seemed calm, which reassured me that Logan wasn't lurking nearby. The lady and her dog disappeared into their apartment as we stepped out.

As we got closer to Marion's apartment, Cynthia said, "Can we stop by my place first?"

"Sure."

Cynthia pulled out a key and unlocked her door. The moment she opened it, her face fell, and I knew something was wrong. I used my Air powers to lift her and quickly move her back behind me. I glanced inside the apartment and instantly knew why she reacted the way she did. The whole place was trashed. The couch had been torn apart and there was stuffing and debris all over the floor. "Go to Marion's now," I said as I called on my Electrical powers.

I didn't take my eyes off the wrecked apartment, and I heard Cynthia frantically knocking on Marion's door behind me. "It's me, Marion. Open up."

The door creaked open, and Marion said, "What's going—"

Cynthia cut her off and said, "Logan!"

The moment the door closed and I heard the bolt engage, I opened the comms. *"Blue, Logan's been to Cynthia's apartment. Scan it from the shadows."*

"Roger. Hold on."

I used my right foot to push the door fully open to get a better view, and my anger surged as I spotted Die Bitch! gouged into the drywall in front of me.

Blue's voice came back over the comms. *"The place is clear."*

"Roger that. I'm going in."

The place was a mess. Beside the couch, the coffee table was upside down, all four of its legs snapped off. The cupboard doors had been torn off in the small kitchenette to my right. Oddly enough, the dishes were still inside and intact. I frowned at that, as it didn't match the rage displayed everywhere else. Then it hit me that Logan hadn't smashed the dishes because they would have made too much noise. That both impressed and frightened me. He had obviously been in a full rage but still retained enough control not to break things, which would have alerted Marion or any of the neighbors to his presence.

I moved to the bedroom and my eyes were immediately drawn to the smashed guitar in the corner. The neck had been broken in four places, and the body of the guitar was in even worse shape. My eyes started to well up, as I knew the loss would be hard on Cynthia due to the connection the guitar had to her grandfather. I forced myself to focus on the task at hand. The rest of the room was just as bad. Her bedsheets, pillows, and mattress were torn to pieces. Her clothes and her luggage had been pulled from the closet and dresser and every piece was shredded. I couldn't spot a single piece of undamaged clothing.

The tiny bathroom wasn't any better. The shower curtain was destroyed and dumped in the tub. Her makeup was dumped out on the counter and smashed. On the mirror, which was remarkably still in one piece, he'd written several obscenities and threats in pink lipstick. Even the toilet seat had been ripped off its moorings.

Blue, though, had been correct that the place was clear. I wondered how long ago he'd been here. If Bree or Olivia were available, I'd have pulled them down here and they'd probably have been able to estimate that based on scent. I opened my visor and fished my phone out of the pouch it was in and texted my foundation Weres to ask if they were available.

Davin and Josh were both in class. Davin added that he was willing to ditch if he was needed. Hunter, though, replied that he was done for the day, as his last class was a spare. I texted him back and asked for his location. When he replied, I told him that Blue would be there soon. I let the other two boys know that Hunter would be helping. Davin sent back a sad face emoji in response.

I let Blue know that I needed Hunter and where he was. She said she would be there shortly.

I double-checked that the hall was clear and then crossed it to Marion's apartment. I knocked, announcing that it was me. Marion cautiously opened the door, and I told her Logan was gone. I explained about Blue and Hunter joining me shortly and told them to relax but stay in the apartment.

Marion nodded and closed the door. I spotted Blue coming down the hall with Hunter in tow.

He'd gotten his hair cut since I'd seen him at our last training session just over a week ago. He was wearing a Blue Jays jersey and jeans, and I could swear his arms had gotten a bit thicker since I'd last seen him. I knew he'd been working out, trying to bulk up a bit. He'd been doing that since Charlie died. I felt sorry for his parents, as it was bad enough just trying to feed a Were, never mind one that was trying to put on weight.

"Thanks for coming," I said to Hunter.

"No problem, what's up?"

I explained about Logan trashing the apartment and told him I needed his nose to give me a better idea of when Logan had been here.

Hunter shrugged and stepped by me into the apartment and whistled. "Someone has anger issues."

"Understatement of the year there," I said as Blue and I followed him in.

When he reached the center of the room, he stopped, closed his eyes, and inhaled deeply. "I have his scent but it's fading. I'm guessing it's been at least twelve hours since he was here. Probably longer than that."

"You sure?"

He shrugged. "It's not an exact science here but I'd be willing to put money on that guess."

"Alright, thank you. Blue will take you home."

He frowned. "You sure you don't need me for anything else?"

"Nah, I just needed a timeline on when Logan was here. Thanks again."

"Alright, see you Sunday then," Hunter said as he and Blue left.

I glanced at my phone and saw it was coming up on three. Hunter's estimate meant Logan would have been here at three in the morning. He tried to break into our place at 1:34 a.m. Based on that timeline, he hit us first and then came here and trashed the place. That didn't feel right to me. While Logan had avoided breaking dishes or the mirror, he still would have made some noise, and at three the morning, those noises would have been more noticeable by the neighbors.

Hunter had qualified that he'd probably been here longer than twelve hours ago, though. So it was possible that he might have come here first. I guessed that Marion might have been his target. Somehow, he found out or knew about the wards protecting her place and didn't make the attempt. His nose, though, would have picked up Cynthia's scent in the apartment from her clothes and things she had come into contact with, and he changed his plans.

He picked the lock, trashed the place, and then decided to go after Cynthia and me directly. He could have been here as early as nine or ten and, at that time, the neighbors would still be up and about and wouldn't be as prone to noticing the odd noise coming from here. That felt more right to me.

I called on my powers as the front door to Cynthia's apartment opened but relaxed when I saw it was Cynthia and Marion. Before I could warn her, Cynthia made a beeline for the bedroom.

"*No,*" she said after spotting her guitar, her voice soft. It was a heart wrenching sound.

I moved over to her and took her in my arms and said, "I'm sorry."

She hugged me fiercely for a moment and then stepped back and said, "The important thing is that no one was hurt." She glanced over to Marion. I nodded and she added, "I'm going to take a quick look to see if any of my clothes are salvageable."

Cynthia disappeared into the bedroom, and I joined a shocked-looking Marion.

In a soft but fierce voice, Marion said, "Get this bastard and keep my niece safe."

I nodded firmly at her words, as I fully intended to do both. Now I just had to figure out what Logan would do next.

Chapter 22

Tuesday, November 29

I got the answer to my question later that night when Detective Little called me at home.

"*Hurricane, I'm on scene at a murder on Victoria Avenue South, under the rail bridge near Charlton Avenue. We suspect Logan Reeves was involved.*"

Charlton Avenue ran parallel to the bottom of the mountain brow. I could picture the bridge in my mind, as I had passed over it many times. That location was also very close to Juravinski Hospital, where Logan's stolen minivan was found.

"*What leads you to believe that Logan was involved?*"

"*He left you a message. It's probably better if you come here and see for yourself.*"

I was a bit surprised that he was inviting me to an active crime scene, but I wasn't going to complain. "*I'll be there shortly.*"

Cynthia cocked a questioning eyebrow at me from the couch we were sharing. "Duty calls," I said and quickly explained what was going on.

I rushed up to my room and yelled for Blue and Stella who had retired to bed just before the call came in.

I had half my armor on when they showed up. I explained the call and asked Blue to find a shadow nearby but outside of the crime scene. She nodded and left while Stella helped me get the rest of my outfit on.

As Stella and I came down the stairs, another thought occurred to me. What if this wasn't just a message but a ploy by Logan?

"Portal's open. You will emerge on Charlton just before where the police have blocked access to Victoria," said Blue.

I shook my head. "Change of plan. I'm going to fly there instead. Use the shadows to check on Marion and the area around her apartment. After that, check the area around us."

Blue's purple eyes studied me intently for a moment and she said, "You believe this might be a ruse to pull us away from the house?"

"Could be. Better safe than sorry. I will check around the house from the air and then fly to the crime scene. Keep the comms open."

Blue nodded and then stared off into the shadows.

"I'll deactivate the alarm system," said Stella.

I smiled at that, as last night we'd forgotten to do that and set it off when I opened the sliding glass door. I reached the back door and paused.

A few seconds later, Stella yelled, *"Clear!"* and I opened the door. I stepped out and scanned the area and was relieved that it seemed normal. Cynthia slid the door closed behind me and I heard her yell to Stella that I was clear so that Stella could reengage the alarm.

I called on my Air powers and lifted myself into the air. I hovered above the house and scanned for any sign of Logan's aura but didn't see anything. I flew toward the small woods behind the house and made a long, slow zigzag pattern over them. I scanned the dense woods for any sign of Logan's presence but came up empty. If he was going to strike at the house, waiting in those trees made the most sense, as he'd be in his element, or at least his beast would be.

I debated making another pass over them and figured I had time. It was a cold thought, but it wasn't like the murder victim was going anywhere soon.

The second pass yielded the same lack of results but made me feel better that Logan wasn't lurking there. I turned towards the center of the city and put some serious air behind me. I let Blue know that I hadn't spotted Logan and was heading to the crime scene.

Flying, with its lack of traffic lights, had some advantages, as I arrived at the scene in less than ten minutes. Even if I hadn't known where I was going, the blue and red lights of the police presence below would have acted as a beacon.

I landed outside the crime scene and approached the police barricade that had been set up on Charlton and Victoria. I smiled to myself as I got closer and saw the officer standing guard was Jim Thompson. Jim was one of Rob's poker buddies and I knew him from those games.

"Hurricane!"

"Good to see you, Jim. How's the wife and kids?"

"They're good. Tommy's fitting in well at his high school this year."

I was floored at that. Last time I'd seen Tommy was at a barbeque party Rob held at his house and at the time Tommy had just been a little kid. "High school? Already? You're making me feel old."

Jim grinned. "You and me both, my friend. Anyways, Detective Little is waiting for you. Don't want to keep him waiting."

I thanked him as he lifted the yellow police tape, and he pointed down the incline towards the bridge.

As I made the small walk down towards the bridge, I saw the flash of a camera going off along its right side. I spotted crime scene techs busily working around the area, and there was a tent erected on the sidewalk near the far end of the underpass. I assumed the victim was inside the tent.

"Hurricane!" yelled Detective Little from the left side of the bridge, waving me over.

I crossed the street and joined him.

"Good to see you again, Detective. I'm surprised I'm allowed on scene; your partner can't be happy about that."

Detective Little worked with a senior detective who was a friend of SWAT Sergeant Murdock. Any friend of Murdock's wasn't a friend of mine. Detective Little, his partner, and I worked together last month on the lich case, but only because the English Vampire Court appointed us as their representatives. Otherwise, I wouldn't have been allowed anywhere near the crime scenes.

Detective Little smiled and said, "He's off on sensitivity training this week, so it's not his call to make. Also, I'm not allowing you directly on the crime scene, just close enough for you to see something."

"Sensitivity training?" I asked.

"He made some very inappropriate remarks about a female officer and was dumb enough to do it in front of her. He was suspended without pay for a week and must complete mandatory sensitivity training before being reinstated."

"Well, at least you get a couple of quiet weeks then." He nodded, and I added, "If I'm not allowed on scene, why am I here?"

"Follow me and I'll show you," he said as he turned and started heading under the bridge.

This was a bit mysterious, but I figured I'd play along. We walked down the sidewalk, and I couldn't help but notice the amount of graffiti lining the darkened wall of the bridge beside us.

Detective Little stopped once we passed the midway point under the bridge and yelled, "Bernie, hit the lights."

I stopped beside him, and a loud click came from the other side of the bridge. A floodlight came on and I frowned for a moment as it illuminated more graffiti, but then I saw the message: *Keep hiding, Hurricane.* It was written in what looked like wet red paint. My stomach churned as I realized that it wasn't paint.

"Seen enough?" he asked, and I nodded, speechless, trying to take it all in. He yelled again and the lights went off.

"I'm assuming that was why you believe this was Logan?"

"That and the victim had wounds consistent with a Were attack," he said.

I wanted to rub my temples, as I felt a massive headache coming on, but my armored helmet impeded me. I'd thought I had all my bases covered. The wards around our house should have been enough to keep us safe, and Marion was virtually on lockdown, her apartment equally warded. What I hadn't accounted for was how desperate Logan had become. He was wanted for the murder of a police officer, and he had nothing left to lose. He was facing a maximum sentence, which meant there was nothing to prevent him from killing whenever he felt like it.

"Details on the victim?"

"You sure you want to know?"

My stomach heaved at that, but this killing was on me, and I wanted to know everything.

"The victim's name was Marty Cheever, thirty-nine, married, father of two. He worked at Steel Co. According to the wife, he took the dog for a walk after he finished his shift and never came home. We found the dog alive but cowering under some trees just down the street. The body was discovered by another dog walker about two hours ago," he finished and then looked at me with concern.

I followed his gaze down to my hands, which were dripping blue sparks at my surge of anger. "Sorry," I said as tampered down on my powers. I had no doubt the bloody wall would be added to my roster of bad dreams in the future. Thankfully, the victim was covered by the tent, so Marty's bloodied corpse wouldn't also be part of my nightmare playlist.

I glanced at the clock on my visor and saw it was just past eleven, which meant the crime had occurred around nine this evening. "Did you interview the wife?"

He shook his head. "Victims Services broke the news; they stopped by here to fill me in and left just before you got here."

"How is his wife doing?"

Detective Little's face fell. "About as well as you would expect. I just hope that she has a strong extended family around her that can help her and the kids through this."

My gut knotted up at the guilt that I was indirectly to blame for their grief.

I wrapped things up with Detective Little shortly after that and headed home. I needed this flight to clear my head. I'd prevented Logan from using anyone close to Cynthia or me, but I couldn't do anything to prevent him from striking at residents of Hamilton at will. He knew I loved this city and its inhabitants and was using that against me. There were two kids that would grow up without a father, and I swore there wouldn't be another one.

Chapter 23

Wednesday, November 30

It was gone midnight by the time I'd gotten home and brought everyone up to speed on what happened. We were now in the office trying to figure out a plan to catch Logan and end this threat to the city.

I was pacing back and forth and made a point of continually checking my hands, as I was seething in anger and frustration. It scared me how enraged I was; the only thing keeping me in check was Cynthia's presence, as I didn't want her thinking I was like Logan. She'd been quiet and withdrawn since I'd gotten back and part of me knew she was blaming herself for Marty's death. "We need to find Logan and put a stop to this once and for all."

"How?" asked Stella. "Everyone is looking for him, yet he has managed to remain virtually unseen."

I almost growled back at her but kept myself in check. I stopped my pacing in front of the map of Hamilton on the wall. I spotted the pinholes all over the map from our last case with the lich as I studied it.

"This change in tactics might give us our best chance of apprehending Logan," said Blue.

Sparks dripped from my hands as I thought through Blue's statement, and I hastily stopped my display. Blue was implying that if Logan continued to attack random people in Hamilton, he might be spotted during an attempt. But a lot more people could die before that happened. "Fuck that, we aren't using people as bait. There has to be a better way."

My eyes lingered on Juravinski Hospital on the map and then the rail bridge, and I noted how close together they were, and an idea popped into my head. "Any reports of stolen cars today?"

"Not since the last time I checked the crime report, but let me check again," said Stella as she spun around on her chair and began tapping away at her keyboard. "Still no reports."

I smiled at that and turned around from the map. "I think I know where Logan is . . ."

Blue frowned but her tail began making happy circles. "Please explain."

"Come here and look at the map."

Once I had everyone gathered around, I pointed at the hospital and said, "Logan dumped the van here, and Marty was killed here—both locations are very close together. What if there's a reason for that?"

Stella tugged her braid and then her eyes lit up. "You think he hasn't stolen another vehicle and is on foot."

I nodded. "Yup, and I think he is hiding out on the Bruce Trail. Think about it. Everyone is looking for him. If he were staying at a motel, hotel, or even an Airbnb, someone would have seen him. If he was hiding on the trail, though . . ."

Blue's purple eyes almost twinkled as she said, "Between the Bruce Trail's trees and light foot traffic and Logan's enhanced senses, it would be easy for him to avoid hikers and dog walkers. Also, at this time of year with the cooler temperatures, there would not be as many people on the trail."

Stella's excited expression diminished, and she said, "The trail isn't very wide, but it runs the length of the Niagara Escarpment between Stoney Creek and Dundas. That is a lot of ground to search if you're right. Also taking on a Were in a wooded area isn't going to be easy."

The Bruce Trail runs close to 900 kilometers from the Niagara River in the south to the tip of Tobermory, Ontario, on Lake Huron and Georgian Bay in the north. Thankfully, we just needed to worry about the part that ran through Hamilton and its suburbs. But Stella was right—that was still a lot of ground to cover.

I kicked around the logistics of an organized search. My team and our foundation members could start at one end of the trail and a couple of EIRT teams with police canine units at the other. We'd also need to have a massive number of police cruisers patrolling above the trail on the mountain and down below in case Logan decided to bolt from the woods and into the city itself when he heard the search teams closing.

That was a lot of manpower and expense, and I wasn't sure I could get EIRT and the Hamilton Police Department to buy into my Logan is hiding on Bruce Trail theory. Even if I could, something like this would take days to arrange. How many more people would die in that time? "Okay, if he is on the trail, how do we flush him out?"

Blue's tail picked up speed behind her and she said, "Napalm?"

Cynthia laughed and then abruptly stopped when Blue gave her an odd look and she clued in that Blue wasn't making a joke.

I worried a little that I'd been around Blue long enough to briefly consider her option before dismissing it. "Effective, but we don't have access to enough planes for that. Also, I was hoping for something a bit more climate friendly than burning down Hamilton's biggest green space."

Stella suggested something along the lines of what I'd been thinking of earlier. Her plan involved our team, the foundation members, EIRT, and the police. I shared my concerns about the time it would take to set up and the possible body count while we waited.

Blue suggested a hybrid approach. While we were waiting for the search to get organized, she could scan the trail from the shadows, and I could fly over, searching it from above. She added that we should modify Stella's monitoring program to add the words *Were* and *attack* in case he struck again. That way, we'd be alerted immediately.

I idly rubbed my chin as I considered her suggestions. It was a bit more proactive than just waiting to organize a massive search, but a part of it still had us indirectly using the citizens of Hamilton as bait. I paused at that thought. "I have a plan."

Stella and Blue both groaned at that and weren't any happier when I explained what we were going to do.

***

Twenty minutes later, I was in my armor and hovering about 500 feet above the center of the Bruce Trail in Hamilton. In the back of my mind, a little voice was screaming at me that this was a very bad idea, but I ignored it.

I took a deep breath and began calling on my powers. I then released a huge showy arc of lightning in all directions around me. While it looked like an impressive display of my power, the light show was more flash than anything else, as the lightning bolts were all low voltage.

I spent a good minute lighting up the night skies above Hamilton and continued the display while slowly lowering my altitude. If Logan was anywhere along the Bruce Trail, there was no way he could miss this.

A minute later, as I reached treetop height, I ended the show and lowered myself to the ground. I knew this area of the trail fairly well, as I'd explored it a lot during my youth. I found the large flat boulder that was just off the main path and sat down.

I turned on my rear camera and the thermals and waited. With the rear and front cameras, I had a 360-degree view of everything around me. Logan's extra-warm Were body would show up like a shooting star on the thermal vision, which meant he couldn't sneak up on me.

"I'm in position. Anything?" I said over the comms.

Blue was scanning the trail east and west of me for any sign of Logan's presence.

"Negative. Keep the comms clear."

I smiled at that last part, as Blue was basically telling me to shut up. She had point. Logan's sensitive hearing would easily be able to hear me talking from a long way off in these quiet woods. We needed him to believe that I was serving myself up for him on a platter and that this fight would just be mano a mano.

I'd hoped between the cameras and Blue's shadow talents that we'd spot him before he got to me. The moment he was in sight, Blue and Stella would pop out from the shadows and the three of us would take him down.

As a bounty hunter, this plan was about the dumbest thing I could do. The key objective of being a good hunter was to take down the target with minimal risk to yourself and the population at large. Sitting on a rock in a pitch-dark wood as bait certainly wasn't the safest thing to do. In these tighter confines, I'd also given up my biggest advantage, which was flight.

The old hero part of me, though, strongly approved of this plan. Better for me to be bait than some helpless victim. In my mind, that was a hundred times better than letting some poor civilian be slaughtered by Logan.

I nervously flicked my eyes between the upper part of my display area, which showed the view from the front camera, and the lower area, which showed the rear.

My heart rate picked up as I spotted a flash of red in the distance on the rear display. I immediately relaxed when I saw its size, however. It was clearly a raccoon, rabbit, skunk, or another small animal.

At least I know the thermals are working, I thought, trying to look on the bright side.

As time ticked by, I was starting to doubt Logan would show up. He might correctly believe that this was a trap. I was betting, though, his beast wouldn't be able to resist my challenge. I idly kicked around the idea of standing up and whistling and yelling, "*Here, doggie-doggie,*" to piss off his beast even more but decided against it. The last thing I needed was an even more enraged Logan.

The hardest part about the wait was maintaining my comms discipline. My nervousness had me wanting to crack jokes, but I managed to keep my immature urges in check.

After about an hour of sitting on the boulder, I decided to stand up to stretch my legs. I'd barely gotten to my feet when a loud roar shattered the silence and something big and heavy crashed into my upper body and drove me face-first into the ground.

The suddenness of the attack caught me off guard. I had just enough time to realize Logan had used the trees around me to approach and surprise me from above.

"*Hel—*"

My cry was cut off as Logan grabbed my armored leg in one of his huge silver paws and swung me face-first into a nearby tree.

A sickening crack echoed in the confines of my helmet as my nose broke against the front plate of it. I was also pretty sure I'd bitten my lip but was dazed so badly by the impact that I couldn't be sure of it.

Heck, I wasn't even sure of my own name at that point.

I had hit the tree so hard that if I hadn't been armored and had the extra support, the impact would have easily broken my neck and killed me. My face had hit the display on my helmet and changed the camera mode from thermal to normal vision again.

Towering above me were two or three silver Werewolves in standing hybrid forms. It took me a moment to realize that it was just one Were, and that my vision was blurry from the impact.

Logan growled again and swung me back the other way. This time the back of my armored head slammed into a tree. The lower display instantly turned to static as the back camera got knocked out of commission.

Oddly enough, this second hit seemed to knock some sense into me and helped me regain my shattered wits.

Another loud growl cut the night, and Logan began to swing me again. In desperation, I lashed out with electricity in all directions.

Logan yelped as the shocks hit home and he released me. I tumbled through the air in an uncontrolled flight. I tossed out a blast of air behind me to stabilize and stop my flight in the nick of time. A split second later, I hit a tree. Thankfully, it was a light hit and I just slid down the tree and landed at bottom of it.

Another angry growl rocked the night air, and I frantically tried to scramble to my feet. I'd only gotten on my knees when I spotted the three Logans in all their silver-furred savagery standing about ten feet in front of me.

I began calling on my lightning powers and planned to fire out a blast wide enough that it wouldn't matter which of them I hit.

Multiple streaks of flame flashed in front of me, and Logan's growl was instantly cut off. I blinked, trying to understand what I'd just seen, when Logan's head rolled off his shoulders and bounced on the ground.

His body tipped forward and standing directly behind him were three Blues, all wearing the same pointy-toothed satisfied grin lit up by three flaming swords.

I released the power I'd been building up for my last stand and sighed in relief. Another part of me, though, prayed the three Blues were due to my impaired vision or a concussion, as there was no way I could keep that many of them away from rocket launchers in the future. "Thanks."

Blue gave me a nod of acknowledgment and gave Logan's corpse an appraising glance. At first I assumed she was just evaluating her swordsmanship, but then I noticed what had caught her attention. The fur, claws, and canine aspects of Logan were slowly changing in front of our eyes.

Twenty seconds later, the Were form had been replaced by his human one. I was relieved that Logan had fallen facedown so I didn't have to see his junk. He'd been with Cynthia, and if things were proportional, that view probably would have given me a minor complex. It didn't help that in another life, Logan probably could have made a mint as an underwear model, which was already feeding my insecurities in my relationship with Cynthia.

Blue pulled me from my musings by offering her hand. Things were improving, as there were only two hands instead of three. I reached up and could feel my hand and arm trembling inside my armor. It hit me that the fight—well, more like the beat down—had rattled me more than I wanted to admit.

I knew the fight with Logan in these woods wouldn't be easy, but I'd kind of pictured lifting him into the air with my powers to immobilize him and then frying him with lightning. Getting smacked around like a ping pong ball being bounced off trees certainly hadn't been the plan. The sheer speed and ferocity of his attack had shaken me. Thankfully, I'd had a deadly blue alien ace up my sleeve, which was the only reason I was still here. My armor had also proved its worth today. Without it, Logan probably could have easily ripped my throat out when he landed on me.

Blue clasped my forearm and yanked me to my feet. I braced myself, my other arm against the tree to stop the world from spinning. I was lightheaded and wasn't entirely sure if I was going to pass out or throw up. The taste of blood in my mouth certainly was encouraging the latter.

Blue must have sensed my lack of stability, as she hadn't released my armored forearm from her grasp. "Do you require more assistance?"

I didn't answer and just closed my eyes and tried to center myself.

After feeling a bit more in control, I blinked my eyes open and was pleased to see that I was down to just one Blue, though she had a slight blurry haze around her. "I'm good now. Thanks."

Despite feeling like hammered garbage, a part of me was feeling pleased with how things turned out. Logan was dead, which meant the threat to Cynthia and the people of Hamilton was over. I was a quick shadow portal away from getting home and getting some much-needed healing. I'd also take this whole experience to heart going forward and embrace the bounty hunter way of doing things with safety as the primary objective of any takedown. I silently thanked Odin that I was still alive to learn that lesson.

Blue and her tail went stock-still, and she cocked her head towards the eastern side of the trail. "Company!"

My heart rate picked up and I went on alert. My concern grew that Logan might have possible accomplices. We hadn't seen any signs or had any indications of that, but I couldn't rule it out.

I turned to face the new threat. Down the path in the distance, I could see multiple flashlight beams bobbing along. My stomach knotted up as around half a dozen people moved toward us. Thankfully, none of them had auras, which meant they were human. That said, it didn't mean they weren't dangerous.

I let out a sigh of relief as the silver SWAT letters reflected in the light for a second. "It's just the police. Don't make any sudden movements."

Blue slowly sheathed her sword, and then held her arms out and away from her body in a non-threatening manner.

The lead officer closed on our position, and I groaned as I recognized Murdock's short bulldog form. My hope of being healed in short order began to vanish like a magician's coin. I also really wasn't in the mood to deal with Murdock's crap at this moment either.

He stopped about ten feet away and raised his weapon in our direction. I did note that his finger wasn't on the trigger and reluctantly gave him points for that.

"Hurricane, is the perp down?" he barked.

"Yes, we're clear." I realized that Blue was blocking his view of the body and added, "Blue, stand to the side so Murdock can see for himself."

I also had to give Murdock points for lowering his weapon the moment I said we were clear. His gaze locked on the headless corpse, and he walked towards it with his guys in tow.

As he got closer, I was both disappointed and pleased to spot the silver paint on the base of his gun's magazine. The paint meant he was using silver rounds, which was the ideal choice for hunting Werewolves. I was glad to see him making the correct choice for a change, but I was also disappointed, as pointing out his flaws was one of my favorite hobbies.

"Good work, Hurricane. You just saved the taxpayers the cost of a pointless trial," said Murdock as his eyes found Logan's severed head lying in the dirt to his right.

I suddenly feared that my concussion was worse than I feared, as that sounded way too much like praise. "Blue should get the thanks; it was her sword work that finished the job."

Murdock nodded, turned to Blue, and said, "Then my compliments to you, Miss Moon."

I smiled both at Murdock's politeness and at Blue's last name. Blue's current identity had been created by Sarah at the English Vampire Court. Sarah always liked to have fun coming up with names, and Blue Moon was certainly an amusing one.

My smile vanished as I gagged when a glob of blood began dripping from my nose down the back of my throat. I popped open my visor and spat it out on the ground.

"Damn, Hurricane, just when I thought you couldn't get any uglier . . ."

There is the old Murdock I know and love, I thought.

I would have made a crack about glasshouses because Murdock certainly wasn't winning any beauty contests, but I was too busy spitting blood.

To my surprise, when I finished clearing my mouth and throat and straightened back up, Murdock was holding out a bottle of water to me.

"You need this more than I do."

I gratefully took it from him and was about to say thanks, but he yelled, "Alright, people! Secure the scene. Jenkins, get on the horn and call EIRT. Wallace, break some chem lights and mark a path so those EIRT pussies can find us."

Once he was satisfied that everyone was doing their jobs, he turned his attention back to me and said, "We'll try and wrap this up quickly so you can get some healing and I can get you out of my crime scene." He cracked a small grin to take the sting out of the comment.

My mouth full of water, I nodded in approval. With that, he wandered off to bark and prod his guys. I spit the water out and was pleased that it cleared the taste of blood from my mouth. I took multiple gulps of water and almost sighed at how good the coolness felt going down.

I watched Murdock and his team work and had confusing feelings about him by this point. While Murdock was as prickly as a cactus to deal with and didn't study up on Enhanceds enough, he was a brave and decent cop. The man had taken the point position and gone into dark woods knowing there was a possible homicidal Were lurking there. The praise and the water were a kindness I hadn't been expecting from him either. Maybe going forward I'd try not to bust his balls as much, and maybe things might be different between us. Of course, that could have just been the concussion speaking.

***

Murdock had been true to his word, and less than thirty minutes later, we were home. EIRT had arrived and taken control of the scene. I hadn't met this squad before, but they seemed decent. I was almost shocked by their lack of questions, and they wrote us up a bounty claim ticket and sent us on our way.

I got the impression from all the cops on scene that they were just happy a cop killer wasn't walking upright anymore.

I was relieved to leave the crime scene in their hands and return home to the couch where Cynthia tended to my wounds.

She moved her hands back from my face and said, "How's that feel?"

I wiggled my nose and smiled. "Much better, thanks."

Cynthia was about to say something more, but Stella and Blue entered the living room and Stella said, "We've uploaded the paperwork for the bounty. Need us for anything else?"

I thought about it and said, "I'll need Blue to take me to Grundy's tomorrow. Logan broke the rear camera on my visor. Tonight, just get some sleep. And thank you both for everything."

I was happy about Stella filling in the paperwork, but I looked at Blue as I thanked them both; I was grateful for her timely save this evening.

They both left and Cynthia said, "Any other injuries hiding under that armor?"

"I don't think so, but you could join me in the shower and take a much closer look. You know, just to make sure," I said with a grin and a lusty expression.

Cynthia giggled and shook her head. "Sounds like you're fine, but I'll join you just in case."

I probably should have jumped at the chance, but something else had been bothering me. Cynthia had been with Logan for a year and a half, and I got the impression that, at one point, she'd cared deeply for him. Yet, since I'd been home, she'd been upbeat. "Um, that would be lovely, but you sure you're okay?"

Her face fell a bit, but she nodded slowly and said, "I'm good. You're worried about how I'm feeling about Logan's death?" I bobbed my head and she added, "I did care for Logan, and maybe at one point even loved him, but that died when his mask slipped six to nine months ago. I'm not even sure the man I cared for really existed, you know?"

Her eyes welled up slightly as a bit of her grief peeked through, so I didn't answer and just wrapped her up in a hug and held her quietly.

I understood where she was coming from. Logan had played a role and put up a false front to lure her into a relationship. The fact that his true personality came out later and she left him for it reassured me that she'd be okay with his death.

I broke the hug and said, "Good news, with me what you see is what you get, though I do have a confession to make . . ."

A look of concern filled her lovely features. "Oh, what's that?"

I grinned and said, "I'm much better in bed than what you've seen so far. I was taking things slow so I wouldn't overwhelm you with my sexual prowess."

Cynthia burst out laughing and snorted at that. The response did hurt my pride a bit, but it was worth it just to hear and see her laugh.

"Thanks for the warning . . . I think I can handle it."

"You sure? There is a reason all the ladies say 'once you go Zack, you never go back.'"

Cynthia shook her head at me but laughed. She held out her hand and I took it and got to my feet. "C'mon, Romeo, let's hit that shower, and you can show me some of your soapy moves."

At that, I wisely shut my mouth and followed her upstairs.

Chapter 24

Friday, December 2

With the threat of Logan over with, the next couple of days were quiet.

While Cynthia was on a call with her mom in the living room, I took the opportunity to join Stella and Blue in the office, looking to get an update on a secret project I had them working on.

Stella smiled when she saw me and lifted a black cardboard box from the desk and said, "We got it done this morning."

I took the box from her and carefully opened it. Inside, nestled in light blue tissue paper, was a picture frame. I smiled as I spotted the polished wood and then frowned in confusion about the thin copper-colored metal around the outside and the inside of the frame.

"We used the guitar strings to finish the inner and outer edges. I hope that's okay?" said Stella.

After Cynthia's apartment was trashed, I had Blue return to the apartment and take the remains of the guitar back to the lab. I asked Stella and Blue if they could mount pieces of wood from the smashed guitar on a picture frame. I hadn't even given a thought to the strings. "It's wonderful, thank you. I owe you both."

I placed the cover back on the box and headed downstairs to wait for Cynthia to finish her call.

My timing was good, as she was coming out of the living room as I entered the kitchen. "Everything good with the family?"

She smiled and nodded. "They're fine and relieved that the whole ordeal with Logan is finished. They were getting pretty tired of having orcs stationed outside their house."

I held out the box and said, "This is for you."

A curious and excited expression flashed across her face as she took the box from me. She opened it and looked at the picture frame resting on the tissue paper.

"The wood and metal around the frame are from your guitar. I thought maybe you could put a picture of your grandfather in it."

My gut knotted up as I watched tears begin to stream down her face, and I worried that I'd upset her by using her guitar this way without asking her.

She put the box carefully down on the counter and wrapped me in a tight hug. "It's beautiful. Thank you."

I wrapped my arms around her and said, "As much as I would like to take all the credit, I only came up with the idea. Stella and Blue were the ones responsible for the craftsmanship."

"I'll be sure to thank them later."

She loosened her hold on me and was about to lean in and kiss me when there was an unexpected knock at the door.

I sighed at the unwelcome interruption and let her go so I could answer it.

I thickened the air around me as a precaution and opened the door to find an elderly man with glasses holding a long white cardboard box.

"Zack Stevens?" he asked.

"That's me."

"These are for you," he said as he handed me the box. He wished me a good day and headed down the driveway.

My confusion grew as I spotted his van with Jean's Flowers written on the side of it.

Who the heck is sending me flowers? I thought.

I took the mysterious flowers inside. Stella and Blue were coming down the stairs in response to the knock, and we joined Cynthia in the kitchen. I opened the box and was greeted by green tissue paper with a small gold sticker on it. I removed the sticker and peeled back the paper to find an arrangement of twelve beautiful long-stemmed roses and baby's breath.

"You got me flowers too?" asked Cynthia with a mixed expression of happiness and confusion.

I shook my head. "They were sent to me."

"There's a card," said Cynthia, pointing to it.

I opened the card, and saw a short message: *One down – Alex*

Any joy I had about having a mysterious admirer or something instantly vanished. My face must have displayed my worry, as Cynthia said, "Zack, what's the matter?"

I wordlessly handed her the card, and she read it out loud. "Oh," she said.

The flowers were a warning that Alex Gray was watching our progress and an implied threat that the clock was ticking on us finding Pierre. I felt that weight of responsibility bearing down on my shoulders again.

Worse, I had no clue how we'd find Pierre. If Detective Grissom's theory was correct, Pierre had fled the country, and the entire world was a big place to search. By the lack of sightings, it felt like Grissom was correct. Either that, or Pierre was dead. I idly wondered if Alex Gray had found and killed Pierre and this whole flower thing was just him playing mind games or trying to establish some sort of alibi. But that seemed like a stretch.

I moved us up to the office for an emergency strategy session. "It looks like Alex Gray's patience is running out, and we need to find Pierre soon or things are about to get a lot more interesting around here."

"It seems the logical course of action is to complete the bargain with Manny," said Blue.

I expected that comment from her, but I wasn't ready to make that deal yet. Finding out the name on Pierre's fake ID would help us track him down. But if Manny was what I thought he was, owing him a favor would be something we'd probably regret. I still wasn't that desperate, but if things didn't change soon, we might be. If it came down to a choice between taking on Alex Gray and the entire Misfit Mafia or owing Manny a favor, the decision would be pretty simple. I shook my head. "Not yet. That is only an option I'm willing to use if we have no other choice."

"I understand your concerns, but we've been looking for Pierre almost nonstop since he became a fugitive and have hit a wall. This might be our only option at this point," said Stella.

"I know, but let's take another look at things. We need to think outside of the box. This is similar to our case with the Master. Remember when the new Acolytes reappeared? The Master hadn't been seen in months, yet we came up with a way to find him. This has to be easier than that."

Stella nodded at that, and the room went silent, as I knew everyone was trying to come up with an idea.

I mentally went over everything we knew about Pierre. TJ's clue about Pierre hiding out at the cabin was a bust, as Blue had been checking it constantly via the shadows and it was undisturbed.

Stella had gone over Pierre's finances with a fine-tooth comb and came up empty. I wondered if she missed something there. "Stella, did Pierre have any foreign holdings?"

Stella tugged on her braid and then shook her head. "No, his only foreign holdings were shares in large public companies that were part of his stock portfolio."

I mentally sighed at her answer. It would have been nice if he owned some land outside of Canada, as that might have indicated where he fled. I wandered over to the whiteboard on the wall and picked up a marker. "Okay, what do we know about Pierre LaPointe?"

"He's a mage," said Stella.

I wrote that on the board.

"He's ruthless, wealthy, and likes young women," said Cynthia.

I left off ruthless but added the other two to the board. I was tempted to make a joke about Pierre being on the island of a certain deceased billionaire that had been in news recently due to his death and allegations of his activities with underage girls but decided not to. To Pierre's credit, the women he'd been with were young but not underage.

Blue pulled my attention back to the here and now when she said, "He has no living family."

I added that to the board as well. The suggestions slowed down after that, but I added *criminal* and *using a fake ID* to the board. Stella suggested *owns property in Quebec and Halifax*, and those went on the board too. Blue added that he had been seen fleeing with two other men. After that, we hit a wall.

I was a bit underwhelmed as I looked at the list but tried to put on a brave face. "Okay, we have a list, what things might be useful in finding Pierre?"

Stella said, "Maybe you can call Walter and see if he can put some feelers out in the magic community about Pierre—he is a mage after all."

I perked up at that. The mage community was a tight-knit group, as it wasn't uncommon for them to reach out to other members when they were stuck on casting or working on a new spell. Pierre might have another mage as a close friend or acquaintance that we didn't know about. "Good. I'll do that when we're finished here. What else?"

The room went quiet again and I studied the list. I honed in on his affinity for young women. "Cynthia, was there a certain woman that Pierre seemed more attached to than others?"

Cynthia got a thoughtful look on her face and then said, "No. Almost without fail, Pierre would have a new piece of arm candy each week. I don't remember him being with any woman for longer than a week."

I mentally cursed at that because it sounded like these women were just conquests for him, and I doubted he was close to any of them or would have let any of them know anything important.

We tossed around random thoughts and ideas for a bit, but none of them were useful.

Cynthia then said, "Besides the club, Logan and I spent a lot of time at Pierre's house. He has this huge house on the lake and would entertain there regularly. He warned everyone that the upper level of the house was strictly off-limits and that entering it would have fatal consequences. He'd even take his latest woman of the week to a bedroom in the basement and not upstairs to his room."

"Mages can be a little odd. He might have had a lab upstairs for his magic projects and didn't wish for anyone to disturb them."

Cynthia shook her head. "I think it is more than that. Logan was his most trusted man. I asked Logan one night if he'd ever been upstairs, and he said he hadn't. With Blue's abilities, isn't it worth a quick trip out there to see if we can find anything?"

I was wondering how much of this was related to the case and how much was just Cynthia's curiosity in finding out what was upstairs but kept that thought to myself. "Even with Blue's powers, it won't be a quick trip. Magic users are infamous for making their dwellings deathtraps. Odin only knows what nasty spells, wards, traps, and defenses he has lying in wait."

Stella perked up. "They might not be there anymore. Remember when GRC13 raided our house?"

"The police raided this house?" asked Cynthia with a shocked expression.

"Twice. Once after we'd robbed the Mint and then again when I was framed for murder."

I swore I heard Cynthia mumble something like, "At least he's not boring," but I'd already shifted my attention to Stella as my feeble brain finally figured out where she'd been going with her comment. "You think that EIRT raided Pierre's house and disabled all the wards?"

Stella nodded and said, "They'd have to. It's only logical to check a fugitive's primary residence in case they are hiding there. I could hack their case files and check."

"No. While I have no doubt about your abilities to do just that, let's try something a bit less illegal first. Cynthia, give Blue the address to Pierre's place, and let's see if Blue can find some sign that EIRT has in fact raided the place first."

Stella looked disappointed but gave me a small nod. Cynthia rhymed off the address to Blue, who nodded and typed something into her computer. I assumed Blue was finding the place on the map first.

While Blue was searching the shadows, I pondered whether or not this trip was even worthwhile. If EIRT had raided the house, they probably took anything that was related to finding Pierre's current location. On the other hand, there was a chance that they missed or overlooked something. As we weren't exactly being overwhelmed by other options, I decided we might as well check the place out and hope that we got lucky.

Less than a minute later, Blue came out of her trance-like state and said, "There is an EIRT notice on the front door."

I smiled and said, "Let's go visit Pierre's house."

Chapter 25

Friday, December 2

We came out of the shadows into a sitting room at the back of Pierre's house and were greeted by the heavy staccato pounding of rain. I glanced out the sliding patio door and was impressed at the sheer volume of the downpour.

I couldn't help but notice the view and the size of the backyard. The wood deck alone was big enough to almost land a plane. I was exaggerating that but not by much. The raindrops pounded the wooden surface and created an almost hypnotic display. There was no deck furniture to be seen, and I assumed it must be in storage due to the lateness of the season. There were a few ornate stone planters lining the edge of the deck.

Beyond the deck, to my right, there was an in-ground pool that caught my attention. I could see shimmering vapors rising from the water. The vapors meant it was heated, but the more puzzling thing was that the rain wasn't disturbing the pool's surface. I frowned at that and then it dawned on me that Pierre must be using a spell to keep bugs and other things from getting into it.

My stomach knotted up a bit, as it also meant not all the magic had been dispelled from the house, and I was starting to regret my decision to bring Cynthia with us. She'd guilted me into it by pointing out that she knew the house better than any of us, adding that if the three of us went, she would be left unprotected at home. The threat from Logan was over, but Pierre and Alex Gray might decide that Cynthia was more useful dead than alive.

I quickly checked out the rest of the backyard from my viewpoint. There was a span of decking that ran down the center of the yard that connected the deck to the dock at the end of the yard. The dock was empty, and the lake beyond was mostly obscured by the rain. The water I could see was cresting sharp three-foot-high waves, and it looked like it would be a rough day to be out there. The only other thing of note was the red and green clay surface of a tennis court that was off to the left side of the yard.

I pointed out the active magic around the pool and turned my attention to Cynthia. "This place could be very different than you've been used to if there are any active traps," I said. "Stay behind me and walk where I walk, okay?"

She nodded and I took the lead as the four of us left the sitting room to explore the rest of the house. The possibility of traps made me glad I'd taken the time to armor up.

We passed a living room, dining room, and a games room with a full-sized billiard table. The games room really brought home the size of the place, as you would need a good-sized room to fit one of those and this one had space to spare. The geek in me approved of the classic arcade machines lining the back wall. I was a fan of Pac-Man, Galaga, and other popular titles from the eighties. A small part of me would have loved to stop and play them for a bit.

A pleb like me didn't know when a house officially crossed the line to become a mansion, but I suspected I could probably use the term to describe Pierre's house. It was easily double the size of our four-bedroom house and probably closer to three or four times the size.

We checked out the main kitchen for any clues, which was large enough to prep for a dinner party of sixty, but the garbage and recycling had been cleaned out. I suspected they were at an EIRT lab being analyzed.

The search of the main level hadn't revealed anything of note. We decided to split up. Stella 'helpfully' volunteered her and Blue to take the basement while Cynthia and I would check out the upstairs.

I wanted to reverse that, but Cynthia protested that she really wanted to see the upstairs, which left me with no choice.

I sighed to myself as I watched them open the door to the basement staircase and disappear. I turned to Cynthia and reminded her to follow behind me and step where I did.

She bristled under my stern tone but slowly nodded in agreement. I hoped that my fears were unfounded, and this trip would be a walk in the park. I'd apologize to Cynthia if that was the case, but for now, better safe than sorry.

I glanced up the sweeping spiral staircase and admired the rich dark hardwood and its craftsmanship. I took a moment to study each of the steps, trying to see if I could spot any obvious traps but came up empty. Taking a deep breath, I made my first step up the stairs.

I let out a sigh of relief when I reached the top stair and nothing happened. I checked over my shoulder to make sure Cynthia was okay, and she paused about six steps behind me. I mentally nodded in approval.

The moment my feet touched the landing, a deep hum filled the air and iron bars shot up around me. My armored hand touched one of the bars of the new cage I'd suddenly found myself in and my body almost shuddered in pleasure as electricity coursed through me.

By the jolt I got, Pierre wasn't screwing around. That amount of juice would have easily knocked out a normal human if not killed them outright.

"Zack! Are you okay?"

I turned around and glanced at a worried Cynthia through the metal bars and nodded. "I'm fine. Thankfully the bars were just electrified, which, other than giving me a nice pick-me-up, didn't hurt."

I looked around the cage and realized that I may have been fine, but I was still trapped. The bars went all the way to the ceiling, so flying out wasn't an option.

I needed help. "Please go find Stella and Blue and bring them here."

"I'll be right back," she said as she pivoted and slowly went down the staircase.

The slow pace had me confused for a moment, but then I smiled as I realized that Cynthia was retracing her steps exactly. I approved of her newfound caution.

While I waited for Cynthia to bring help, I kicked around options for getting out of this trap. Stella's Hyde form could probably tear it open, but I wasn't sure how she'd handle the electricity. Blue's magic sword could easily cut through the bars and free me, and I was leaning towards that as the solution but then remembered the cage was magic. Using magic to break something magic can have unpredictable results. A flashback of Blue using her sword to destroy a magic portal during our adventure with rapkeys at the Dundas golf course came back to me. The resulting explosion had blown a huge crater in one of the greens and ended any chance I had of ever getting a membership there.

The idea of being at ground zero of another explosion like that didn't appeal. I desperately tried thinking of another way to get out of this cage. My eyes lingered on the umbrella stand at the front door and I smiled.

Blue, Stella, and Cynthia appeared in the hallway. Blue, upon spotting me and my predicament, shrugged and drew and ignited her sword.

Just as she stepped toward the stairs, I said, "Wait!" Blue froze and I added, "Let's go a different route . . ."

Once I explained what I had in mind, Blue sheathed her sword and turned to retrieve one of the umbrellas from the stand. She stopped at the bottom of the stairs and asked, "Ready?"

I nodded and she gripped the umbrella like a spear and threw it up the stairs at me. I blinked in astonishment as her throw put the tip of the umbrella right between the bars in front of me and I grabbed it.

"If bounty hunting ever goes cold, you could make a nice living as an NFL quarterback," I said to her, an amused smile on my lips.

Though, I'm not sure the NFL is ready or would allow a female blue-skinned alien on the field. Screw 'em if they didn't; it would be their loss, I thought.

Blue shook her head. "I have no interest in that sport. The protective equipment they wear takes all the enjoyment out of it."

I laughed at her answer and then focused back on the task at hand. I shifted the umbrella around and opened it. The shadow it created wasn't as large as I hoped, so I crouched down to make sure my entire body was engulfed.

I waited for Blue to open a portal, happy that this time using an umbrella was much better than the last. The heist at the Royal Canadian Mint had been a desperate and hairy ordeal, and I was grateful for the lack of poisonous gas, machine guns, and angry guards.

A blue arm popped out of the shadows and grabbed me. I rolled out of the shadows in the same sitting room where we had arrived. I was starting to feel like I was playing Portal.

I got up and said, "Thanks."

Stella said, "The basement is a bust. Nothing of interest other than enough BDSM equipment to film the next *Fifty Shades* movie down there."

Cynthia laughed but I just stood there dumbfounded.

"What?" said Stella with a coy smile. "You aren't the only one that can make movie jokes on this team."

"How? When?" I sputtered, still not believing Stella had seen that movie.

"It was Liv's pick for movie night. You were out at a poker game. To be truthful, it really wasn't my cup of tea. The books were much better than the movie."

I lifted an eyebrow at the last part. This was a side of Stella I hadn't been aware of and, quite frankly, didn't want to know about. I hastily said, "Well, looks like this trip has been a waste. Let's go home."

"What about the upstairs?" Cynthia asked.

I pointed at myself and said, "Hello, I just escaped a lethal trap. I think that is enough for one day."

"Where's your sense of adventure?" said Cynthia with a grin.

She turned to Stella and Blue and I felt my shoulders slump as I noticed their expressions and knew we weren't done yet. I was going to claim that with the iron cage blocking the way, we had no access to the upstairs but dismissed that thought as soon as I had it. Blue's shadow travelling abilities would gain us access to the upstairs.

"Okay, fine, but we are doing this my way."

A few minutes later, I came out of the shadows, hovering about a foot off the floor. As I looked around the quiet bedroom, I nodded in approval. I'd asked Blue to find a shadow in a little-used room on the upper floor. This room was obviously a spare bedroom by the sparse decor. I spied a bit of dust buildup on the top of the table lamp and in a few other places around the room, which confirmed for me that it was seldom used.

I opened the comms and said, *"Arrived safe. Commencing my sweep now."*

"Roger that," Blue replied.

I called on more of my Air powers and pushed a heavy gust of wind towards the floor six feet out in front of me. My thinking was that by stepping on a certain point of the floor, I'd activated the trap earlier. I hoped that by shooting air at the floor, I could trigger any other traps.

I came out into the hall and rattled some pictures on the wall, which made me jump. I was sweating a bit in my armor, wondering if this was what it felt like to clear a minefield. I went down the hall towards the cage, pouring out the air in front of me.

I reached the cage without incident and backtracked. The air almost smashed an expensive-looking vase off a small display table in the hall, but I shunted the air quickly under it before it hit the ground and saved it. I focused as I carefully used my powers to lift it back up, rotate it, and gently place it back on its table.

I smiled to myself as I finished and knew that my departed mother would have been proud of me for that sort of fine-tuned control. She used to train me using an egg that I had to get through a small obstacle course with just my powers. I usually had to clean a lot of yolks off the floor and sometimes the walls after those sessions.

It took another five minutes, but I swept the entire upper floor and nothing exploded, shot at me, or erupted into flames. I returned to the spare room I'd started in and dismissed my powers.

The rest of the team came through the shadows and joined me. There were seven rooms on the upper level but the only two that were of interest to us were the main bedroom and the home office. The bedroom didn't yield any clues other than Pierre's love of retro porn magazines. The man had a Smithsonian-worthy collection of them.

Cynthia made a face at that discovery, and I said, "Maybe he just likes reading the articles."

She rolled her eyes at that but did let out a small giggle.

The office was next on our list. The entire room was lined with floor-to-ceiling shelves of leather-bound books. The subjects of the books covered a wide variety of topics such as magic, history, military conflicts, science, and even religion. Stella's face lit up when she saw them.

"Focus. We're looking for clues. We're not here to add to your library back at the lab," I said.

The solid oak desk in the center back area of the room pulled my attention, and I figured it would be a good place to start. The top of the desk was clear other than a paper blotter. I cursed at the sight of a loose power cable sticking out of a hole in the desk, as it meant there'd been a PC here, but that was probably at EIRT being examined for evidence. The lack of papers on the desk meant either Pierre had been very neat, or they too were with EIRT.

I reached for the top right-hand drawer on the desk and frowned when it didn't budge. I realized it was locked. The smell of smoke alerted me that something was wrong. I cried out as I felt a burning sensation on my fingertips and pulled my armored hand away.

"Zack! Are you okay?"

I glanced down at my gauntlet and saw that the armored tips of my forefinger, middle finger, and thumb had melted and been deformed. I hastily popped the release to the gauntlet and pulled my hand out of it. The skin on the three digits had already begun to blister. I blew on them, which didn't seem to help much.

Thankfully, Cynthia saw my dilemma and took my hand into hers and started healing me.

By Odin's hairy balls, I hate mages, I thought as Cynthia finished healing me.

A sharp crack filled the room, and I looked over and saw that Blue had used her sword like a crowbar to pop open the drawer.

So much for not using magic to disrupt other magic.

The good news was that the trapped drawer hadn't exploded or consumed us all in flames. The bad news was that it was empty. Either Pierre had cleaned it out when he fled or EIRT had during their search.

"Feel better?" asked Cynthia as she released my hand.

I nodded and thanked her.

The rest of the desk drawers weren't trapped but didn't contain anything of use in our search for Pierre. We looked for another few minutes but came up empty and decided to call it a day.

As we were leaving, Cynthia seemed a bit down. "What's up?" I asked.

She shook her head and said, "By how protective Pierre was about the upstairs, I was sure we'd find something good."

"Stella, Blue. Hold up for a moment. I want to show Cynthia something."

I took her hand and led her to a room we hadn't searched together as a group and stopped her at the doorway. As there were no visible papers or anything that might contain a clue to Pierre's whereabouts, I hadn't felt the need to do a more thorough search. Inside the room was a stout wooden table with beakers and a Bunsen burner on it. There were wood cabinets with glass doors lining the walls. Inside the cabinets were various bottles, vials, and assorted magic components. There were runes etched into the floor, which was why we hadn't searched this room, but I had flown around to check it out.

"I suspect this was the room that Pierre didn't want people to find. Inside those cabinets are some priceless spell ingredients. One was labeled ground unicorn horn; another one was labeled phoenix feathers. Those were just a couple I looked at. Those components are extremely valuable and worth a small fortune on the open market. I also suspect those runes on the floor are containment runes. If someone had disturbed one of them, and Pierre hadn't noticed it, that could easily be a life-ending mistake for him when he went to cast his next spell in there."

Cynthia brightened up and said, "Thanks. At least I now know why he was so paranoid about people coming up here."

I smiled. "Let's go home."

The nice thing was our adventure was early enough that, with Blue's help, I was able to get my damaged gauntlet to Grundy's for repair. They promised to have it fixed by tomorrow morning.

We wrapped up the day before dinner with another strategy session in the office.

"It looks like we have no choice but to make that deal with Manny now," Stella said, her shoulders slumping.

I was about to agree with her, but ever since we left Pierre's house, I had this feeling that we were missing something. I still viewed the deal as a last resort and wasn't ready to pull the trigger on it yet. I stared at the list on the whiteboard hoping to get some inspiration. "Let's hold off on that for now. What about the two accomplices that were seen leaving with Pierre, do we know anything about them?"

Stella spun around in her chair and typed something and then said, "Not much. The descriptions are pretty vague. Both men are in their thirties, brown hair, average weight and height. No visible tattoos or markings. EIRT still hasn't released their names either."

"Not much to work on but why don't you and Blue look into them further and see what you can come up with? Pierre isn't likely to make a dumb mistake like posting to social media, but maybe his two companions won't be as sharp."

Stella nodded and said, "We'll look into it. In the meantime, remember to call Walter."

I hadn't done that before I'd left and decided now was a good time. Walter picked up after a couple of rings.

"*Dude, what can I do for you?*"

"*Looking for information,*" I said and then explained about Pierre LaPointe.

His tone told me he was less than excited. I realized he was hoping I'd called to commission a new magic device. I decided to sweeten the pot for him. *"If you can get me a solid lead on someone who knows where he is or might be, I'll pay $25,000 and waive that favor you owe me."*

"I'll see what I can find."

I smiled as the interest level in his tone had picked up considerably at that. I ended the call.

The Manny deal was lurking in my mind, but maybe Stella and Blue could dig up something on Pierre's companions, or Walter might get lucky and find us a lead. I was annoyed about that feeling I was missing something but couldn't narrow it down. I hoped that my subconscious might puzzle it out sooner rather than later.

Chapter 26

Saturday, December 3

When I got up, I saw that Mother Nature decided to make sure everyone knew it was December by bringing snow. The snow squall didn't last long and stopped before I'd finished my first coffee for the day. A light blanket of snow covered the grass and trees, but the road and sidewalks were clear. We usually didn't get much snow in Hamilton this time of year. It wasn't uncommon for the first snowstorm not to arrive until January. I hoped that the early snowfall wasn't an omen for the rest of winter. Especially since my relationship with Cynthia hadn't reached the point where I could ask her to shovel.

As Cynthia and I had a quiet breakfast together, I pondered Pierre's house. I found myself comparing our dated kitchen to his state-of-the-art one. Our kitchen badly needed a refresh. But, as this house was just temporary, until our original one next door was rebuilt, it wasn't high on my list of things that had to get done. At that thought, I had a eureka moment.

Cynthia gave me a curious look as I sprang to my feet, probably because half my food was still on my plate. "I'll be right back."

I tore up the stairs to find Stella and Blue in the office.

"We still haven't found anything on Pierre's companions," said Stella, not looking up from her screen as I entered.

"Never mind that. Can you dig through Pierre's finances for the cabin at the lake? I'm looking for building expenses, materials, contractors, etcetera—anything related to the cost of building the cabin."

Stella gave me an odd look but shrugged and said, "Give me a few minutes and I'll see what I can come up with. Care to share what you're thinking?"

"It might not be anything, but I'll know if it is when you get me those numbers. I'm going to finish my breakfast and will return after that."

Cynthia lifted a questioning eyebrow when I rejoined her. "Your mood suddenly got much better," she said.

I was busy stuffing food down my throat and just nodded. I swallowed and said, "I have a theory on where Pierre might be but need Stella to run some numbers first. It might not be anything."

Ten minutes later, Cynthia and I were loading the dishwasher when Stella yelled down, "Zack! I have your numbers."

We joined Stella and Blue in the office and I asked, "How much was the total number?"

Stella glanced at a spreadsheet on the screen and said, "He expensed about 3.5 million dollars in building costs."

I fist pumped the air at that answer. All three of them looked at me like I lost my mind. "Our visit to Pierre's house wasn't a waste after all."

"Care to explain that?" asked Cynthia.

I smiled and said, "After we left the house yesterday, something was bothering me, and I couldn't put my finger on it. The one thing that struck me about our visit was that Pierre had a taste for the good life. That house was beautiful, and he didn't spare any expense. Now compare that to the cabin."

Cynthia's eyes widened and Blue's tail started circling rapidly behind her, and I knew they'd figured out where I was going with this. Stella, not having seen the cabin, was still confused.

I turned to her and said, "The cabin is a small single room number with a bathroom, and there is no way it cost three and half million to build. Not even close."

Stella perked up and said, "You think there's another cabin?"

I nodded. "Yup. You said Pierre had bought up all the land around the lake. What if somewhere around the lake is another cabin? One that is more in line with Pierre's upscale lifestyle?"

"Looks like TJ might have been right after all," Cynthia said.

I tried to contain my excitement, as this was just speculation on my part. The large building expense might just be Pierre laundering money via tax expenses, but I was leaning towards my second cabin theory.

***

An hour later, after picking up my repaired gauntlet from Grundy's, I was armored up and Blue opened another portal for me. I came out of the shadows in front of the cabin to a cold, blustery day. I could see my breath in front of me as I exhaled and was grateful my secondary Ice powers kept me from feeling the cold. It seemed December was making its presence felt here in Quebec too. At least it wasn't snowing yet, but by the dark clouds above, that might not be the case for long.

I called on my powers and lifted myself into the air. As I flew over the lake, I kept my eyes peeled along the left bank, hoping to spot something in the trees. I kept my altitude to about twenty feet over the water. If there was another cabin somewhere out here, I hoped by staying low I was less likely to be spotted. The last thing I needed was to locate that cabin and find Pierre gone because I'd spooked him.

The cabin we'd been taken to when we were kidnapped was on the west end of the lake. When I escaped from Logan, I'd swum south. I hadn't seen a hint of another cabin around either of those two areas, so I was betting that if it existed, it was either to the north or east. I was currently flying along the northern coastline of the lake.

Being back over this lake again reminded me of how happy I was to have my powers back. Even the cold windy day couldn't dampen my joy as I streaked over the lake.

My joy did fade a bit when I curved around the far eastern end of the lake and still hadn't found anything. That area had been my best guess about the other cabin's location. I wasn't giving up hope, though, as there was still a chance it might be in the southeastern area I was about to fly by.

A few minutes later, I spotted the small stream I'd walked along after coming ashore during my escape. My hopes about finding the second cabin had dropped dramatically at this point.

I kept my eyes peeled along the shoreline as I flew the final leg towards the cabin, but I was already debating how bad making a deal with Manny would be.

As the cabin came back into view, I felt defeated. I'd been so sure that I'd been on to something. I studied the simple cabin as I got closer and shook my head. There was no way that cost three and a half million to build. By buying and, unfortunately, destroying houses over this past year, I had a pretty good idea of building costs. That cabin couldn't have been more than a quarter million, max, and it was probably much less than that. If Pierre had been inflating the numbers for a tax expense, he had been taking one heck of a risk. A quick visual inspection would rapidly expose his fraud.

I knew in this day and age most companies and government agencies wouldn't do an in-person inspection. Usually, they'd just call up Google Street View and check a property that way. The remote location meant it wouldn't be on there, but it would show up on Google Maps in satellite view. Was he banking that Revenue Canada would see it there and not look any deeper? That seemed thin to me. Pierre, with his mage background, would be a cautious person by nature; add in his criminal enterprises and this thinly veiled scam seemed way too risky.

I decided to throw caution to the wind and put some height under me as I flew back out towards the center of the lake for one last look. The dark clouds were low in the sky today, so I went as I high as I could without having them obscure my view.

When I reached the center of the lake, I stopped and hovered there, high up in the air. I turned towards the original cabin and slowly rotated clockwise from there. As I faced the northern most point, my heart beat faster as I spotted a large cabin tucked back among the trees. Even from this height and distance, I could tell the place was closer to what a 3.5-million-dollar building would look like. It was easily twice the size of my house, and I wasn't even sure if I could still call it a cabin.

I instantly realized how I missed it on my earlier flight. I'd seen the small gap between the trees but had assumed it was a feeder stream and ignored it. That 'feeder stream' ran for about twenty feet and then hooked around to the right and opened to a small cove. A dock sat on the far end of that cove and the cabin was set back from that. The entire cove, dock, and cabin were hidden from view by the trees around them.

I didn't want to be spotted, so I decided not to linger and dove hard back to the surface of the lake.

As I skimmed over the water on my way back to the original cabin, I had a huge smile stuck on my face.

We've gotcha now, you son of a bitch.

***

I shared my good news with the team when I got back. I used a laptop to show Blue where the cabin was on a map and asked her to observe the place from the shadows. "But be careful. We don't want to spook Pierre, and Odin only knows what anti-spying spells he might have in place."

Blue gave me a sharp look and said, "Relax, not my first cow convention."

Cynthia giggled and was about to say something, but I sharply shook my head at her, and she stayed quiet. I noticed Stella had turned away but hid her amusement with a cough.

Blue was incorrectly paraphrasing Liv's favorite "not my first rodeo" line and had done this in the past. Every time she did, I knew I should correct her, but I didn't, as I got way too much enjoyment out of it. Stella must have felt the same way because she too refrained from correcting her.

Blue was already in her trance-like state, gazing into the shadows, and she either missed or ignored our amusement.

Stella said, "Once Blue gets us intel, are we going to storm the cabin?"

I shook my head. "What is one of my key bounty hunting rules?"

"Never mess with any member of the God class?" said Stella.

"That is my number one rule, but not the one I'd been thinking of . . ."

Stella tugged her braid for a moment and said, "Never attack a magic user in their home?"

"Bingo!" I said. "We've already had a taste of Pierre's traps at his house, and that was after EIRT had cleared most of them. I shudder to think how many he'll have around that cabin knowing he's a wanted man. Hitting him directly would be suicide."

Stella nodded. "So, what is the plan?"

That was the million-dollar question. At this point, I had no clue how to flush Pierre out of that cabin. "Let's see what Blue finds out and then we'll go from there."

I was getting warm standing around in my armor but didn't want to take it off in case Blue's spying alerted Pierre and we had to go at a moment's notice. I retreated to the kitchen to find a bottle of water.

I joined Stella and Cynthia on the couch while we waited for Blue to complete her recon. We didn't chat, as Stella and Cynthia were watching Blue closely, and I was pondering how to get Pierre out of that cabin.

I'd just finished draining the last of my water when Blue gave herself a slight shake and tore her gaze from the shadows.

"Pierre and his two companions are at the cabin. I focused on trying to determine what powers the two of them had. The taller of the two moves with inhuman grace and his speech is archaic and formal. The other one, from what I could perceive, appears to be just human, but I only had that small window to observe him."

Between the inhuman grace and formal speech, I guessed that we might be dealing with a vampire. And an old one at that. It was still daytime, though, so I dismissed that thought. A Were was my next thought, but that also didn't add up. While Weres had extended lifespans over humans, they generally lived no longer than 200 years. Witnesses described Pierre's companions as being in their thirties, which would put a Were at somewhere between fifty and ninety in actual age. That was nowhere near old enough for the formal archaic speech Blue had observed. "Your first suspect sounds like they might be fae. Elves have that type of inhuman grace to their movements and that fits with the formal speech."

"Drow?" asked Stella.

"Possibly, or wood elf. At least I hope it's one of those two."

Cynthia frowned. "Drow or any elf with their speed and magic are dangerous. Why would you hope for that?"

I let out a long sigh and said, "I'm not arguing that elves aren't dangerous, but there are a lot of different fae types, and some of those make elves look like kittens by comparison. Thankfully, I can't see one of those types serving Pierre. The ones I'm thinking of would either enslave him or eat him."

We could deal with an elf. I was more concerned about the second one, but there was a chance he was just human and the most we'd have to worry about was him being armed. "Was the second one eating when you saw him?"

"He did not consume any food during the entire time I observed him," said Blue.

"Well, probably not a Were then. I don't like not knowing what his powers are. My fear is he's a Super with some unknown power that could give us trouble. For now, we need to figure out how we want to do this takedown. I've been giving it some thought and have come up with an idea that Blue will like."

Stella looked shocked and said, "The cabin is isolated but isn't a rocket launcher a bit much?"

It was Cynthia's turn to look alarmed, and Blue's tail suddenly started moving excitedly.

I shook my head. "No, not a rocket launcher, anti-tank missile, or anything along those lines. Do we still have those water cooler jugs filled with gas at the lab?"

In our case against the lich, Stella had saved the day when we were fighting an undead T-Rex by converting her water cannon into a flamethrower. The original cannon hadn't survived that encounter, but Stella had built another one. The original purpose of that cannon had been to spray down a demon with holy water. I knew we had water coolers filled with holy water in case of another demon, but I was pretty sure Stella had also added a couple of coolers filled with gas as well.

"There are two full ones at the lab," said Stella.

"Good. My thought is that I'll fly above the cabin and empty it over the roof and then ignite it."

Cynthia gasped, Stella looked unsure, and Blue nodded firmly in approval at my plan.

"Isn't burning down a cabin a bit extreme?" asked Cynthia, shaking her head.

I was going to argue that it was less extreme than a rocket launcher but decided on a different approach. "Yes, but these are fugitives wanted for murder, and entering that cabin isn't an option. We'll be doing this during the day, so it's not like we are burning them to death in their sleep. My idea is that they will quickly notice the fire and flee the cabin. At that point, we can take them down in their panicked state, and hopefully there will be enough time I can use my Air powers to smother the blaze."

Stella looked relieved at that, and Cynthia slowly nodded too.

We had about four hours of daylight left, and I wanted to get this over sooner than later. "Blue, you have another hour to observe Pierre and company. Try and figure out what powers that second one has. We'll go shortly after that."

Chapter 27

Saturday, December 3

I swore under my breath as we stepped out of the shadows. My teeth instantly ached, and a feeling of wrongness surrounded me.

"The mystery companion is an Earth elemental," I said through clenched teeth as I put down the water cooler full of gas I carried.

Our plan of burning them out was probably out the window by now, as I had no doubt the Earth elemental had sensed my presence. Without having made a single move, our element of surprise was gone. I turned to Blue and said, "Use the shadows and see if they are going to fight or flee."

Blue nodded and went off into a trance.

We were partially hidden in a wooded area facing the left side of the cabin, but we also had a decent view of the front from this vantage point. The clouds above had thinned out and lightened up. It looked like the threat of a snowstorm had passed.

My mind raced to come up with a new plan for both a fight and flight scenario. I hoped they were going to flee. There'd be a chance that they'd all run in different directions, which meant we could just go after Pierre and not have to deal with the elf and Earth elemental. Even if they stuck together, there was a chance that with my Air powers or Blue's shadow power one of us might just be able to pick off Pierre and his companions might just decide to keep running.

I figured, though, that we probably wouldn't get that lucky, and I was willing to bet they'd fight. Once the Earth elemental told Pierre there was an Air elemental nearby, he would assume it was me. I doubted he'd pass on a chance to eliminate a key witness to his kidnapping and attempted murder charges. The Earth elemental would also be itching for a fight just to stop the feeling of wrongness around him. If the elf turned out to be a Drow, he wouldn't pass on a chance for murder and mayhem.

I'd just finished mentally going through the best way to play this out if we were going to have to fight, when Blue came out of her trance-like state and said, "They are planning to engage us and will be out the front door shortly."

"Blue, you take the elf. Stella, stay behind me and when the Earth elemental comes after me, you take him. Pierre's mine. If any of us finishes off our opponent, assist whoever needs help the most."

Stella's Hyde form grunted in acknowledgment and Blue nodded. She opened a portal and disappeared. For a moment, it felt like she was abandoning us, but I knew she'd be watching from the shadows and then use them to strike at the elf when the time was right.

The feeling of wrongness grew in strength as the front door of the cabin slammed open and a fully rocked-up Elemental came stomping out. The Earth elemental's aura was about four inches in size, which meant he had decent power but nothing amazing. Brock, an Earth elemental and one of my foundation members, had an aura that was more than six inches. He and Stella sparred regularly, and Stella's Hyde form usually won against him more often than not. The smaller aura made me feel better about our chances.

In this case, size does matter, I thought with a grin.

The elf was directly behind the Earth elemental and the rainbow, black, and purple aura around him confirmed that we were indeed facing a dark elf.

I opened the comms and said, *"The elf is a Drow."*

"Roger that," answered Blue.

Pierre came out of the cabin last. He was wearing a mage's robe that was such a deep shade of purple it almost looked black. He carried a thick six-foot-long staff with what looked like many intricate runes etched along its length. He was clean-shaven like he'd been in his photos, which was a disappointment, as I always wanted mages to have full Merlin-like beards. I did give him points, though, for skipping the traditional mage's pointy-brimmed hat, as I'd never been a fan of them.

The Earth elemental stopped in his tracks once he was off the covered front porch and his granite head swiveled around as he searched for me. The elf acrobatically climbed one of the pillars and then swung up onto the porch roof like a spider monkey. He slipped a longbow off his body, nocked an arrow, and began scanning for targets. Even from here, I could see the putrid green substance covering the arrowhead, and I thickened the air in front of me as a precaution against the poisoned arrow. I doubted the arrow could penetrate my armor or Stella's thick skin, but it was better to be safe than sorry.

I decided to get on with the fight and stepped out of the woods to expose myself. The moment I did, the Earth elemental shook his fist at me and charged, and the Drow shot his arrow. The arrow stopped in the thickened air and hung there in front of me. I'd played this game before and manipulated the air to flip the arrow around, using my Air power to shoot it back at the elf.

Pierre lowered his staff in my direction, but he frowned as the Earth elemental was blocking his shot.

The Drow's next shot was disrupted as he dove down to avoid the incoming arrow I'd returned to him. I nodded in mental approval as I spotted Blue suddenly appear from behind a stone chimney on the roof and crept down it towards the Drow on the lower roof.

The Earth elemental was almost on me, so I blasted myself into the sky and away from his massive rock fists.

I was about twenty feet in the air when I heard a crash and grunt below and behind me and assumed Stella had engaged the Earth elemental. I had no time to check, as a noxious green ball of acid shot from the end of Pierre's staff directly towards me.

I pushed a huge blast of air underneath me to quickly gain some altitude to avoid it. I blanched at the sizzling sound that followed. I glanced over and saw the top of the tree that the acid ball had hit wither and disappear in blackish smoke. It had gone through a four-inch-thick tree limb like a plasma cutter through butter. I shuddered to think what would have happened if that acid ball had hit me.

Out of the corner of my eye, I saw Stella and the Earth elemental exchanging powerful blows, but Stella seemed to be giving more than she was receiving.

I focused my attention back on Pierre but spotted Blue and the Drow engaged in a whirlwind of swordplay as they both danced along the porch roof. The Drow's silver sword almost seemed to sparkle in the sunlight, and as it was able to take blows from Blue's ignited blade, it too was magically enhanced.

The arrival of another green acid ball brought me back to the here and now. I jinked right and down to avoid it. I was tired of playing defense and sent a blast of lightning towards Pierre. The acid streaked by me overhead, and I was disappointed to see a light blue energy shield appear around Pierre, preventing my lightning from striking home.

Between the lich's energy shield, the Master's lightning-proof suits he'd made for the Acolytes, and now Pierre's magic shield, I really missed the old days where I could just shoot a blast of lightning at a villain and they'd go down just like Odin had intended.

I did note that my blast had caused Pierre to flinch, and the acid ball he released ended up shooting a good ten feet behind me. He also clenched his left fist like the impact of the lightning had caused him some pain.

I fired another blast of lightning in his direction and put a little more power into it. The light blue bubble appeared around him again, but I clearly heard him curse. He shook his left arm in pain, and I spotted a gold bracelet on his wrist with a large glowing blue gem on it. I swore I spotted a small wisp of smoke escape from around the gem on the bracelet.

I was about to follow up with another blast of lightning, but Pierre was quicker. He fired off three acid balls at me in rapid succession. I almost gave myself whiplash as I sent a massive gust of air to push me around in the opposite direction and away from the incoming barrage.

My ploy worked and all three acid balls missed. I sent another bolt of lightning downrange at Pierre as he fired off yet another noxious ball. I exhaled in relief as I barely managed to fly above it.

I smiled as the gem in the shield bracelet was now glowing like a small sun on his wrist. Pierre lined up another shot with his staff and I quickly flew higher. The moment the acid ball was launched, I dove towards him and the ground and let out rapid blasts of lightning. Pierre cried out in pain and dropped his staff as the first blast hit the energy shield. Smoke now billowed from the glowing gem. The second blast of lightning hit the shield again and Pierre screamed and yanked the bracelet off. The final blast of lightning hit Pierre directly in the chest.

His whole body shook like he was having a seizure, and his eyes rolled up in his head before he dropped to the ground like a puppet with its strings cut. Pierre twitched on the ground once and then went still.

For a brief moment, I worried I'd killed him, but there was still an aura around him, which meant he was alive.

Blue appeared on the ground about fifteen feet behind Pierre's unconscious form and gave me a nod. She sheathed her magic blade and seemed unconcerned.

My eyes shot up to the porch roof and I spotted the Drow lying in a pool of blood with a gaping wound in his chest. He had no aura and the glamor that had made him look human was gone, revealing his pointed ears, slender frame, and purple skin.

I banked towards Stella to go help her and instantly understood why Blue hadn't rushed to Stella's aid.

Stella's Hyde form was straddled across the chest of the downed Earth elemental and was continually pounding her huge right fist into his rock-covered face. The Earth elemental wasn't even using his hands to protect himself or fight back.

The rock covering suddenly disappeared, and he cried out, "St—"

I looked away as Stella's fist descended. My stomach churned and my lunch almost came up at the wet popping sound that filled the air. The feeling of wrongness around me instantly disappeared, which confirmed the Earth elemental was dead and saved me from having to look. Even without the visual, I suspected that this would be added to Zack's wake-up-in-a-cold-sweat nightmare playlist.

I banked around to fly back towards Blue. I felt bad for Stella. She wasn't a stone-cold killer, and I knew she'd regret killing the elemental. In her defense, his change back to his human form had been so quick that she'd had no time to pull her blow. I made a mental note to keep a close eye on her and make sure she was okay.

Blue had already gotten out a pair of power-blocking cuffs from her pouch and had flipped Pierre over on his front. I sighed in relief as she secured them around his wrists and put the fight to an end.

A few minutes later, Stella joined us near Pierre's unconscious form. She was back in her small human form, her face pale.

I was about to tell her that the death blow was an accident when a low groan from Pierre filled the air. I blinked in surprise as he began to stir on the ground. I'd figured with the amount of electricity I pumped into him, he'd have been out for much longer.

I moved closer to him, and he was already shifting up onto his knees.

Tough old bastard, I thought with grudging respect.

He had a dazed look on his face. I reached down to grab his upper left arm and helped him to his feet. I kept hold of him, as he was a touch unsteady, but he seemed to be making a rapid recovery.

A split second later, his entire head exploded, and my view was obscured as blood and brain matter splashed over my visor.

Chapter 28

Saturday, December 3

A loud *boom* echoed in the air as the sound of the shot caught up with the impact.

For a split second, everything froze and I was overwhelmed by the sudden and unexpected violence. Pierre's headless corpse slipped from my grasp and collapsed back to the ground, shaking me into action.

My heart pounded in my chest and my adrenaline spiked, which seemed to slow down time around me. I turned towards the direction I'd guessed the gunshot had come from, which was from the woods on the opposite side of the cove, and thickened the air around me as a precaution. I pushed a bit more power into it to make the air shield wider and taller to hopefully provide more protection for my teammates.

"Stella, change! Both of you get behind me!" I yelled as my eyes frantically scanned the woods for any sign of the sniper.

Fear gnawed at me as I waited for the next shot. I was pretty confident that between the shield and my bulletproof armor, I'd be fine, but my worry was for Stella and Blue. Stella's Hyde form could resist low caliber rounds but whatever had taken out Pierre certainly wasn't low-powered. Blue's scale mail armor wouldn't even slow down a round like that.

"We are in position behind you," said Blue.

A part of me longed to take to the air and go after the shooter, but my priority was my teammates' safety. "Blue, put your hand on my shoulder and have Stella do the same with you." I felt the weight of Blue's grip and added, "We are going to slowly side shuffle to the woods where we arrived. Once we get there, open a portal and get you and Stella out of here, understood?"

"Understood."

I stepped to my left, keeping my eyes locked on the woods across the cove.

As we slowly shuffled towards safety, the hardest part was keeping a slow and steady pace to make sure the Air shield was covering us. Each second dragged by, as I kept waiting for the next round to arrive. My heart thundered in my chest. I hated feeling this exposed.

I almost tripped on a rock at one point but Blue's grip kept me upright, and I exhaled as I'd also managed to hold the Air shield.

I let out a deep breath of relief when we finally reached the woods, and I felt Blue release her hold on my shoulder.

Ten seconds later, Blue's voice came over the comms. *"We are clear."*

"Roger that. Scan the woods across the cove for signs of the shooter."

I was already in the air before I'd finished my instructions to Blue. I reduced my Air shield, as it was just protecting me now, and angled it between my body and the ground. I also increased my speed and randomly changed my direction to make myself a harder target to hit.

I scanned the woods below, looking for an aura or any sign of the shooter. I didn't have much hope of seeing an aura, as most Enhanceds didn't use weapons, so there was a good chance our sniper was just human. Humans were less of a danger, but as Pierre demonstrated, they could still be a deadly threat.

The leaves had fallen off the trees, but the woods were quite dense with pine trees, which limited my visibility from above. The upside was that that lack of visibility worked both ways, so it would be harder for the sniper to get a good shot at me.

"Anything?" I asked over the comms as I banked for another pass over the woods.

"Negative."

My powers were starting to get tapped out, and I decided to drop the Air shield to conserve them. I figured between my speed, my random flight pattern, and the cover of the trees, I was pretty safe.

The search from the air wasn't proving fruitful, as it was hard to spot anything in the thick woods. I considered dropping to ground level and attempting a search on foot but decided that was a bad idea.

In the back of my mind, I'd been trying to figure out who had taken that shot. I'd initially thought it might be another bounty hunter trying to snatch the half-million bounty on Pierre from us. I dismissed that for a couple of reasons. We had Pierre in power-blocking cuffs, and I'd recorded everything on video. The moment he was cuffed, that shot became murder and not a legitimate bounty. I also doubted a single hunter would dare to take us on to steal that bounty.

The logical candidate was Alex Gray, as he had the most to gain from seeing Pierre dead. That sniper had to be either on his payroll or under contract to him. Pierre had probably hosted Alex Gray here, and Alex would've known how much this cabin meant to Pierre. He could have just used us to flush Pierre from it. The sniper was his insurance that Pierre wouldn't be alive to testify against him.

If Alex was involved, I wanted to avoid a ground search. Alex Gray would have hired the best. The sniper had been disciplined enough to wait until the moment we had Pierre in cuffs and defenseless. They had probably been camped out for days, waiting for us to arrive, and would have planned for our presence and their own escape. I was willing to bet there were traps or explosives in those woods. Tripping a claymore would be a shitty way to end the day.

After my third pass over the woods, my powers were running on fumes. I hadn't spotted anything and assumed the sniper was long gone.

I opened the comms and said, *"I haven't spotted anything, have you?"*

"Negative. No sign of the shooter."

"I'm running low on juice. Open the portal in the woods where we arrived, I'm coming in hot."

"Roger that."

I banked around and headed for the portal. A cold part of me realized that the sniper had actually done us a favor. With Pierre and Logan dead, any threat to Alex Gray was over, which meant Cynthia and I were safe. I'd have much preferred to take Pierre alive and let Grissom build a case against Alex Gray, but a small, selfish part of me was glad this was over.

While things might be done with Alex Gray for now, another part of me suspected our paths would cross again in the future.

***

I sighed in pleasure as I hovered between the two Tesla coils in our secret lab and let the electricity flow over my body. After the shit show the afternoon had been, this Air elemental hot tub equivalent was like a small slice of heaven.

It was hard to relax, though, knowing the day wasn't over. Blue was currently calling into EIRT the GPS coordinates of Pierre's luxury cabin. I made sure she added that there was the possibility of an active shooter on site and that there might be booby traps in the woods he was hiding in.

With the remote location, the threat of a shooter, and possible explosives, I suspected it would be at least an hour before EIRT was on scene, which gave me more than long enough to recharge my powers and join them.

I wasn't looking forward to the conversation I'd be having with Detective Grissom. I knew he'd be devastated that his best chance at taking down Alex Gray was now a headless corpse.

I pushed that thought from my mind. For now, I was just happy to let that wonderful electricity make my entire body tingle. I was glad Cynthia wasn't here. By my visible arousal, she might be a bit concerned about how much I truly loved these Tesla coils.

About twenty minutes later, Blue popped out from the shadows and said, "EIRT is en route, ETA thirty minutes. They will have canine and explosive ordinance disposal assets on hand."

I sighed to myself, as it looked like my fun time was over. I had just enough time to get some food, armor back up, and get back on the scene.

I flew down from the Tesla coils and joined Blue at the Food-O-Tron. Thankfully, by the time it was done making our food, I was, um, presentable to see Cynthia again without her raising any questioning eyebrows at me.

With food in my belly, my armor back on, and my powers topped up, I returned to the site of Pierre's cabin. EIRT hadn't arrived yet, but I could hear the sirens way off in the distance, and they were getting louder by the second.

The sun was low in the sky, and we probably had just over an hour of daylight left. I suspected that was why EIRT was responding a bit quicker than I'd estimated. It would be much easier to search the woods with natural light than at night.

I figured I had time for one quick pass over the woods to do another search for the shooter. My hopes of finding him were low, and I was willing to bet he was long gone, but I might get lucky.

As the convoy of law enforcement vehicles pulled up, I completed my unsuccessful search and headed over to join them. I opened the panel on my gauntlet to expose my green hero ID and landed slowly in front of the lead vehicle with my arms wide apart to appear as nonthreatening as possible.

Four heavily armed EIRT officers got out of the lead black SUV and all of them headed toward me. None of them had auras, which meant they were all human. I spotted auras on two of the officers getting out of the second vehicle, however. The first was large with a red and white checkered pattern, which meant a tank—someone who could dish out and receive massive amounts of punishment. The other was a smaller but much more common aura—purple, brown, and silver—which meant Werewolf.

Both would be valuable in searching a possibly trap-infused forest. The tank could probably take a claymore blast and shake it off. The Werewolf's nose would be even more useful for tracking and finding the shooter, and their keen senses would be unlikely to fall for a tripwire or trap.

"Bonjour," said the lead officer as he reached me.

The officer had sergeant stripes on his sleeves and the name *Latour* stitched onto his uniform.

"Bonjour. I apologize but that is the extent of my French. Do you speak English, Sergeant Latour?"

"But of course. Please call me Henri. It's a pleasure to meet the Hamilton Hurricane."

I blinked at that, as I wouldn't have expected a fan out here in Quebec. I also smiled at his pronunciation. As an English speaker, I found French to be annoying, as directions on packages were in both French and English. For some reason, I always seemed to hit the French side first.

There were times, though, when I appreciated the language. Henri in English sounded so plain and boring, but in French, it was pronounced *on-ree*, and I always found that had a much nicer ring to it. Henri had dropped the *H*'s on Hamilton Hurricane, which certainly gave a more exotic feel to it.

"Please call me Zack. The Hurricane has been retired for years. I also hadn't expected anyone here to be familiar with my former identity."

Henri smiled and explained that his brother-in-law was the Hamilton cop who had been injured trying to disrupt an attack by a rogue vampire on a homeless person about six or seven years ago.

Small world, I thought in astonishment.

Stopping that attack had been my last official act as the Hamilton Hurricane. Rob had filled out the bounty on that one on my behalf. That check had been a miracle, as I was flat broke and about to be evicted from my shitty apartment at the time. It also was the start of my bounty career.

With introductions out of the way, Henri got down to business. He and his three officers stayed with me to get the details of what had happened. Another group of officers had fanned out and were searching the woods for the shooter. Two others, though, had stayed behind and were currently on top of the armored vehicle in a counter-sniper position.

They had a laptop that one of Henri's men had set up on the hood of the SUV. I felt a bit nervous and exposed as I took off my helmet and tried to forget the memory of Pierre's exposed head exploding like a ripe melon. I was betting the sniper was long gone.

I connected the helmet to the laptop to show the recorded video of our engagement with Pierre and company. My stomach knotted up the moment I did this, as I remembered Stella's fight with the Earth elemental and worried that I might have gotten her in trouble.

The Earth elemental had tried to surrender, but there hadn't been enough time for Stella to pull that last punch. With the helmet connected, I had no choice now but to cross my fingers and hope that Henri and company would see it the same way.

The four EIRT officers watched the video mostly in silence, but they occasionally made a comment to each other in French that went over my head.

Once the video was over, Henri said, "Why do you suspect there might be explosives or traps in the woods?"

I explained that I was probably being overly cautious, but the shooter was a pro and had waited until the best possible moment to take out Pierre. That type of patience made me believe they'd have an escape route and ways to slow down any pursuit.

"Agreed. Better safe than sorry, eh?" he said and spent the next few minutes asking me more questions about the encounter and what had led us to Pierre.

The rest of our conversation was put on hold when his radio squawked on his tactical vest. He answered it and a long string of French followed, going back and forth between Henri and whoever was on the other end. I wished I'd brought Blue along, as she would have been able to translate it for me.

Thankfully, the moment Henri ended the communications, he said, "One of my team is a Werewolf. He tracked the shooter's scent through the woods and out to the roadway in the distance where it ended. There were tire tracks in the dirt but that was the only sign of someone being there. The shooter is in the wind."

"Well, at least no one will be taking any potshots at us from the woods."

He nodded. "Other than the scent, there was no sign of the shooter's presence. No shell casings, no cigarette butts, no food wrappers, nothing. The shooter didn't even pee on a tree out there . . . I think your theory about the shooter being a pro was right. You're a lucky man that the target was Pierre and not you."

I was about to joke about dodging a bullet, but that was a bit too on the nose, so I just gave a silent nod in response. Henri was right; I was lucky. The moment Pierre was cuffed, the sniper could have taken me out first and then finished Pierre with the next shot. I wouldn't have even seen it coming. That shook me a bit.

There was a tendency in the Enhanced community to dismiss normal humans as real threats, and I had been guilty of that at times. It was always things like this that slammed home how dangerous that line of thinking could be. The sniper could have ended my life just as quickly as a vampire or Were could have torn out my throat.

The sun was down before Henri and his team were done with me. I had three bounty claim tickets for Pierre and his two companions. Henri didn't even mention or question Stella's accidental fatal blow to the elemental, and that probably meant she was in the clear.

I thanked Henri and had Blue open a portal for me and headed home.

Chapter 29

Saturday, December 3

Later that night, I found myself in Detective Grissom's basement office at EIRT headquarters in Toronto. I took him up on his offer of a drink and felt the burn of his budget bourbon on the back of my throat. It was strange having alcohol again after avoiding it for the last month or so. I'd usually never been a big drinker and that bourbon was rough enough that I doubted I'd even finish it.

I'd put the video of our encounter with Pierre on a USB drive and sat there in silence as Grissom watched it. I knew he would want to know what happened and this was probably easier than me explaining. At least this showed that we'd tried our best to take Pierre alive for him.

Grissom blanched when he reached the part where Pierre was killed and then clicked with his mouse to end the video.

I sat there in silence as he emptied his coffee mug in one swallow and topped it up with another healthy pour. "Thanks for trying to bring Pierre in alive."

"Sorry that it ended like that."

He tipped his head towards me and went quiet for a moment and then said, "We found our leak."

I perked up and said, "That's great, who was it?"

"An IT guy who was head of our network security. He'd been with the department for close to thirty years."

It would be easy for someone in that position to monitor emails and phone calls for any mention of the Misfits or Alex Gray. He probably had a program set up to do just that. "I'm glad the leak is plugged. Congrats on catching him."

Grissom took another drink and shook his head. "It wasn't me. It was the internal task force that Acting Director Cooper put together who found him," he said. Grissom paused and then sighed and said, "I'm embarrassed to admit he wasn't even on my suspect list. I figured it had to be another detective or agent that was the leak."

"How'd they catch him? Unexplained money in his account?"

"No. Since the leaks began, his finances were clean and accountable. The task force looked further back and found that just before the leaks happened, he made a lot of large cash withdrawals and had maxed out his credit cards. That's what tipped them off. Once the leaks started, those withdrawals ended."

I frowned in confusion. Usually if someone was getting bribed, money was coming in. The light went on and I asked, "Drugs?"

Grissom shook his head. "Gambling. He'd gotten himself in deep with some bad people."

"Alex Gray bought up his debts and he paid them off with information?"

"We're not sure. He said he dealt with someone named Mr. X, and he was instructed to report any mentions of the Misfit Mafia, the primary Italian mob family in the province, or the Russian mob. He never dealt with anyone other than this Mr. X."

I thought about that and realized that this was a better play for Alex Gray. By using an information broker, it provided a layer of deniability for him. Ditto by adding in the Italian and Russian mobs. "Were there any operations against the Italian or Russian mobs that were disrupted by leaks?"

"We don't think so, but that same team that found the leaker is looking into all past cases involving those two parties to confirm that."

"It's strange that this IT guy never gambled again. Most addicts can't help themselves," I said.

"This mysterious Mr. X cured him of his gambling addiction by showing him what would happen if he so much as played a lottery ticket. The IT guy was forced to watch as Mr. X's men tortured and killed another gambler who hadn't paid his debts. We've opened a new homicide case, but we don't even have a name yet. Detectives are going through missing persons cases from that time period and trying to match it against the description he gave them."

Damn, I thought. *Certainly an effective way of curing someone of an addiction. Somehow, though, I didn't see Gambler's Anonymous adding it to their program.*

"Any leads on this Mr. X?"

"No. He wore a mask on the rare times they met. All we have is average weight and height and the phone number to a burner phone, which led nowhere. Most of their conversations were on a gaming server that is hosted in China, so we have almost no chance of even getting an IP address for Mr. X."

It sounded like EIRT's chances of catching this mysterious Mr. X were pretty slim. There was also almost no chance of them building any sort of case against Alex Gray over this.

Grissom drained his mug again and looked longingly at the open bottle but didn't reach for it. He turned his attention to me and said, "I think I'll use the next few months here to wrap things up and take retirement in the spring."

I blinked in surprise at his statement. "Acting Director Cooper forcing you out?"

He shook his head. "No, this is my decision. It bothers me that I missed the IT guy completely. Maybe it's time for someone younger, better with technology, and with a fire in their belly to go after Alex Gray. I've spent almost two decades and have lost good people and a marriage to this case. I just don't have any more to give."

I could tell by the look on his face that this hadn't been an easy decision. "Any thoughts about what you'll do in retirement?"

A small smile appeared on his face. "My daughter lives up in Barrie and has two kids that I'd like to get to know better. I've had my eye on a nice cottage on a lake up in that area for a bit and think I'll pull the trigger on that. I met a lovely lady earlier this year and things seem to be going well. She's retiring at the end of the month. I'm hoping she might be open to joining me up there to spend our days fishing, hiking, and entertaining grandkids."

I smiled at that. "Sounds like a nice plan. You've got good people here and Alex Gray is on my radar now. He'll make a mistake one of these days and we'll make him pay."

"That would make a great retirement present," he said as he raised his empty mug and toasted it with mine.

Chapter 30

Friday, December 10

We went almost a week before running into another crisis. It was finally time for Olivia's trial at the English Vampire Court, and I was anxiously awaiting the verdict. I paced back and forth across the office floor while Blue and Stella worked on their computers and ignored me.

Neither of them was currently on my good side at the moment. Since we'd wrapped up our case with Logan and Pierre, I'd been pestering them nonstop about Liv, or at least it was nonstop when Cynthia wasn't here.

Once Logan was no longer a threat to Cynthia, Marion had gotten contractors in to fix her wrecked apartment in record time. And now that Pierre was dead, Cynthia moved back in and resumed her apprenticeship.

Other than the first night, Cynthia had spent all of her nights here at the house with me. Blue had been kind enough to shadow travel her to and from her apartment each day. We had been together almost continually, other than during the days when she was working with Marion like she was today.

I kept my inquiries about Liv's welfare to a minimum when Cynthia was around so as not to arouse her concern that I was pining over Liv. Cynthia was decent and relaxed about Olivia and our history, but I didn't want to push my luck.

For the whole week, Stella and Blue had brushed off my concerns about the trial.

"She's a grown woman, and she's dealing with it herself," said Stella.

"You must trust her judgment," Blue had agreed.

I loved and respected both Blue and Liv but didn't fully trust either of their judgment. Blue was usually levelheaded but had a propensity towards violence, which needed to be monitored. Olivia was, well, Olivia, and prone to doing Olivia-like things.

Also, no one at the English Vampire Court or even Liv herself would take my calls. My frustration about the lack of information on how things were progressing was driving me nuts. I'd been tempted to book a plane ticket and visit them in person, as Blue had refused to take me there.

The only thing that kept me from getting on a plane or losing it entirely was that Stella was fully backing up Blue. Stella loved Olivia and Bree like daughters and would do anything for either of them. If Olivia was truly in danger, there was no way Stella would just sit back and do nothing. The only thing keeping me sane was my trust in Stella's love.

I cursed as I watched blue sparks drip from my hands and tamped down on my powers as I continued wearing out the line of carpet I was pacing.

Stella said, "Found us a possible bounty case. Jewel heist from a museum in Paris. Ten million in stolen gems. No alarms were triggered, no sign of how the thieves got in and out, and no video of the thieves. The jewels just disappeared one night. Authorities suspect the thieves were Enhanced due to traces of magic at the scene. There is a million-dollar bounty for their capture."

It sounded like the perfect heist, and I knew why Stella was interested. She adored a good mystery and loved solving them even more.

I was intrigued by the case but said, "Pass."

Stella spun around in her chair and said, "Why? A million dollars is certainly worth our time."

"It's not the money; it's the location."

Stella frowned for a moment and then resignedly shook her head and turned her chair back around to find us another case.

Roman, the current head of the French Vampire Court had his position because we'd killed his predecessor, Giselle, but that didn't mean we were friends. Many of Giselle's supporters at the court would like to see us dead. To go traipsing around Paris would be like poking the hornet's nest. North Korea would probably be a safer place for us to work than Paris.

It was a shame, though, as the case did sound interesting. "Try finding something a little smaller scale and more local. Remember, we are technically supposed to be on hiatus until Bree and Liv are back."

Stella nodded and continued searching. Earlier in the week, Blue had argued that since I had my powers back, there was no reason we couldn't resume bounty cases. We discussed it and decided it wouldn't hurt to look at what cases were out there. I was more interested in small, simple ones just to keep in practice. There were too many times I'd missed having Bree, Liv, and Alteea around during the Logan and Pierre affair. I didn't want to get into something big without them.

I halted my pacing when Stella's other phone rang. This was the one she used to contact the English Vampire Court. It was the call we'd been waiting for.

Stella answered it and I listened intently to her side of the call, trying to infer how things were going from her tone. Annoyingly, Stella's responses were short and neutral.

She spun her chair around and my stomach knotted up at the expression on her face. Stella didn't say anything for a few long seconds and glanced sadly at the phone in her hand.

Suddenly, a huge smile lit up her youthful face and she said, "The case has been dismissed; Olivia will face no consequences."

Relief filled me, but another small part of me was tempted to send some static electricity at Stella to pay her back for playing up the drama of the moment. "How did she win?"

Stella shook her head and said, "That is her story to tell. Sarah has invited us to visit so Olivia can tell us herself."

"When?"

"As soon as we're dressed," said Stella.

I groaned to myself at having to wear my formal monkey suit again but didn't dare risk going casual and exposing us to Elizabeth's ire, especially after Olivia had just gotten herself out of hot water.

I headed to my room to get changed and, with it being late in the afternoon, realized that Cynthia would be done soon and looking for Blue to pick her up.

The gods were smiling on me as I sent a text to let her know that we were visiting the English Court and dinner tonight would be delayed. She answered that Marion had an unexpected patient just arrive at her door and she too would be running late.

Now I just need to remember how to tie my tie.

***

Sarah was kind enough to allow us to shadow portal to her office directly. I always loved visiting Sarah's office due to the sheer number of things to see. I spotted what looked like a new bastard sword on her wall of weapons, but she may have just rearranged the display. I always got a kick out of the turtle-themed knickknacks tucked around the place. I was pleased to see Romeo and Juliet, her two pet turtles, in their aquarium.

I had less than a second to take all of that in before Liv cried out my name, blurred across the room, and embraced me in a hug. I wrapped my arms around her and just enjoyed being in her presence again.

I felt her body stiffen against me, and she broke the hug and said, "Did you get a girlfriend?"

Her green eyes studied me intently with a neutral expression. I'd hoped this topic would be something that we'd talk about later.

"Yes, how did you know?"

"I can smell her on you."

Vampire senses never ceased to amaze me. I'd taken a shower after Cynthia had left for work today, and despite that, she still was able to detect her.

My nervousness grew as Liv's expression hadn't changed and she asked, "Is she treating you right?" I smiled and nodded. "Are you treating her right and not being too much of a perv?"

"Yeah, I've been good. I haven't even brought up the topic of a threesome with her yet."

Liv giggled and shook her head at me. "I'm happy for you. Does this mystery woman have a name?"

"Cynthia. She's Marion's niece."

Olivia nodded and said, "We'll talk more about Cynthia later; I have more hugs to give."

Before I could even bob my head or answer, Olivia blurred over and wrapped up Blue in a hug. Sarah was currently in the process of hugging Stella and gushing about how she missed her.

I spotted a small familiar rainbow aura hovering just in front of me and said, "Hello, Alteea."

Alteea dropped her glamor, and I suddenly had a naked redheaded pixie before me.

"Master Zack! Lovely to see you again."

I blinked in surprise as Alteea delivered that line in an impeccably crisp English accent. "You've gone native I see."

Liv laughed and broke her hug with Blue and said, "Yeah, it's so classy and shit, and totally adorable."

We all swapped partners and Liv scooped up Stella and told her that she'd missed her. Alteea flew over to Blue and greeted her. I was glad that Stella was only hesitant about physical contact with males. Between Sarah and Olivia, she didn't stand a chance.

Sarah ended up in front of me and shook her head. "It's bad enough that she marked you, but now you have a girlfriend too. I'm starting to think I'll never get my tasty Air elemental snack . . ."

Dealing with Sarah was always an interesting experience, as she both aroused and frightened me. It really didn't help that she was almost a dead ringer for the lead actress of my favorite vampires versus Werewolves movies. I'd been drooling over that actress for years. Even the black leather Sarah wore was a close match to the outfit in the movies. Sarah was as deadly as she was beautiful. I knew that if Elizabeth ever ordered my death, Sarah wouldn't hesitate, and I'd be dead before I could even blink. Seeing her in action during our last fight with the Master and his new Acolytes had been an eye-opening and terrifying experience that I was still having nightmares about.

While Sarah in her role as court champion was scary, she had a softer side that we were privileged to see. She genuinely cared for Stella like a mother would for a daughter. I was sure that Stella's extended lifespan was part of that. Sarah was five hundred years old. I couldn't imagine what it must be like to care for people that you'd outlive by centuries. It had to make it easier for Sarah knowing that she had at least a couple hundred years to enjoy Stella's company.

"A pleasure to see you again, Sarah. You are looking as ravishing as always."

She smiled at that and said, "While this is fun, time grows short, and we should get to what brought you here."

Sarah turned and sauntered back to her chair, and I tried my very best not to check her out in those black leather pants and mostly succeeded. I really hoped looking wasn't considered cheating and probably should have that discussion with Cynthia soon.

I took one of the two seats in front of the desk and Stella took the other one. Liv took up a spot to the right of Sarah, and Alteea fluttered over Liv's shoulder. Blue moved and stood protectively behind Stella.

I looked at Sarah and said, "Can someone fill me in on everything that has gone on?" I shot a pointed glance at Stella and Blue and added, "I've been kept in the dark by certain people."

Sarah shrugged. "Not my story to tell. I'll let Liv-kebab fill you in."

"Liv-kebab?" I asked.

Liv gave me a half smile and said, "It's her pet name for me. She's run me through with her sword twenty-seven times—"

"Twenty-eight," said Sarah with a smug grin.

"Sorry, twenty-eight times now during our training sessions."

I sat there speechless for a moment. Liv had only been here six weeks, yet she had managed to get stabbed twenty-eight times. I managed to compose myself and said, "And you're good with this?"

Liv shrugged. "It hurts like a bitch, but what can you do? Like Blue always says, 'pain is a great teacher.' Besides, it makes Grandma here happy—"

"Soon to be twenty-nine times," said Sarah under her breath.

Liv frowned. "—and that is better than her being grumpy. You should see how good my sword work has become."

"Yes, I'm now confident she can go into battle without stabbing herself," said Sarah in a droll tone of voice.

I mentally shook my head at the two of them. They were like oil and water. It was probably a miracle Sarah hadn't killed Liv by now. "Unorthodox training methods aside, you were charged with violating court protocol and the charges are now dropped. What was that about?"

"I was baited into it by Agnes, who wasn't happy that I'd become Sarah's temporary apprentice. The protocol I broke was the code of respecting your elders. It has a fancier term, but it means that a younger vampire isn't allowed to disrespect an older one."

Sarah jumped in and said, "That particular protocol has fallen out of favor in recent years. The last time it had been used in a charge before this was 173 years ago. The main reason it has gone by the wayside is that all vampires at court have an older vampire they report to. If someone like Agnes brings charges against Liv, she risks offending me. Annoying a higher-ranked vampire isn't the brightest thing to do."

I pondered what Sarah had said, and it made sense to me why the code hadn't been used in a long time. I focused my attention back on Liv. "What did you do to offend Agnes?"

A coy smile appeared on Liv's face, and I mentally groaned. "She made a snide comment at me, and I told her she was an ass-faced loser that would only ever get laid by wearing two paper bags over her ugly mug."

I winced at that, and Sarah said, "She was also dumb enough to make that comment in a hall packed full of witnesses."

"Whatever. They all laughed," said Liv. Her grin got bigger, and she added, "The only thing more hysterical than that was when Elizabeth read that out in court today during the trial."

Sarah's stern face cracked a grin. "Yes. I never believed I would ever get the chance to hear Her Majesty use the term 'ass-faced.'"

I broke out laughing at the image of Elizabeth using that line. The rest of the room broke out into giggles as well.

When Stella composed herself, she said, "I'd have loved to have seen that."

Liv beamed and perked up. "The trial was video recorded, and I have a copy. I'm thinking about making it my ringtone."

Sarah looked sharply at Liv and said, "Do not do that until after you've left. Assuming you survive that long." Liv nodded, and Sarah added, "Getting back on point. While Agnes is a suck-up and toad, she has her uses. She is one of our leading scholars on the twenty-seven volumes of court protocols and laws. Something I pointed out to Liv-kebab when Agnes filed the charges. Agnes would be acting as the prosecutor in the case. So, to summarize, Liv managed to screw up in front of witnesses, giving Agnes an airtight case, and Liv would have to act as her own defense against one of the English Court's best prosecutors."

Laid out like that, I wondered how Liv managed to beat the charge, but another thing popped into my head. "What was the penalty if Liv lost?"

"Like all court cases, it depends. Elizabeth can impose any penalty ranging from a fine up to death. Though death was unlikely, Liv did face the real possibility of banishment," said Sarah in a casual tone.

"Okay, the case seems like a slam dunk for Agnes, so how did Liv beat the charges?"

Sarah glanced pointedly at Liv and gave her a small nod.

"I went through all the twenty-seven volumes looking for a way out. After a week of pulling my hair out and not finding anything to help, I found a way to change the game."

I saw Blue's tail begin to move in happy circles and realized Blue already knew the answer. I suspected she knew it before the trial even began. It hit me that this was why Blue and Stella were so unconcerned about the trial.

Liv smiled and said, "One of the oldest laws on the books is the right to trial by combat. I invoked that right today."

I gasped out loud at that. "You dueled Agnes to the death?"

Liv shook her head. "No. I discussed this option with Sarah before the trial and she agreed to help me. When I declared I wanted to have a trial by combat, Sarah immediately announced that she would be my second."

"Second?" I asked in confusion.

Sarah said, "It is customary that in any duel, a second is nominated in case something happens to the primary combatant. It is also the right of the primary duelist to defer combat to their second. Trial by combat is an ancient custom, and the last time it was used was over 300 years ago. Elizabeth had brought treason charges against a vampire that was making a play for the throne. He demanded trial by combat, and Elizabeth nominated me as her second and deferred the fight to me," she said, pausing and pointing at the scar on her face before continuing, "and that was how I got this little souvenir."

"So, you fought Agnes?"

"No. Liv-kebab and I had agreed beforehand that if Agnes showed a spine and was willing to fight, Liv would face her. The reason I went along with the plan was to stop Agnes from passing off this fight to *her* second."

I was confused again but thought it through and smiled. "Let me guess, once you volunteered to be Olivia's second, no one stepped up to be Agnes's second?"

Sarah nodded. The arrangement was brilliant, as it meant that if it went to trial by combat, Agnes would have no choice but to fight Liv herself. She also had to weigh the fact that Liv might defer, and, therefore, Agnes would have to fight Sarah, which would have been a death sentence. "How old is Agnes?"

"She is just past her seventy-fifth year of being turned."

I whistled at that and looked at Liv. "You were taking a hell of a gamble."

Liv had a powerful sire, which made her a potent vampire in her own right, but she was less than two years old. Agnes would have gained a lot of power and experience in those seventy-five years and would have been a dangerous opponent for Liv.

Sarah said, "Not really. While Agnes has had basic arms training, as all members of the court are required to, it is not her forte. Between Blue's and my instruction, Liv is more proficient with a sword than Agnes is. I'm fully confident that if it would have come to a fight, Liv would have won. As it happened, once Agnes realized she'd been outmaneuvered, she dropped the charges and apologized for wasting everyone's time."

Liv had played a dangerous game but had managed to come out okay in the end. I was proud of her for finding a way to beat the charges. I looked at Liv and said, "I can't think Agnes is very happy at this moment, and you still have six more weeks here—watch yourself."

Sarah suddenly got an evil smile on her face, which made me nervous. She said, "That won't be a problem. Agnes is currently on a flight to Cold Lake, Alberta. She will be spending the next two months there scouting possible locations for a new safe house."

December and January in Cold Lake Alberta. It is a good thing that vampires don't feel the cold like we do, I thought with a smile.

Even with the cold not being a factor, Agnes, as someone used to the amenities of London, would probably hate being there. "Nasty."

"Agnes just learned why the respect your elders protocol hasn't been used in 173 years," said Sarah with a satisfied smile.

Epilogue

Even the brisk minus twenty-degree temperatures of late January couldn't dampen my excitement. Bree, Olivia, and Alteea were all coming home this evening. I'd spent yesterday running around picking up food for their welcome home dinner. Well, food for Bree, as Olivia would just be having her usual liquid dinner. I had some juicy-looking steaks marinating in the fridge that I knew Bree would kill for.

Cynthia had taken the day off to help me prepare the welcome home festivities.

She glanced at me over her morning coffee and said, "Someone is excited today."

"Of course I'm excited—we're getting the band back together!"

Cynthia smiled. "*The Blues Brothers* was such a great movie."

It was so awesome having someone in my life that got my movie references without me having to explain them. "I love you!"

Shock flashed across Cynthia's face and my heart pounded in my chest as I realized what I'd said. I'd never used the *L* word with her before today. I'd just said it because she caught my reference, but another part of me knew I meant it for more than just that.

The last six weeks with Cynthia had been like a slice of heaven for me. The more I got to know her, the more I cared for her. She was bright, funny, kindhearted, and beautiful. Most days I had to pinch myself to confirm that life wasn't a dream.

My spirits soared and my worries vanished as a warm smile spread on her lovely face. "I love you, too."

Hearing those four simple words put me over the moon. I got up and Cynthia did too, and we embraced in a hug and a deep kiss.

A moment later, Stella and Blue walked in from the living room, and Stella said, "Get a room."

We broke apart and wished both of them a good morning.

Blue's tail began moving at a rapid pace and she said, "If you wish to fornicate, we will leave to give you your privacy. I would suggest utilizing the counter, as the table's shoddy construction might not survive your amorous attention."

Heat filled my cheeks at her words and Cynthia just giggled. "There won't be any kitchen, um, fornication—" I noticed Cynthia had a slight look of disappointment at my words and hastily added, "—today." That got me an approving smile from her.

Images of us using the kitchen in naughty ways popped into my mind, and I felt myself starting to react. I decided to quickly change the topic and said, "Today the only thing on the agenda is to finish prepping the welcome home party. How's the decorating going?"

Stella smiled and said, "Come see for yourself."

We moved to the living room, and I stopped at the threshold to take everything in. Stella and Blue had been busy. There was a big *Welcome Home Olivia, Bree, and Alteea*, banner strung over the TV. There were streamers and balloons everywhere. The balloons brought a smile to my face, as they were orange with black cats on them. Bree would love them. They were Halloween balloons, and I wondered where they'd gotten them since it was January, but Blue and Stella were masters at finding hard-to-find things.

The Halloween theme continued, and I noticed white plastic vampire fangs with red tips tucked all around the room as well.

I spotted a brightly colored box sitting on the coffee table that I recognized as the Sugars of the World collection, which meant our returning pixie would be happy. There were four large snack bowls, each with a different large sealed bag of chips in it. "Will four bags be enough?"

Stella giggled and said, "They should be. I didn't want Bree to fill up and not have room for your dinner."

I nodded and spotted Cynthia nodding as well. She'd dated Logan, so she was keenly aware of Were appetites.

I turned back to Stella and Blue and said, "The room looks amazing. The girls will love it. Thank you."

A glance at my phone showed it was just past eleven. Bree was expected to arrive back at the Barrie pack compound by five and Blue would bring her home from there. The sun would set just after six this evening, and then Blue would retrieve Olivia. That gave us just under six hours to prep.

Stella and Blue left us and we got down to the business of getting dinner ready. Cynthia had helped me plan out tonight's menu and had graciously agreed to bake a German chocolate cake, which was Bree's favorite. I was a good cook, but baking wasn't my thing, so I was grateful for her help. Cynthia was a great cook in her own right. Over the last six weeks, we'd puttered around together in the kitchen several times, and I always enjoyed those experiences.

We put on some tunes and got to work. I found myself checking out Cynthia as she started precisely measuring out her ingredients, and I couldn't help but feel like I was the luckiest man in the world. Saying we loved each other today was a big step in our relationship.

I suddenly pictured two cherubic kids tugging at Cynthia's apron, wanting to help her bake. I smiled to myself as I saw my imaginary kids giggle and scream as Aunty Liv appeared and announced that she wanted some delicious veal and chased them around the kitchen. I envisioned Cynthia rapping her spatula over Bree's knuckles to stop her from snacking on the ingredients, and Blue and Stella sitting at the table having tea and shaking their heads at us in amusement.

I shook my head and cleared those pleasant thoughts and focused back on cutting up the bacon for my potato salad.

One step at a time. I need to get through tonight first.

While I was excited at having Bree, Olivia, and Alteea home and back with us, there was another part of me dreading tonight. Bree was easygoing, and I was sure she would like Cynthia. The chocolate cake pretty much ensured that Cynthia would be loved by Bree. Alteea also wouldn't be an issue.

My biggest worry was Liv. There was possible awkwardness from our romantic past together, which might create friction between Cynthia and Liv. Cynthia had been pretty cool about it so far, but I worried that might become an issue. My main concern, though, was Liv. I loved her dearly, but Liv could be a bit prickly with new people. I thought back to her and Charlie meeting for the first time and how poorly that went. Liv tolerated Charlie but never really warmed up to her. Liv seemed really good when she found out about Cynthia, but it had been six weeks, and Odin only knew if her feelings had changed on the matter. The last thing I needed was for Liv and Cynthia to be at odds with me stuck in the middle.

I just had to hope things would go well.

***

"Welcome home!" we yelled as Bree came out of the shadows and into the living room with Blue just behind her. Bree smiled and wrapped Stella in a hug. The two exchanged soft words that I didn't catch but Bree's grin grew.

I checked her out and decided she looked good but tired. Her blonde hair had grown a lot in the three months she'd been gone. She had it tied back in a ponytail and the end of it came down past her shoulders. I usually liked long hair on women, but it didn't seem to suit Bree like her usual short hair did.

Her face seemed a bit thinner, and I wondered if she'd lost weight. I'd actually expected her to put on a few pounds due to her visiting various Were packs. The couple times I'd gone to the Barrie pack, the food had been both exceptional and plentiful. I remembered that she was visiting the lowest-rated packs on the Were Council's survey, though, and maybe they didn't put out the same type of spreads that the Barrie pack did. I wondered if they couldn't put out decent food for their members, how bad these packs really were.

Bree broke her hug with Stella and Cynthia, and I stepped forward. "Welcome back, Bree. It's so good to see you." I paused and with one hand gestured toward Cynthia. "This is Cynthia."

Bree nodded and said, "Nice to finally meet you in person." She then enveloped her in a quick hug.

I'd introduced Bree to Cynthia on the video chat we'd had at Christmas. The call had been too brief; we'd barely had time to say hellos and get a quick update on how each of us was doing before Bree had to go. The only communication we'd had from her after that was a few days ago when she confirmed she was coming home.

She ended the hug with Cynthia, and it was my turn. I wrapped my arms around her and said, "I missed you."

"I missed you, too."

Even with the thick winter jacket she was wearing, I could feel her large chest being pressed up against me and said, "I've missed these even more."

Bree quickly broke the hug, pushed me back slightly, shook her head, and laughed. "Nice to know you haven't changed." Bree shifted her attention to Cynthia and said, "You haven't beaten that out of him yet?"

Cynthia shook her head. "No, it's too much a part of him to even try."

Bree laughed at that and unzipped her coat. She took off the long black Canada Goose jacket and exposed what I considered the standard Were attire, which consisted of a grey hooded sweatshirt and matching track pants. Bree ditched her boots and then liberated a bowl of chips and the three of us took seats on the couch.

"Go easy on those; we have a huge dinner menu that will be happening as soon as Liv gets here," I said, looking at the rapidly shrinking bowl of chips.

Bree laughed. "That won't be a problem," she said. She paused, lifting another handful to her mouth and added, "So you got your powers back. Did Agent Chambers get his back, too?"

I was impressed that Bree remembered Doug Chambers and his power issues. He'd been a member of GRC13 that we worked with to take down the lich. During our final battle with the lich, he'd been hit by the same spell I had and lost access to his Fire elemental abilities. Immediately after the battle, we called each other daily to check if either had gained them back.

After about a week, he announced he was done with GRC13 and was joining a friend's company that did private security. That allowed him to spend more time with his family and exposed him to much less danger. We'd agreed only to call if something changed and we got our power back.

"I called him after I got mine back. That was six weeks ago, and he hasn't called, so I'm assuming he still doesn't have his powers."

Bree nodded resignedly. "How did you get yours back?"

I took a deep breath and went over the whole adventure with Logan and Pierre. Bree stayed silent through all of it, though she did shake her head firmly in disapproval over the whole getting-hit-by-lightning-on-purpose part of my story.

When I finished, she said, "Sounds like the world is better off with both of them not in it." The moment she finished she shot an alarmed glance at Cynthia and added, "No offense."

Cynthia gave her a slight smile and said, "None taken. I'm probably happier than anyone that Logan is no longer walking around."

Bree relaxed as she studied Cynthia for a moment. "So, you two are now a couple?"

"Yup," said Cynthia.

"At least we might get some girl scouts coming by the house now to sell cookies without being scared off by his horny vibe."

I covered my heart and gave Bree a wounded look, but she and Cynthia were too busy laughing to even notice my antics.

Once they finished, Bree started to exchange her empty bowl of chips for a full one, and I said, "Not so fast. It's your turn to spill what you've been up to. You were nervous about taking this assignment; did it end up being as bad as you feared?"

Bree got a faraway look on her face for a moment and then said, "Yes and no. Four of the five packs we visited weren't as bad as I thought they might be. The fifth one though . . ." She paused and shuddered. "Tonight is for celebrating, so we'll discuss that one some other time."

For the next half hour while we waited for the sun to go down, we all chatted. Stella brought Bree up to date on how things were going with training Emma. Their progress had been slow, but they were making some. Emma was now able to project her power for a few seconds before being overwhelmed by it. Earlier this week, she made it to five seconds, which was something.

The moment the sun went down, Blue got up and disappeared into the shadows to get Olivia. I took that moment to dash outside and fire up the barbeque, as the chips were rapidly vanishing.

I arrived back in the living room just as Liv and Alteea emerged from the shadows with Blue in tow. She spotted Bree and yelled, "Bestie!" and hugs were exchanged.

I almost moaned at what Olivia was wearing but managed to keep that impulse in check. She was wearing a set of black leathers identical to those that Sarah usually wore. She even had a katana sword sheathed over her shoulder.

I really hope that outfit was a gift, and she didn't steal it from Sarah, I thought.

I moved beside Cynthia who leaned into me and whispered, "Wow, she's even hotter than in her pictures."

I caught Olivia's smirk out of the corner of my eye, as I had no doubt she'd heard that. I ignored Liv's reaction as my stomach tightened and my heart rate picked up.

Danger, Will Robinson! I thought.

This was one of those deadly situations similar to *does this dress make me look fat?* How I answered her statement could make or break this evening or possibly worse. My first inclination was to deny it or compliment Cynthia instead, but I ruled that out. There was no denying Liv was hot, and I also risked pissing Liv off if I went that way.

Pointing out that Logan hadn't exactly been chopped liver in the looks department was my next thought, but I really didn't want to bring him up on a night we were supposed to be celebrating. I decided to play to my strengths. "If you want a threesome, I'm sure with your tasty healer blood, Liv would be up for it."

Without missing a beat, Cynthia said, "Threesome? You can barely keep up with me in bed."

Even though Bree and Olivia were still engaged in hugs and greetings, both laughed and flashed thumbs-up gestures in our direction. Cynthia had a big grin on her face at her joke, and while she'd impinged my honor that was a price I was willing to pay. I also had no response to that. "Alteea, drop your glamor and come say hi."

I watched the rainbow aura dart towards me. She seemingly appeared out of thin air in front of us.

"Oh my God! You told me about Alteea, but you didn't tell me how adorable she is!" said Cynthia with a beaming smile as she studied our tiny fae.

"Thank you, Mistress Cynthia," said Alteea, with a British lilt to her words.

"Just Cynthia, please."

I shook my head at her and said, "You're fighting a losing battle with that one." Cynthia frowned at me, and I added, "We've all been trying to get her to drop the whole *Mistress* and *Master* thing since she arrived."

An expression of understanding crossed her face, but I also noticed a little determination there. I assumed Cynthia wasn't going to take my word for it and would try to convert Alteea.

Liv was getting closer to us but was currently gushing over Stella. Bree had managed to return to the couch and was finishing off the last of the chips.

"Did you enjoy your time at the court, Alteea?" I asked.

She bobbed her head. "It was a great adventure, Master. Her Majesty liked me being there, as she wasn't the shortest one. She even called me her mini-me."

I blinked at that but as both Elizabeth and Alteea had almost matching shades of red hair, I could see it. My shock was that Elizabeth had made an *Austin Powers* reference. Between that and using the term *ass-faced*, I wasn't sure I even knew who she really was anymore.

Alteea fluttered off to say hello to Bree, which was impressive, as she was never truly comfortable around Bree. I did notice that it was just a quick greeting, and she quickly landed on the coffee table and used her claws to open her collection of sugars, which might have explained her new sudden bravery.

I suddenly had my arms full of my favorite vampire. "Welcome home."

She squeezed me tight and said, "Good to be home."

Liv broke the hug and then turned her full attention to Cynthia. She smiled and said, "It's nice to finally meet the woman who has Zack here so smitten."

"Great to meet you as well. I love your outfit," said Cynthia.

Liv preened. "It was a gift from my trainer for not getting stabbed fifty times."

"What was the final count?" I asked.

Liv glanced away and mumbled, "Forty-nine."

Cynthia looked at us both like we were nuts, but Stella said, "Zack, go cook the steaks. Blue and I will get out the rest of the food."

I nodded. I glanced at Liv and said, "Can you explain the whole stabbing thing to Cynthia?"

Liv took Cynthia by the hand and joined Bree on the couch. I gave them one last glance as I left the room and hoped the two of them would get along.

All three of them were laughing when I cut through the living room with the platter of uncooked steaks, which I took as a good sign.

As I laid out the ton of meat on the grill, I prayed Bree still had her legendary appetite, as we would need it to get through all this steak.

I spent the next fifteen minutes alternating between monitoring the steaks and stealing peeks into the living room. Bree, Olivia, and Cynthia seemed to be laughing and chatting away happily each time

I looked. I was overjoyed that my fears about them not getting along seemed to be unfounded.

With the steaks done, I entered the living room to hear Liv saying, "Does he thank you nonstop during—"

I loudly cleared my throat, knowing where Liv was going with that question and said, "Dinner's ready!"

Cynthia giggled and gave Liv a quick nod as all of them got up from the couch. As I headed to the kitchen, I realized that my new problem might be Liv and Cynthia getting along *too* well. I sighed and figured it was better than the alternative.

I placed the heaping platter of steaks in the center of the table between the huge bowl of my rustic potato salad and the platter of roasted veggies Stella and Blue had made. They had done an amazing job of laying out the table. It looked great.

We all took our seats and began loading up our plates, except for Liv and Alteea who were content just to drink their dinners. I was impressed that Cynthia didn't even bat an eye at them drinking blood. I'd been a lot more squeamish when I had first witnessed it. It made sense that a little blood was no big deal for her I supposed; she was a healer and a nurse after all.

Liv used this time to tell her tale about her troubles with Agnes and how she'd turned the table on her.

Once everyone had built their plates, I raised my champagne glass in the air and said, "To the team being back together!"

I got a rousing chorus of "Cheers!" and we began eating. As I ate, I glanced around the table at the smiling faces and animated conversations going on and felt truly happy. I'd enjoyed my time with Cynthia these past weeks, but with Bree, Liv, and Alteea gone, it hadn't felt quite right. Now it was perfect.

As Bree finished her first steak and was reaching for another, I said, "Save room for dessert. Cynthia made German chocolate cake."

Bree used the tongs to lift the steak onto her plate and said, "I always have room for cake."

Towards the end of the meal, Cynthia mentioned that she was spending most of her nights here, and Bree said, "Great, I hope my noise canceling headphones are where I left them."

Cynthia frowned in confusion. I grinned and said, "She wears them to avoid being jealous about our hot lusty sex."

Liv coyly glanced over at Bree and said, "At least with Zack you won't need to wear them for long . . ."

The ladies all laughed, and Cynthia fist bumped Liv. I let that comment pass without responding for fear of digging myself into a deeper hole.

Once we'd finished dessert, Cynthia and I started doing kitchen cleanup while the rest of the team relaxed. I wasn't paying attention and managed to stab my finger with a knife enough to draw blood.

I cursed and spotted Liv and Alteea turn their heads like someone had just rung the dinner bell. The rest of the table went quiet as well.

Cynthia was quicker than any of them and grabbed my hand and healed me.

"Thanks," I said as the pain disappeared.

Bree smiled and said, "I hope you're not just dating her for free healing."

"Of course not. It's for the free sex," I said with a grin.

Cynthia playfully smacked me. Everyone groaned, and I was showered with crumpled paper napkins and other debris for my comment.

Once the cleanup was completed, we retired back to the living room.

As I sat there with my arm around Cynthia, and her snuggled against me, I took everything in. Liv and Bree were rapidly chatting back and forth with smiles and giggles; Alteea was doing her best to make sure no sugar was left behind in the box on the coffee table; and Stella and Blue sat drinking tea and just quietly watching everything.

In short, it was perfect.

I had no idea what future adventures awaited us, but with the people I loved most around me, I knew it would be fun.

THE END.

Author Notes

I want to take a moment here and thank the fans of the series for their warm response to *A Bounty of Darkness* (Book 7 of The Bounty Series). As of writing this, the book has been out for a month and the comments and responses to it have been overwhelmingly positive. I had been very nervous about how it would be received. The book ended with Zack losing his powers, the team breaking up, and Liv ending her and Zack's relationship. Add in that it ended on sort of a cliffhanger due to those unanswered questions, and there was a lot there that had the potential to upset readers.

I hope that *The Misfit Bounty* has answered those questions, and you, dear reader, are happy where things have ended up.

If you want to keep up to date on what is happening with The Bounty Series, please visit my Facebook page (https://www.facebook.com/TheBountySeries). It is updated weekly. There is also a link there to my website (www.markusmatthews.com) and links to all the other social media I'm on (Goodreads, BookBub, Instagram, etc.). Lastly, if you have comments or suggestions for the series, please email me at me@markusmatthews.com.

- Markus Matthews
August 19, 2022

www.ingramcontent.com/pod-product-compliance
Lightning Source LLC
LaVergne TN
LVHW091537060526
838200LV00036B/650